MISS 'NILLA'S LIBRARY

MISS 'NILLA'S LIBRARY

JOE DILLSAVER

THE PAPER HOUSE
PUBLISHING

I dedicate this work to my best friend and wife of 50 years, Jackie. Also, to my children, Matthew and Carrie plus to my grandchildren Savannah, Knox, Molly, Colin and Luke. Special recognition to my College High friends, the "Geezers."

Contents

Introduction

W ell, I started this thing. Lord knows where it will end. This first page may be all I write. If I ever finish, I have no doubt it will immediately rise to the level of other great works like *A Tale of Two Cities, War and Peace, Lady Chatterley's Lover,* and *Riders of the Purple Sage.* My reading was never quite the same since they quit making Classic Illustrated Comic books. I cannot imagine how students get their book reports done although one of our local sages told me about something called Cliff Notes. Miss Nilla kept a substantial number of the Classic Illustrated Comic books at the library. I spent a lot of time there especially during summers. When I was growing up, that was about the only air-conditioned place in town.

Huh, the first paragraph is done and I seemed to stray a little bit from what I started out to say. I wonder if this happens to other great writers besides me. If I remember right, critics call it writer's block. Don't have many critics left around here. Grandma Bessie used to present her musings in the local paper years ago about some new novel. I especially remember her talking about *Desire Under the Pecan Tree.* It stirred quite a controversy about censorship in the rag. I stole the book from the library and hid under the creek bridge to read it. I was eight at the time and couldn't figure out what the fuss was about. An article appeared saying the book disappeared from Miss Nilla's library but I was able to sneak it back in. Mae Reba's great Aunt Millicent commented she had to keep a fan near by while she read the book to hold down the hot flashes. Mae Reba gave us boys a hot flash. That is another story. After the uproar about *Desire Under the Pecan Tree,* Grandma limited her future columns to reviewing the Sunday sermons at the local Methodist church for the benefit of Hogshooter's shut ins. She did get a few stares and snickers when she added the minister should preach a series on the meaning of Song of Solomon.

We lost Grandma Bessie several years back. Being a critic took a toll on her. She was only ninety-four when she died. Her eldest daughter insisted the inscription on the tombstone read: "Beloved mother, grandmother, Christian and critic. May she rest in peace." I sure hope she does because over the years people reported numerous sightings of her ghost.

I decided a while back (no more than forty years ago) that I needed to tell the story of our little place in the sun. Why? Because. I can't or won't tell you exactly where it is, but it's somewhere. I will narrow it down to either Missouri or Oklahoma. Why? Because I don't want to get anyone mad at me. Besides, this way Grandma Bessie's ghost will have a harder time finding me if I lie just a little bit. I thought about some names for the place like Coodys' Bluff, Niangua, Matoka Junction and the real racy Climax Springs. Instead, I am going to name my non-fictional, fictional place, Hogshooter. There is a Hogshooter Creek east of Bartlesville, Oklahoma, but saying a town is located there ain't accurate. As I look back on my life, I cannot think of anyone who is more qualified to tell the story of Hogshooter than me. I did take into consideration the fact at one time Sensible County (where Hogshooter is located) did have the highest illiteracy rate in the state. That fact may or may not be true now.

I was raised in Hogshooter.

Moved away for several years.

Came back to live and enjoy my golden years (more like copper penny years now days).

In addition, I am highly learned.

Or, as we used to jokingly say, "I am highly edumatcated." Since it is a joke, please feel free to laugh.

People always said I had a way with words. For the most part, I ignored the comments that I am a windbag, liar or a prevaricator. I learned that last word on *Jeopardy*. It's amazing what I learned watching that show. I rate it right up there with *Sesame Street* for its educational value.

I do plan to lie extensively during this story because I don't want to get sued. So, if you don't like what I say, remember it's your fault and not mine. In other words, I do plan to make up a lot of this stuff and lie about a bunch more.

Hogshooter, Sensible County

Hogshooter has a long and glorious history. The Sensible County Hysterical Society taught me the idea. Excuse me but that should be the Sensible County Historical Society. When I was in elementary school, the society came each year and presented a program to the third graders. The group used to have a large and varied membership but the number and quality of the organization shrank considerably over the years. When I reached that magic grade the five individuals who spent time with us were for the most part still lucid and really could remember the county's history. Those who now come are of questionable ancestry and mental capacity. On my return home, the Hysterical Society invited me to join and I am considering lending my expertise and credibility to the Hogshooter third graders.

After I was invited, I learned a set of notes in outline form existed and would provide guidance for a presentation. There is even a rumor something on the computer called PowerPoint might keep the attention of those little buggers.

I remember bits and pieces of the history lesson given to us. The presentation took place in late October and the weather started to turn cold. If we paid attention, we received hot chocolate. Lil' Billy Boston didn't get any one day because he kept sticking a pencil up his nose. The teacher sent him to the principal's office. Billy had problems with where he put things. Eventually, he did five years in prison. Bill became quite a folk hero to some of the local gentry years later. He swears he fell in love with a ewe and named her Alice. When Bill got out of prison, he lost his mind. He swore someone else took Alice as a lover and wouldn't tell him. Alice's owner stated there was no truth to that rumor and she simply became lamb chops. Lil' Bill spent years looking for Alice. Finally, he mistook a ram for the ewe and was critically injured. The local judge felt it was time for Bill to be put out to pasture so to speak. Apparently, he fared well in the district institution for the mentally disabled until the federal government decided to close it for community-based treatment. Bill died and someone said his ghost roams the fields looking for Alice. No one has seen Grandma Bessie with him yet.

Sure are a lot of ghosts around here.

The presentation from the Sensible County Historical Society is contained in a large black notebook. If I help with the program, I will get to use the notebook. In a way, then, the history of Sensible County has remained unchanged for all those years since the black notebook was first prepared. There is probably more truth to that statement than the few remaining members of the society admit to or can remember. I was assured that while the notes have faded a bit over the years the ink is still fairly readable on the now yellow pages. The notes aren't too brittle to handle and won't disintegrate any further.

I asked the keeper of the notes why they hadn't been transcribed to new paper and she told me you can't change history. When she said that, I figured I shouldn't press the subject any further.

Whatever the yellow notes say, I am convinced Hogshooter has a glorious past. The present prospects do not look too good but that subject is for another day.

The history of Sensible County is spurious at best. Old timers would not call it that but say it's unique.

The original settlement location of the village sat near a low water crossing on Hogshooter Creek. Actually, that was the first non-Indian settlement. The Indians used the area for hundreds of years. The land had good water, plenty of game and passable soil if the natives chose to grow a few crops. The river ford lay in a protected valley with a plateau rising in the west and north. In the winter, the heights seemed to cut off some of the bitter wind the whipped down from Santa Claus land.

This part of the United States was in later years called tornado alley. Myths hold a twister will never strike where an Indian camped. This myth was challenged years ago when a tornado struck part of a tribal campsite. The old chief declared the twister hadn't hit them because the only damage was to the local poo-poop. For lack of a better definition, that was where the tribe did their business and was an annex to the camp. Some of the younger braves said the chief's declaration was full of crap.

Years later, a tornado clipped Hogshooter again. The area hit was about the same as the tribal twister. The rest of the town did not receive any major destruction. Maybe both the old chief and the young braves were right.

One nuisance did plague not only the early natives but the early settlers as well. You see, there was this black stuff that kept oozing from the ground. Someone tried to dig a water well and hit this stinking stuff. In later years, this black nuisance became an economic blessing and a curse at the same time. You guys ain't dense. I expect you figured out what that black stuff was. If you haven't I have a few things I need to sell you.

The first non-Indian in Hogshooter was a French man named Pierre Something. No, I am not lying to you. According to the yellow notes of the hysterical society that is his real name. No one really believes it especially since it is doubtful he could read. He showed up one day, made friends with the Indians and stayed. Before anyone could figure what he was really doing, he built a little shack and took in some goods from the tribe. This initiated commerce on the creek. His trading power became legendary as did something else he was good at. A substantial number of babies were born in the area possessing a distinctly French appearance. When the young ladies were asked about his magic, most just smiled and grinned. Because the dry goods business was good, Pierre could afford luxuries and the resulting prodigy who appeared.

For a number of years, there was a controversy in the Sensible County Historical Society concerning where the Pierre Something moniker came from. Some members maintained he was an adventurous entrepreneur who traveled areas where no white man had been. When he found the Hogshooter Creek valley, he recognized a marvelous opportunity to establish a trading relationship with the natives.

Another division agreed he saw an opportunity to establish a relationship with the Indians but it had nothing to do with commerce. They said it was more likely based on the premise that French men like Pierre were interested in other kinds of connections. One local scholar challenged his lineage by quoting from the annuals of a history of the French exploration of this area of the country. The commentary stated many of the members of the expedition abandoned it because of various criminal acts they committed. Rather than face punishment for their actions, they deserted. This, the scholar concluded, was the reason for Pierre's unusual last name. The mystery remains until today.

As the numbers of the Something family grew, so did the non-Indians who drifted into the valley. The tribe on the other hand, viewed this occurrence as disturbing and moved onto the plateau west of the creek. Far as I know, they weren't struck by a tornado there either. This area later became the home area for the tribe as designated by the US government. But that is another story.

A particularly unsavory group of individuals wandered into the Hogshooter area during this time. Pierre carried about all the goods they needed and he didn't ask any questions. The shopkeeper kept plenty of whiskey and that made his location a special selling point to individuals of questionable character. Another attraction was the lack of a regular law enforcement presence. Any law came from a distance away and their officers didn't really want to be in Hogshooter anyway. So, for the most part the strangers were left alone. Everyone left them alone except the female residents who also filtered into Hogshooter. For the lack of a better word, the men were a horny lot and always seemed to have money. To me, that might indicate a certain other business prospered along the creek. The yellowed pages of the hysterical society specifically tell the reader not to make such a judgment. I guess things changed over the years.

Always on the lookout for a business opportunity, Pierre slowly began to expand his empire. In addition to his small store, he added a saloon, a blacksmith's shop and a bank. Some visitors to Hogshooter thought it unusual in that wild day and time such a small place had a bank. This sentiment seemed remarkably on point considering the rather rough nature of those who flowed in and out of the settlement. Such feelings were reinforced by the fact that the law enforcement was at best spotty since the area was still a territory.

To such speculation, the wily Frenchman only smiled.

Give Pierre some credit here. The money in the 1st Bank of Hogshooter was safe. No one ever robbed the institution even in the desperate days of banditos and ne'er do wells. Another explanation surfaced several years ago as to why the money was safe. The reason was Pierre's bank kept the outlaws' valuables. This reasoning is hearsay. In fact, the hysterical society voted by a 3 to 2 margin that the rumor was a despicable lie and it would not allow such a blot placed in the annuals of Sensible County. I am only presenting it here for the sake of telling both sides of the story. Since I am now a member of the society, I am not endorsing said rumor. It does make some sense though.

Some of the worst of the western bad men called Hogshooter home from time to time back then. One of the most famous was Wilbert 'Big Butt' Seymour. Legend has it he was a large man known to go through a horse in just a few months. He originally came from Virginia and chose the wrong side of the civil war. His relatives kicked him out of the family. Over the years, 'Big Butt' became an expert chicken stealer and rose to number 150 on the list of most wanted desperados.

Whisperin' Charlie Williams made his name by attempting to rob churches. He got the name Whisperin' because he took a drink of some bad moonshine and it ruined his vocal cords. Notice that I said above he attempted to rob some churches. He was never successful and got the stuffing beat out of him on numerous occasions. Charlie wasn't wanted for those attempted crimes. Several people felt sorry for him and wanted him caught so someone could take care of him. An anonymous individual posted a reward for his capture. At one point the amount rose to $11.12. I have speculated this is the reason he was never caught.

Another famous Hogshooter outlaw turned out to be a woman. For a long time most people thought she was a man. She went by the name of Cicero Two Noses. Speculation centered on Cicero being a member of the tribe that abandoned the creek for the plateau. That turned out to not be true. An itinerant cowboy discovered her true sex when she made a drunken pass at him. He escaped after she passed out and was last seen riding as fast as he could out of town muttering something about her being so ugly she would cause a train to take a dirt road. No one knows what kind of crimes Cicero really committed. She was the only one who knew what they were, if any, and she wasn't telling. After she died, the mystery of the two noses was settled. It seemed Cicero didn't have two noses at all. The one everyone assumed was a second nose was in reality just a big growth. Sure looked like a second nose.

Back to the banks in Hogshooter...

After that black stuff was found on the creek banks, several other banks popped up in and around the town. The story of the big boom will be discussed later in this epistle.

A few years ago, the last bank moved out of Hogshooter. It was a sad day. Miss Nilla, the librarian, wisely stated in the local paper that a bank does not a community make. Everyone marveled at such a profound statement. Delbert (Del) Martin snorted in rebuttal, "Sure as hell helps though." Both philosophical statements possess a modicum of truth.

Now, one has to drive ten miles to Violet for a full-service bank.

They tried a limited-service office is Florinda's Grocery but it just didn't work. Next, they will be taking our post office. What is the world coming to?

I do have to give the bank a nod for trying. They put an ATM at Burl's Quick Stop and Bait Emporium. They had a little trouble with it because several people wrote their PIN numbers on the wall next to the machine so they had them handy when they needed them. The real disaster hit when Shoe Bob Something (a direct descendent of Pierre) got drunk over at the Pink Pigeon in Violet and came back to Hogshooter when he ran out of money. They found him and the ATM in the back of his pickup the next day out behind the Dairy Dilly. No one including Shoe Bob had any idea of how both got there. The ATM was unharmed and Shoe Bob's mom wouldn't let him come to town for a while. The paper said Shoe Bob is 47 years old.

So much for the early history of Hogshooter...

The Hygiene Disaster, the Railroad and That Black Stuff

Hogshooter was not very large when its first major problem arose. For some reason, many of the population began experiencing severe digestive problems. A death was noted around this time, attributed to 'loose bowels.' An asterisk was added to the yellow notes stating that such a cause was never substantiated because there was no medical examiner at the time. Duh! They didn't even have a doctor yet. Sounds to me the hysterical society tried to cover up this morbid vignette in the history of our town. Why they wanted to do that I have no idea.

It should be noted, the yellow notes say, that an expert was brought in, found the cause of the problem and suggested a solution.

I know the real reason. One day several weeks ago, I was sitting in the cafe one morning having my cinnamon roll and a cup of coffee. Willy Willowblossom came in and sat in the booth with me. Willy is a card-carrying member of the Indian tribe that moved to the plateau to get away from the crazy white men living next to Hogshooter Creek. I have known him just about all my life and I consider him to be a good friend.

Willy asked me why the concerned look on my face and I told

him of my tentative appointment to the hysterical society for the purposes of instructing the children of the glorious history of Sensible County and Hogshooter. He smiled and asked if I knew most of what was told the kids was unsubstantiated. I did but pointed out to him I was not going to tell those old ladies that. Willy said he saw my point and he wouldn't either.

I was vexed about a certain part of the history. I relayed the part about the loose bowels. He heard about loose bowels sinking ships during WWII but not about those on Hogshooter Creek. I reminded him the saying was loose lips not loose bowels. On further musing, I do suppose that loose bowels could sink ships.

Willy was joshing me and told me what really happened. One of the elders of his tribe related the story of an ancestor being asked one day about the cause of the local misery when he came to town to buy supplies. He spent about fifteen minutes nosing around the little village and returned to the person who quizzed him. The ancestor took the villager to the shores of the creek. There he pointed to the fast-flowing water.

"Poop, wash and drink—make you sick. Indians always drink, wash and poop and don't get sick." About that time, a rather large 'floater' came by and the white man's face lit up. He now understood. You get water up stream to drink and then for the clothes. Nature accommodated downstream.

There was an expert as outlined in the notes and Willy identified him although he wasn't sure of his name.

After this incident, the leaders decided to post the appropriate signs along the creek for those who could read and pictures for those who couldn't. A more important and completely unintended development occurred as the result of the belly woes. More modest individuals came to the area and the open facilitation of nature couldn't be tolerated especially among the womenfolk. Outhouses began to dot the reaches of the community. The local store secured a simple set of plans and cut the lumber to the proper specifications. A buyer erected the facility anywhere he desired. Or, the labor could be contracted. The digging of the appropriate size hole cost extra. However, a good hole might last for a while although many folks wanted a new one especially during the summer. A good catalog was always in demand not only for reading but for other functions as well.

Designer thunder jars began to appear about this time. Finding your way in the middle of the night to the outhouse could be a dangerous proposition given skunks and other varmints in the area. I remember visiting my grandma and making the trip in the dead of winter. That was an enlightening and quick experience. I was told not to dilly dally because a local drunk fell asleep on the throne and woke up with a frost-bitten butt. Reflecting on that advice, I am not sure it was true but it sure made an impression on my young mind.

I once heard an anthropologist give a talk on the excavation of outhouse pits. Apparently, an expert can get the history of an area from its crappers. The pits became repositories of other trash items as well. Some jars found are worth thousands of dollars. Well, you can have that money because I ain't going to be digging in hundred-year-old crap for anything.

With the advent of the outhouse, a new and exciting sport developed: tipping. This exercise was especially prevalent around Halloween. Many an anxious individual was faced a momentous decision the morning after the holiday because their outhouse was tipped. This practice continued even into my lifetime though I swear I didn't do it (my fingers are crossed). One outhouse mysteriously appeared on the courthouse lawn the same day a big murder trial was to begin. The newspaper story commented on the outhouse and not trial. I don't believe the story on the crapper rather than the legal proceedings was a comment on the current state of the law. I do suppose it does merit some thought.

I am aware of only one injury as the result of outhouse tipping. One Halloween night some youngsters identified their victim, studied the ingress and egress carefully and accomplished the deed. Unfortunately, the edifice was occupied at the time and a violent scream was heard as it hit the ground. The injury was more to Mrs. Eden's pride than the small scratch she received. For some reason, no one ever admitted culpability for the deed.

One of the defining moments in the early growth of Hogshooter was the railroad coming to town. It didn't last long but at least it came for a while. For those of you who are not aware of its history, railroads received incentives to build in certain areas. The magnates became rich from the land given them for right of ways and grants next to the tracks.

The location of Hogshooter had some distinct advantages that made it an attractive location for a spur. It sat in a valley with easy access to surrounding areas. So, a railroad had to make slight adjustments to connect to a major line. While the local industry was largely agricultural, it still provided enough activity to support an investment of a new spur.

The Ottawa, Burlington, Glen, Yankee and Northern decided it was worth the risk to come to Hogshooter. The OBGYN (for obvious reasons the name was simplified to the Ottawa and Northern) came to town. It built a span across the creek and attached an accompanying wagon bridge as well. At first, the local ranchers kept the railroad busy shipping cattle and horses. Once that black stuff was discovered, a boom in machinery and people flowed on the railroad. The company erected a beautiful Spanish style depot.

After restoration a few years ago, it became Miss Nilla's library. The spur is now used a couple times a year but that is about it.

The Sensible County hysterical society tried to get one of those old locomotives for the Hogshooter Park. At the last minute, some bigger town stepped in and stole it from us. We did get a kiddie train ride for the park. In retrospect, that is probably more of a draw than the locomotive ever was. Every year, the local Rotary Club cleans up the ride and operates it during Founders Day. The smile on the faces of the kids is something to see. They come from all over the county for that little train.

I will have to say that the original coming the railroad gave rise to some unique entrepreneurial efforts. Probably the noblest attempt was Joe Randle's idea for chicken and turkey herding. Joe, also called flathead, looked at the cattle business and figured that if ranchers could raise cattle on the range and then herd them to the railhead, he could with the birds. Not the brightest flapper in the flock, flathead went to great lengths to get the chicks and try to raise them in the wild. He got a bunch hatched and fed. When he figured it was time for the great round up he learned birds won't herd, many were eaten by varmints and what was left was tough as leather. Flathead delivered 30 birds to the railroad and most of them died before they got to market. He felt disgraced and left the area. Rumor has it flathead did become a successful moonshiner and politician.

Another noble attempt to use the railroad came from the widow, Mrs. Bertinna Northcut. Rose rocks occur in and around Hogshooter. Bertinna's idea was to use the railroad to transport the rocks back east where she was convinced they would be all the rage. Unfortunately, she was never able to get enough mined to fill even a portion of a boxcar. And, she didn't have anyone on the other end to sell them for her. To Bertinna's credit, in later years she became quite successful with the rock of the month club. She put an ad in the Grange magazine and the business took off. Geology sure was in her blood.

There was only one close call anyone is aware of as far as the railroad being robbed. Seems a transient group of nogoodnicks pulled off an attempt before the turn of the century. They made their living as they moved about robbing mail trains in the belief a considerable amount of money was always in the envelopes. The varmints stopped the train after it left Hogshooter and demanded the mail. To their chagrin, only 3 letters were mailed that day and it was obvious none contained money. In disgust, they stole a cow instead but were caught the next day because the animal wasn't in a hurry to go anywhere. The sentiment in the village was to hang the desperados but instead they were condemned to a year of hard labor in the Sensible County jail. After the year, two ended up staying and marrying local girls they met while serving on the chain gang. A third criminal left muttering something about being too embarrassed to stay.

Only one wreck of note occurred involving the train track. It was several years after the first automobiles arrived in Hogshooter. A young oil speculator came to Sensible County to try and buy up oil leases from the Indians. His name was Ibby Crank from St. Louis. Ibby drove a new Ford and dressed in the latest duds including spats. He considered himself to be a model of fashion for the backward hicks of Sensible County. All the men simply dismissed him as a fop and a sissy because of his looks. On one occasion, Ibby was made fun of and forced to defend himself against one of the violent Loyal boys who wandered over from the town of Blue Gnat. To everyone's amazement, Ol' Ibby put a whipping on the intruder. He didn't even get his clothes messed up.

To say the least, this made an impression on the local harem of female possibilities. Ibby felt it his duty to sample the squeezins of the area over the next few months. Thus, the stage was set for the almost disaster on the railroad track.

A handsome little filly lived in Hogshooter by the name of Emiline Capps. Em just graduated from high school and considered her career opportunities. Without doubt, they were limited for a vibrant young lady in Hogshooter. Em saw this rascally young cad flittering around town and decided he might just be the answer to her dilemma. Over a two or three-week period, she made sure to catch Ibby's eye whenever he came into the café where she worked.

Like I said, Emiline was a looker and the young would be Casanova couldn't help but notice her. One evening after she got off work, the two happened to bump into each other as Em left to walk home. Always the gentleman, Ibby asked her if she would like to go for a ride in his new Ford. She did and the next thing he knew a certain stirring began to occur in a certain place.

Now Em had planned well. She suggested a rarely used road

crossing over the railroad tracks. The location was supposed to provide a very special view of a neighboring lake. Em was right. The scenery was very nice along with another view Ibby soon enjoyed. Nature began to take its course and neither Ibby nor Em saw or heard the train approaching. The crossing was just around a curve and the engineer had no chance to stop before the train cut the back half of the Ford off. In all the confusion thankfully neither of the car's inhabitants was hurt. The situation turned very embarrassing for Ibby because he was not able to find his pants and wallet.

When Emiline's father heard about the happening at the railroad crossing, he and his two oldest sons visited Mr. Ibby Crank. Honorable man that he was and not being able to get out of town because of the wrecked Ford, the young speculator agreed to a visit to the local justice of the peace. Ibby pled his innocence but knew his fate was sealed. The union turned out to be a profitable one for him. Now being a respectable family member in Sensible County led to many a contract and a very comfortable living.

Em did not have a child until a year later. In fact, as the family expanded to 6 children, she grew with it mirroring her rather substantial mother. Over the years, it became clear just who ran the Crank family and it wasn't Ibby.

A rumor soon popped up after the great train wreck of Sensible County that Emiline herself hid Ibby's trousers. When she asked about it by one of her friends, Em just smiled.

In the early years of Hogshooter and Sensible County, that black junk gummed up a bunch of stuff. For one thing, that old sulfur smell stunk up (that is when it really stinks up something) everything around. At times and when the wind was just right, if was difficult for the populace to tell the difference between it, rotten eggs, Big Al's feet (there was talk that his socks were such a hazard that they were burned), a visiting skunk, or the passing of gas after eating beans and onions. The local water well digger hit the goop about as much as his did water.

The US hadn't entered the industrial age yet so the black stuff had limited demand. That wouldn't last long. Oil was first discovered around Bartlesville and down around Tulsa in the Glenpool field. Soon a market for oil sprang up. In Sensible County Jake Something, relative of Pierre, saw an opportunity if the black stuff could be extracted easily. He contracted with an oil guesser to find the right place to drill for the goop. Using a divining rod, the old boy pointed to a place on the banks of Hogshooter Creek. A derrick was built and the process of literally poking a hole in the ground began. The sand level was shallow as indicated by the oozing black stuff.

Jake hit oil and the black stuff, often called gold, now flowed from the hole. Obviously, the strike attracted attention and all kinds of speculators came to the Hogshooter area to get in on the action. Much was written over the years about these turbulent times and the yellow notes don't spend too much time on all that stuff. I do know as I grew up in Sensible County, I heard stories from the oldsters and some of them are interesting. So, even though not in the yellow notes, I like them anyway.

The oil boom brought an interesting and diverse group to work the oil fields. People called them roughnecks for a reason. These men worked hard and then played hard. Hogshooter struggled to find an infrastructure to support these people.

My great uncle, Henry, came to Sensible County in 1919. Oil was discovered several years before and the boom was already waning. He came to help his brother in a grocery store but soon soured on that. Henry worked on the railroad and for an oil company that set up an office in Hogshooter. The old man he started with became its CEO later in life. My uncle would have nothing of it. He believed the area would get over the boom and return to ranching. And, he was right.

Uncle Henry told about a riot that almost occurred one Saturday night. A promoter sponsored a group of wrestlers who toured the area putting on matches. These 'fights' were big money makers. A place was picked in Hogshooter and a ring complete with ropes was constructed. For seats, concrete blocks were stacked and then 2x12's were put on them to serve either as seats or for standing room. The participants arrived complete with their tights and masks. There were good guys and bad guys. The villains were despicable. The audience really got into the matches. In those days, a match might last an hour and nothing like the junk you see nowadays. Of course, a little liquid libation was served to the fans so it wasn't unusual to see a drunken audience member attempt to crawl into the ring to save the good guys.

Anyway, on this one particular Saturday night the place was packed. The bad guys were very evil that evening. It was a good night of matches and some of the rowdies stayed around after they were over to try and get a shot at the bad guys. Their car was a huge roadster. Suddenly the doors opened and all the wrestlers came out together. A roar began to grow in the crowd. How could this be, all of these people, the good and bad guys, together? They hated each other. That was clear from the match. The wrestlers saw something was amiss and they all piled into the car and departed with screeching tires. A few of the stragglers shouted obscenities. Some more hurled rocks after the roadster. For the first time, a few realized it was all show business. The next time they came to town the exit was handled differently.

Grandma Bates handled it herself as I grew up. Those were the very early days of television. On Monday night at 6:30, wrestling from the Coliseum in Chicago came on. Grandma was a big woman and she was exhausted when the matches were over. One of her son-in-laws tried to tell her the wrestling wasn't real. She set him straight in a hurry. From time to time, he would irritate her with the same fake rumor. Good thing he could move faster than she did.

In the days before spousal abuse, an old man and woman showed up one day at the local doctor's office. When asked what happened, the story went something like this. Every week, the couple pulled down the shades and turned on the radio to listen to the wrestling matches. As the action progressed, the couple got carried away and tried to mimic the moves they heard. There was a lot of screaming and such but the two old codgers could pretty well follow the action. Anyway, one day they got a little carried away and an arm got broken. The reason they came to the doctor was to get the arm set. The day was one of the more memorable ones at the office. It seems the old lady proudly announced she usually won at least 8 out of the last 10 times they wrestled and the old man had the broken arm. They were both in their 80's.

Now, don't tell me wrestling isn't real!

The Indians possessed enough sense to get away from the while folk and ended up benefiting from the oil. The federal government ceded the mineral rights of the county next to Sensible to the tribe. Rather than divvying up the rights to the individual members, the tribe held the rights in trust for those on the tribal rolls at the time. Unscrupulous individuals did everything they could to get those rights. Non-tribal members courted young tribal girls with the idea of marrying them to get hold of their wealth. Before the Indians figured out what was happening, car dealers sold new cars to them. Many could not drive so they hired somebody to chauffeur them. When the car ran out of gas, some thought the car was no longer good and they bought a new one.

The trust soon worked and benefited those who lived on the plateau.

This oil activity and money didn't last too long. The roughnecks moved on when the boom ended. Even today, the pumps still rock up and down squeezing the black stuff out of the ground.

For the most part, unless you owned the mineral rights, the average person didn't really benefit from the oil. The population of Hogshooter skyrocketed during these days, and then began to fall as the people left for other oil fields. This activity cemented the existence of the community and many of its businesses.

The railroad's activity spiked also as the yellow notes talked about before. However, once the demand for raw materials began to wane, so did the usefulness of the line.

One unexpected impact did occur in Sensible County. All over there were salt-water ponds and oil spills. Many of these areas are still unusable today. These scars will last forever.

Every time the price of oil or natural gas spikes now a days, companies come back looking for more oil applying new techniques to get at the stuff still there. Now, it's not unusual for a well to go down thousands of feet to reach pockets of natural gas. They can even drill at an angle. When I was a kid, you'd probably get shot for doing something like that.

I just don't know how this works. I watch in amazement when they talk about using corn or even prairie grass for energy. Companies now pile up trash in heaps and then use the garbage to get natural gas for electricity.

As some of you have figured out by now, I am a dynamic individual and I ain't a dummy either. I thought long and hard about how a common person could get in on this energy industry. However, I came to the conclusion long ago that most of the major companies aren't going to let a little guy like me mess with their bottom line. Years ago, I heard about a guy up in Vermont who came up with an idea to have a motor run on water and water vapor. Did you ever hear anything about it? NO. Ain't a major corporation going to let someone like that rain on their profits.

Personally, I have a marvelous idea about how to solve several crises at once. I haven't been able to work all the problems out with this idea yet but I believe what I am suggesting has promise.

Our population is aging. More and more facilities dedicated to us older folks are going to be needed. We all know that. Sometime in the future we will have an energy problem. Also, there is a health care cost crisis. Some people cannot pay for everything they need.

I have discovered that as I grow older, I expend great quantities of gaseous materials. In other words, I seem to fart much more than I did. My modest suggestion is for the government to supply legumes (beans you idiots) to various extended care facilities, nursing homes, etc. This action would increase the passing of even more quantities of natural gas. If we can figure out a way to capture these passages and recycle them just think of the benefits to mankind. Our older population including myself could pay their way and benefit society at the same time.

I have yet to figure out how to capture the expulsions but I am working on it. If pads for incontinence were designed then why can't we capture the natural gas especially at night. I hope to have a working model in the near future with the proper patentable materials ready.

Miss Nilla's Library

Miss Prunilla Jacobs.

That is her full name. I, like so many others in Hogshooter, didn't know for a long time her given name. I learned it by looking at the yellow notes of the Historical Society. I knew her as Miss Nilla.

You have figured out that I am not a spring chicken since I returned to retire. I knew Miss Nilla all of my life or at least all I can remember. You can imagine how old she was before she died. I suppose one could make it his or her calling to try and find out her true age. Me, I was smart enough not to get that woman riled up. There was a time or two when she has looked over those half glasses at me and smirked. That smirking from Miss Nilla was one of the worst things that could happen.

Anyway, one could find out her age if you had some magical ability. The courthouse burned down years ago and most of the vital records of Sensible County were stored there. The fire probably started from a smoldering cigar butt of one of the sheriff's deputies but no one admitted it. The destruction devastated many because if you wanted to join the Daughters of Union or Confederate Veterans you had to provide proof from the courthouse records. Since they were gone, Mabel Blessing came up with the idea church records would do unless you were an atheist. Then you could swear on the Bible your application was correct.

Miss Nilla's birth certificate was on file at the courthouse. In the days when she was born, no one trusted the state government so there wasn't a central depository in the capitol. An unexpected boon of the courthouse burning was two men who swore they weren't married since no marriage licenses existed. One of them got away with it and disappeared a free man. The conductor on the train as he left town stated he sure had a big smile on his face. Cody Durbin was not so lucky. He finally admitted he was married to Cinabobia and the pair resumed their wedded bless along with the ten kids that graced their union. After Cody reconsidered his state of bachelorhood, Cinabobia's assault and battery charges were dismissed by the sheriff. The local district attorney gave two reasons. First was their ten kids might become wards of the county and it wouldn't be able to find foster homes for the little darlins' since everyone knew the brats. Second, the government's budget could not withstand the hit of feeding them while Cinabobia served any time. I guess there was a third reason as well. It appeared all of the county jailers threatened to quit if she became a prisoner.

Back to the story...Miss Nilla didn't have a birth certificate or at least one she would admit to. Now that I think about it, she had something because she got social security. I didn't ask her because, again, I am smarter than that.

On a whim, I asked Burl (the truth) Moon, editor and owner of the local newspaper about Miss Nilla's age. Burl was resplendent in his light blue seersucker suit the day I stopped by. It was a wee bit mussed but not too bad. He snorted when I woke him as I entered the front door. Undoubtedly, Burl was dreaming of all the Pulitzer prizes he might win. The door had one of those little bells on it that jingled when you disturbed it. Burl's tie didn't exactly match his suit and the short part was actually longer than the fat part. The food stain on the tie was pretty much the color of the suit but I am not sure if that was the tint of something dropped or it had cured to that shade.

I asked Burl about Miss Nilla's age and he sat up and cleared his throat. Then he scratched his head and his faced twisted as if he was having trouble passing gas and replied he wasn't right sure. He smiled and told me he'd never get involved in such a touchy subject. That answer I could accept. Besides, years ago a rumor linked Burl and Nilla romantically while Mrs. Moon was still alive. I sure ain't going to go there. I will return to Burl Moon later on in this brilliant expose.

The upstart of this is Miss Nilla was older than about everyone left in Hogshooter.

I heard whisperings about Miss Nilla's lineage. The story of her birth is of some interest. The rumor is when she was born her daddy took one look at her and said, "That is the ugliest child I have ever seen in my life. That little bugger can't be my kid. Who have you been messing around with? She looks like a shriveled up prune so I am going to name her Prunilla."

No one except Miss Nilla's mother can verify the veracity of the above and she's been dead for years. Just after he visited his new daughter, Nilla's daddy disappeared and was never seen again in Sensible County. Some say he simply went out in the woods and killed himself because of the shame of fathering such an ugly child. The coyotes supposedly ate his body. Other rumors had him heading anywhere away from Hogshooter. One of the most persistent musings is that he and Nilla's mother weren't married anyway. With the courthouse burning down, no one could confirm if that was true or not.

Years later, Myrtle Abscess said Prudence Splittail said Nilla's mother told her before she died that the gentleman went to South America to seek his fortune and found it. And, he quietly deposited a large amount of money for Nilla's benefit in the Remarkable State Bank. I know that you are thinking there ain't no such thing as the Remarkable State Bank. Well, you are wrong. The father of the twin Remarkable brothers, James and Jimmie originally owned it. I will tell you more about them later.

Bottom line, Nilla always had money.

As a baby, Nilla's mother proudly pushed her through the streets of Hogshooter. Some said as they passed the sun always went behind the clouds. And, the population of our village was afraid to look on Nilla's face. In fact, one statement (unconfirmed of course) stated that the baby curdled milk if she looked at it just right. I have heard that dogs bayed constantly until the buggy was a good distance past them. All this is just rumor.

I don't hold any truth to these matters. From personal experience, I can relate that she ain't a contender for Miss Sensible County. The title is awarded on Saturday night at the county fair. The honor lost a wee bit of its luster since Sue Bob Willie cast aspersions on the process when someone discovered she actually "entertained" all of the male judges on the evenings leading up to the final choice. The real give away was when Sue Bob's talent, singing a duet with her pet rooster, Rooster, won the talent category. Under intense questioning from one the judge's wives, her husband admitted he was enamored by the rooster. His black eye portrayed another possibility. While the favors Sue Bob delivered never became public knowledge, several witnesses described the judges having big smiles.

Sue Bob was stripped of the title and it was given to Randy Simile because the duet with her canary sounded like as if it came from heaven. Sue Bob left in disgrace but with a smile on her face. One of the local young men believed he saw her in Las Vegas at one of those topless revues. While she didn't sing, Sue Bob could win a swimsuit contest hands down. Hands down probably isn't the right word to use here.

Miss Nilla attended Rainmiller School a couple of miles outside of Hogshooter. Several smaller schools containing grades 1-8 supported the high school. I know this because my dad taught there. In those days, this elementary school got minimal support from the county. A county superintendent of schools oversaw the rural learning establishments in Sensible County. For the most part, the responsibility for running the school remained with the parents.

Rainmiller School had such a group of parents. They hired,

fired and made sure the teacher was paid. These rural schools wanted young men to teach because the women often came for one year and got married. The families provided the books for their kids and this posed a problem for some of the poorer students. The library books were the responsibility of the school. The building and its upkeep was their duty. My daddy earned a little extra money because he served as the janitor as well.

A big wood stove sat in the middle of the room. Usually, one of the older boys got there early and make sure the fire was going before the little kids came in. If it was very cold, the kids crowded around the stove to get warm. Everyone hoped that no one had been out catching skunks because the smell on someone's boot was nigh unbearable. Dad was especially proud of the fact he talked the local parents into separate boys' and girls' outhouses on opposite sides of the school's back lot. Not all schools had such a luxury.

Nilla was the star student according to my daddy. She led the class in about everything. With all eight grades in one room, it was at times difficult to keep the different levels apart. Didn't make any difference to Miss Nilla 'cause most of the time she tried to do the older kids' work as well as hers. She was able to do the lessons better than the older kids. Daddy let her because she was his best student. He made it a point to have new and challenging workbooks for Nilla.

Rainmiller had a crazy habit in its early days of covering two grades the six-year-old year and two more the next. The reason was kind of interesting and stupid at the same time. The area around Hogshooter was largely agrarian and the kids needed to work on the farm. By the time a kid was eight years old, he/she was ready to start the fifth grade. A lot of them never went beyond the eighth grade anyway so cramming all those grades didn't make much difference.

Miss Nilla was an exception to the rule.

She whizzed right through the grades and wanted more. The high school really frowned on the country school's two-year arrangement for four grades so Nilla went through the eighth grade a couple of times before the high school let her enroll. Dad said she turned out to be a blessing because during these years she took over teaching the younger grades.

One interesting occurrence took place during one of those first two years. There was an old stump on a hillside back of the school. No one remembered when that gnarled knot of roots wasn't there. For some unknown reason, Nilla got the idea she was going to dig until the stump was free. Then she was going to push it down the hill. Day after day, she worked on freeing those roots. Some of the kids at first made fun of her but as time went on more and more joined her obsession. Every chance they got and the weather allowed, those little buggers dug. Finally, just before school was out one year, Nilla and her fellow diggers gave a mighty push and the stump broke free from its long predicament. She just took one-step back, clapped her hands together and headed off for new challenges.

There really isn't anything remarkable about that stump except to illustrate the Nilla's grit and determination. Over the years, many people came face to face with this spunk.

My father never saw a competitive spirit like Nilla's. Each year, the county superintendent got the schools together for a day of play and academic games. The activities started with competition between the school grades in different math skills and spelling. You know who always won. That should come as no surprise to anyone. But what did shock many people were Nilla's athletic abilities. She won the running contests for girls with her skirts flying as she left the other girls in the dust.

The biggest prize of the day was the boys' fast pitch softball tournament. Rainmiller only had nine boys. One year, the catcher got hurt in the first game. The pitcher and captain of the team strode over to Nilla and told her to come on because she was going to catch. She simply grabbed the injured player's glove and started playing catch. There were gasps of disbelief and a murmur of protests began to arise from the other teams. My daddy stated there was no rule that said she couldn't play and he allowed it. Her squatting behind home plate in her dress catching those pitches was quite the sight. Oh, by the way, Nilla hit a home run to put

Rainmiller ahead. What the other teams didn't know was she played softball after school and during the summer for years. The boys on the team knew how good she was and didn't mind her at all.

Things weren't always easy for Nilla during those years. It was one thing to play softball with the boys but being around them for anything else was another matter. Remember, she wasn't the kewpie doll of the county. Each year, the school hosted a special night where its students demonstrated what they had learned in school for the community. It might be a play like *Aaron Slick from Pumkin' Creek* or the recitation of a piece of prose or poetry or a famous speech. The fund-raiser included cakewalks and carnival games. The biggest event was the selling of the food baskets. The young ladies bought a basket and shared it with the person who was the highest bidder. All the young men knew which basket belonged to a particular girl even though they weren't supposed to.

One year there were no bidders for Nilla's basket. Even though she kept smiling, it hurt her. Finally, Mrs. Engleman slapped her son fat Freddie upside the head and he bid. The food was great and Freddie learned something else from Nilla that evening. It seemed they disappeared for a while and Freddie came back in with a grin on his face. The lesson many a young man later learned was if you were nice to her, Nilla would be nice to you.

I tried to find out about her high school years but there isn't much information. The only one who knew for sure was Nilla and for the umpteen time I wouldn't ask her anyway. I didn't have my father there to tell me about her doings at Hogshooter High. Still, I have picked up a few pieces along the way and I will probably make up a few as well. Hell, Nilla was so old she probably couldn't remember anything anyway. I will just lie say what I said is in the yellow pages of the hysterical society. If they ask to see them, I will just tell them that I gave an oath to keep what is there secret. If I suddenly feel a slap across my head I will know that Miss Nilla's ghost didn't approve. Won't be the first time she did it to me and even though I am retired it may not be the last. I am amazed at how a little old lady can hold sway over someone as long as she has. Oh, well, such is life in the mini-metropolis of Hogshooter located in Sensible County.

Who was valedictorian of her high school class? Apparently, it wasn't even close. I found a few things out about Nilla while she was in high school. I stumbled across an old yearbook for her senior year. That book was absolutely astounding. You have to remember Hogshooter was not an affluent area by this time. The oil boom disappeared and the population of Sensible County declined. The school didn't have much of anything especially money. The yearbook was handwritten. You have probably guessed who the editor-in-chief was and who wrote the thing out. I don't know how everyone got copies. For me, there has to be some mysteries in life.

Each class had a section. Some of the classes were longer than other grades. This leads me to believe someone from each grade at least helped Nilla. By the way, her penmanship was remarkable.

The section on the sophomore class was particularly interesting. I am just going to use first names to shorten this. Three headings appear: cognomenia (Latin for name?), Descriptive Adjective and Ambition.

CognomeniaDescriptive AdjectiveAmbition
AudraAdmirableHousekeeper
GraceFrankTrained Nurse
OthaLovableGov. Teacher
BessieAmiableFarm Life
BeaulahAdorableBookkeeping
CorrineGarrulousMusician
EdnaConsistentSpinster
WinnifredJealousTelephone Operator
EltonSlowEasy Life
NevaDignifiedSchool Marm
OpalMirthfulWashing Dishes
JakeCongenialFloor Walker
JohnnieInimitableOutlaw
TheodoreTopmostJanitor
LeonaFlirtationsBeauty Shop

. . .

Isn't this listing wonderful? I can say with some authority that some of these ambitions were pretty close to what happened.

The written history of the sophomore class contained some jewels as well:

"The Sohomore (yup, that's the way it was spelled) Class of 1926-27 wishes to mingle its voice with that which is forever sounding through the ages, the records of achievements of man."

"The second event of importance was on the first day of April when we ran off and had an exceedingly good time exploring bluffs and woods."

"A new method of grading was adopted by the teachers much to the satisfaction of the (lazy) scholars."

"The old schoolhouse doors were locked, one last look was taken and we sophomores (right this time) passed to higher level-Juniors."

Interestingly, there is nothing about a junior class. They must have not gotten there stuff in on time or made Nilla mad. Again, that will just have to remain one of the mysteries of life because I ain't asking.

The senior class part of the yearbook has Miss Nilla stamp all over it. Of course, she was the class president.

The class motto: "Aim ever at the best."

Class colors: Old rose and silver gray

Class flower: American beauty rose

How do you go about describing what a senior is? Nilla used a mathematical formula to explain.

Given: Senior

To prove: that a senior is a darling

Proof: a senior is stuck up

Stuckup=proud
Proud=lofty
Lofty=high
High=costly
Costly=dear
Dear=darling
Therefore: a senior is a darling.
I'd say that is pretty novel.

The highlights according to the seniors included a pie supper on December 17th; February 12th, a Lincoln Program; March 25th sophomore class play, "Aboard a slow train through Missouri; April 21st, senior play, "Eyes of Love; and May 6th, "the seniors put their diplomas under their arms, bid each other 'farewell' and depart to all four winds."

A cryptic class history followed written in terms of a dream, a class will and a senior prophecy. The most interesting part of the senior class was a description of the personalities. Now, I don't know how these were arrived at. Nilla could have done it herself or they might have been arrived at it collectively.

NillaAlways looking for the best
    HerbertAlways going but never getting there
    LettieA busy bee that never stings
    ClarenceClimb on, the top is just ahead
    EverittThere is just one girl for me
    RubyAt the foothills climbing
    MarieLife is what you make it
    LamoigneWhat I am to be, I am becoming

I am sure there are other copies floating around Hogshooter. Shoot, Miss Nilla might even have one in the library.

After some real snooping, I was able to find out some other stories about her high school experience. Miss Hestor Fordyce had an impact on Nilla's life. There can be no doubt about that. Miss Hestor knew Latin and taught a class at Hogshooter High for a number of years. The course was an introductory one except that Nilla always took it but the material presented reflected her advanced desire to learn the ancient language.

The teacher believed the class should be much more than just an introduction to *veni, vidi, vici*. For you uneducated heathen, I think these mean I came, I saw, I conquered. These are famous words spoken by the good Caesar himself. Anyway, as part of her "extra work" for her later Latin classes, Nilla assisted other students in the intro class with Roman culture. She got this idea to have a Latin club that would make a presentation every month or so to the language students. The idea worked pretty well for the first month or two until it came time for Verbal Something (yes, another descendent of Pierre). He created a poster of the typical Roman house and told everyone the use of each room. Well, Verbal left off a title for one of the rooms and it the omission spied by Silly Cindi Spurlock. Silly Cindi was notorious for trying to show up other students and cause them embarrassment. She never realized she was usually the one who looked stupid.

Anyway, Cindi's hand shot up and she asked Verbal the use of the room. Now, Verbal while not the fastest pony in the herd possessed a little wit of his own. He remembered a previous Latin club presentation on Roman lifestyle on their gluttony and orgies. Verbal smiled and replied that room was the Barfitorium, the room where during an orgy when they couldn't eat any more the Romans went to throw up. The rumor was Nilla inflicted serious bodily harm on both of them. That rumor was unconfirmed.

Rumor also has it Verbal got in much deeper trouble with Miss Hestor because of an answer he put one of his Latin tests. The question was Julius Caesar's greatest contribution to ancient Rome? Verbal's response was keeping the teenage charioteers off the Appian Way. Miss Hestor warmed her paddle on a particular part of Verbal's anatomy for that answer.

Something of great consequence did occur during Nilla's high school career. In fact, I heard her speak of it. One year during the spring, a circus came to town. In those days, most shows still used tents for their performances. Everyone is Hogshooter was excited about the prospect of seeing the animals. The circus manager, being an especially entrepreneurial fellow, offered a matinee just for the schoolchildren at a reduced rate. Hogshooter and Sensible County were extremely poor in those days and even the reduced rate was too much. Nilla helped at the local bank after school a couple of days a week. She wanted to go to the circus badly. She woke up one of the Remarkable brothers (owners of the bank) and convinced him what a noble venture it would be for the bank to send the kids to the circus. One of the community members was making a deposit in the bank at the time and said the brother was almost nasty telling Nilla to go stuff it. Something happened though and the bank did foot the bill for the matinee performance. The paper gave a good spread on the generosity of the brothers. Privately, Burl (the truth) of the paper said he figured Nilla had something on the old coots and threatened to make it public if they didn't fork up the money for the kids.

Whatever she had, it must have been something. The Remarkable brothers became solid supporters of the library once Miss Nilla took it over.

One summer during her high school years, Nilla got a part-time job at the city/county library. Silence Troth (what a great name for a librarian) was the only employee. She wanted to go visit her sister in another state. If Silence was to do this, the library board would have to shut the place down until she got back. One of the Remarkable brothers suggested Nilla work there while Silence was gone. Burl (the truth) Moon holds they wanted her out of the bank because she caused them unmentionable problems.

Anyway, money appeared in the library budget for her to work the rest of the summer there as a substitute for Silence.

The library at this time was composed of one building with only one room. The "facility" was a one holer out back. In later years, the library would undergo a completely different look. The genesis of how the library came about was interesting. In the middle of the oil boom, one of the magnates came to Hogshooter and noted how rustic the area was. He also noted the lack of cultural opportunities for the roustabouts working the oil fields (rather unusual to note such a thing since many couldn't read). Being a civilized man (well, except the time he got into a fight under the leasing tree during an Indian session on the plateau with another of the richest men in the country), he announced the establishment of a library for the betterment of the people of Hogshooter. He bought a small building, gave money to renovate it and something for books. A local library board oversaw the venture. The money didn't buy much but the citizens of Sensible County believed the library was critical in portraying the image the local people wanted.

You guessed it. The oil money and men disappeared. As a result, the library struggled greatly. The board was undaunted and rightly determined the library should prosper. They raised money the best they could and bought a few new books every year. However, they depended on volunteers to man the building until they finally secured a modest stipend from Hogshooter and Sensible County. That was when they finally hired someone to oversee the place. Silence was a good librarian for the money. She would remain on the job until Miss Nilla took over. But, I will add more about that later.

Anyway, Silence visited her sister in another state. Nilla plotted changes she would make while the librarian was gone. Now, remember, she is still in high school when the vacation occurred. The Monday after Silence left things began to change. She visited several of the Sunday Schools the day before and informed everyone that she would have a children's story hour on Wednesday with refreshments. The venture was an instant success. She provided the cookies and milk the first time and the mothers took turns after that. Nilla began visiting shut-ins and bringing books to them. The newspaper got wind of all these activities and ran a nice article. The kids all felt comfortable coming to the library and their folks didn't mind them visiting on their own. Remember, this was small town American and no doors were locked.

Nilla started bringing fresh flowers to the library and a dish of cookies for anyone who wanted one. The newspaper article ran in the next county and a box of new books soon arrived from an anonymous donor. She also received a world globe and a map. The kids sat and listened in wonder as Nilla pointed to a place and told them about it.

Now all this was fine and good but when Silence returned, the manure hit the fan. She resented what this high school girl accomplished. It simply made more work for her. Nilla was informed that school was starting so her assistance was no longer needed.

The library board got wind of Silence's actions and a rather testy closed-door meeting took place to discuss the matter. There weren't any Sunshine Laws in those days. The long and short of the matter was the Board told Silence if Nilla wanted to work part time at the library she was welcome to do so. Those familiar with the situation said the intrigue for lack of a better word was heavy for a while. A stubborn Nilla wasn't backing down from Silence. The rumor spread the two had a physical confrontation as evidenced by a knot on the side of Silence's head. I don't know if that is true or not and I sure didn't ask. Makes a good story, doesn't it?

Silence remained the librarian for some time after this. Then Nilla replaced her. That is another story.

You will remember I told you Nilla's father left some money for her. When she graduated from Hogshooter High, Nilla enrolled at a teacher's college in a nearby state. I can't really tell you a whole lot about what happened there because the yellow notes are silent on it. Very discreetly, I asked some of the older and more prominent citizens of the area and got stonewalled. The reason is a subject of some speculation. I am probably trying to dig up something where there is nothing to dig. I stopped by the nursing home and visited with Jerry Horvach. He told me about Nilla and her escapades with a couple of young men. When I asked him about the time of the incident, Jerry believed it was right about the civil war. I guess I have to discount his story. Jerry also told me that he expected to be Caesar after the next election. I wonder who his campaign manager is? Brutus?

I caught Burl (the truth) in his office working on an editorial for that week's paper to see if he knew anything about Nilla's college career. He seemed quite agitated that I woke him up so he wasn't any help at all. I guess I'll have to wing it with what I know.

You will remember my father was a teacher in a dependent school outside of Hogshooter. He got his teaching certificate with only one year of college. That was quite allowable in his day. He took some sort of test to get it. I do know Miss Nilla was able to get her teaching certificate. I assume she got a degree from the teacher's college outside of state. Again, I didn't ask her. I don't want that slap upside my head. Now, that whack might drive my hearing aid clear to the other side of my brain.

Nilla didn't come back to Hogshooter when she finished her degree. Instead, she took a job at Violet. As I mentioned before, Violet is just a few miles from Hogshooter and is in Sensible County. When I was a kid, some people used to call Violet a suburb of our town. No one can call it that now because it has both a bank and a Wal-Mart store. There was a lot of grumbling about that Wal-Mart store because it has put Violet on the map.

Even though she taught at Violet, she still lived in Hogshooter with her mother. During these years of teaching, Nilla went through her robust years that can be directly attributed to eating home cooking. About this time a terrible event occurred in Hogshooter almost forever altered the town.

The library burned down.

Nilla was the only female member of the local volunteer fire organization. The department lived up to its motto: "We have never lost a lot."

The impact on the community and Nilla was profound. The message was a town without a public library was not a town. Silence stoked the flames so to speak by announcing that since the fire destroyed her livelihood, she would leave town and go live with her sister, Essie. A large hunk of locals begged Silence to stay but she had none of it.

After this announcement, Burl (the truth) ran a front-page story outlining the dilemma the small town faced. Should the library be rebuilt or should Hogshooter admit it was of no significance? The discussion at the cafe became hot and heavy with both sides refusing to buy the other a cup of coffee. The controversy was made more intense than when Brother Dooby of the Apostolic Brethren Church of the Holy Spirit was asked to leave town. But, that is another story.

Vehement against the rebuilding or having a library at all were the boys from the pool hall. The most vocal of that group was Samuel (Slim) Smith. He was viewed as the leader because most of that crowd at the pool hall owed Slim money. This relationship based on money owed was significant. Those pool hall boys should have been wary of him since he owned a custom-built two-piece pool cue. The rumor was Slim changed his mind about the library when a certain young lady came into the pool hall (unheard of at the time) and asked to see the man. Now Slim was sitting next to the snooker table drinking his double cola when Miss Nilla entered. No one is sure what she said and Slim refused to disclose the truth. Anyway, he dropped his opposition toward the library after this meeting. Years later when pressed on the issue, Nilla confirmed she talked to Slim but there was no truth to rumor she was going to stick that two-piece pool cue up his (!!!!!) if he fought her. Remember again, this alleged incident supposedly took place during her robust period.

The whole county including both Violet and Hogshooter soon became aware of what took place next. Nilla decided there had to be a library in Hogshooter serving the entire county including Violet. She made it appear there was a formidable campaign to reestablish it. In reality, the vast majority of the people in Sensible County could have cared less. The appearance of support was all that was needed. Miss Nilla was a student of politics. She realized if you said something enough times people believed it whether it was true or not.

Her plan was simple: start overwhelming the area with the argument of the necessity for a library if Sensible County was going to grow. There was some real meat to Nilla's argument. She stumped everyone who would listen. Burl (the truth) knew she was right. He inserted story in every issue of the paper about the need for the library. Nilla talked to every organization that would listen from church circles to the Brotherhood of the Mastodons.

I think we need to be honest here. Do you really think anyone would be dumb enough to oppose a lady dead set on bettering the community? Then add the fact the lady was one Miss Nilla and the whole community was hooked like a snapping turtle on a trotline.

One thing she didn't do at this point was a masterful bit of strategy. Most people she visited with were either polite or wanted to get rid of her as quickly as possible. What Nilla didn't mention and only a few people thought of was how the community going to pay for the new expense. There was no insurance money from the fire to rebuild the destroyed old library. Some people wondered about the money but they were probably afraid to bring it up to her. Remember, Nilla was in her robust part of life and most knew about her run in with Slim Smith.

Both the city officials and the county government gave tacit approval for the idea of rebuilding the library. Burl (the truth) made a big deal out of this support. He knew exactly what Nilla had in mind and gave his approval. This may have been during one of the times the two were on "speaking" terms.

There was a building on the edge of Hogshooter owned by the Remarkable brothers' bank. It was a sturdy building with an indoor bathroom. The brothers readily agreed to deed it to the library board with little or no threats from Nilla (that we are aware of). I still wonder what she had on those old coots.

The real coup of getting this building was the fact it was partially in the city limits of Hogshooter and partially in Sensible

County. No one could argue that everyone had a small stake in the new library.

The building was just a shell with nothing in it. That would not be a problem. One of Nilla's best friends and supporters was Teeny Robertson, whose husband owned the local lumberyard. Teeny was a nickname from her younger and less formative years plus before her five kids. The friends plotted so when Nilla walked in the front door of the lumberyard Teeny's husband simply asked what she needed. Nilla's list didn't leave anything out. It was a sizeable collection of everything from lumber to paint.

The plot then thickened considerably. Who was going to redo and pay for the inside of the building? The finest finish carpenter in the county was Flip (nailhead) Dozer. Nailhead was truly the best and willing to do the work at a discount (thanks to alleged threats from his wife). The work was in the evenings and on the weekends. Then a few of the businesses in town ponyed up some money to pay him for the work. Burl (the truth) made this campaign front-page news for several weeks. Soon, the crew working on the library grew as volunteers came to assist nailhead. Some of the ladies in town threatened abstinence if the men folk didn't show up to help with the new library.

For the first time in the history of Hogshooter and Sensible County, the Ladies Auxiliary of the Ministerial Alliance agreed to hold a rummage sale to raise money for library supplies and books. Most of the time these women folk were barely tolerant of one another because of the heresy beliefs each believed the other held. The Alliance agreed to have the sale on the neutral ground at the high school to avoid endorsement of a particular religion by hosting it at a church. A bake sale accompanied the rummage sale and was an enormous success. Teeny's twice dipped iced cinnamon rolls were especially in demand.

Miss Nilla's scheming came together nicely. You will remember she was teaching at Violet at this time. If this all worked out, she'd be able to become the full-time librarian for the city-county organization. She needed to figure out how to get the books plus supplies for the library and get money to keep it open. The main courthouse for Sensible County moved to Violet some years before for reasons I have already mentioned. At the time of the building of the library, the county had no representatives in Hogshooter. Once again with full support of the women of Sensible County she asked to speak to the county commissioners. Nilla's backers packed the meeting room. Before they knew what happened, she was justice of the peace and a notary public. The library was designated as a location for paying Sensible County taxes and assessments. Nilla charged a small fee for her services.

A like arrangement was added for the town of Hogshooter. Before long, the city's utilities allowed their bills being paid at the library. Over the years as Hogshooter continued to shrink, most of the services of the city came for Nilla to collect. She even served as the municipal judge after a while. Many a big city lawyer got an education in the library with Nilla presiding. When she became the city clerk, Nilla took care of the receiving and paying of the municipal bills and receipts.

I don't know if this is true, but one vendor who came to the library to pick up a check told me that had to go to Nilla's house after work to get it. Others said they observed gentlemen exiting there in the night carefully carrying their shoes and closing the door gently. Just the mention of this may get me another whack upside my head from her ghost. This is probably the first time the "don't ask don't tell" policy was instituted.

In later years, the funding problems for the library disappeared because of a joint tax millage levied by both the city and county. This regular money allowed the library to grow and prosper. The problem would reappear later as the county shrank in population.

Miss Nilla had a furnished building and a funding source. She didn't have any books. When she knew she had money for running the library, Nilla resigned her teaching job at Violet and became the "real" librarian of the city/county library of Hogshooter and Sensible County. Silence was jealous when she found out what her rival accomplished.

Nilla had to find a way to get those books.

You figured it out? Nilla wouldn't do anything without a plan. Because of the bake and rummage sale, she had money to buy basic reference materials. Nilla explored the statewide library association and she asked its members to send her duplicates and outdated materials. They complied with boxes of stuff. While a lot of it wasn't the most germane materials, it began to fill up the shelves. Nilla started an adopt-a-book project in the community. Several of the civic organizations helped with projects for the library. Burl (the truth) wrote an excellent article on the library's needs and got it released on the statewide news wire. Several newspapers including the state's largest ran the story and donations of both books and money came in.

Nilla took a step back and looked at what she accomplished. The county Chamber of Commerce honored her as citizen of the year for her library work. I believe this was one of the few times in her life when Nilla was surprised. Such status assured she would manage and expand the library over the next few years. Nilla was in control and she liked it a lot. However, about this time, her mother died. Nilla prided herself in being able to face a situation or a person and control it or them. She couldn't control death and Nilla now was alone for the first time. That seemed to change everything for her at least for a little while.

Before long the library became a beehive of activity. The story hour was back and the kids came to visit in droves. She worked with the teachers in both Hogshooter and Violet to make sure she had the books needed to support their activities. Nilla enlisted help to see that the nursing homes and shut-ins were included. She enlisted a reading "corps" who visited them a couple of times a week to read to the folks.

Elmira Bittle decided to make the library the hub of everything in Hogshooter and the surrounding area. Little Bit as she was called growing up was born in Sensible County but like so many others got married and moved out of the area. Elmira raised a family and then her husband died. With her kids raised and gone, she decided to move back to Hogshooter. One of the reasons given or at least rumored had to do with her ability to get around. For most of her life, she didn't drive a car. While her husband was still alive, Elmira did get a driver's license. She decided to start driving so she went out to practice one day. Little Bit put the kids in the back seat and took off. She was doing well until another driver honked at her. She went home, put the car in the garage and never drove again. Moving back to Hogshooter allowed her to get around much easier.

Now Little Bit considered herself socially adept. She learned to play bridge and other evil card games after she moved away. When she came back, there just wasn't anything to do except sit on the porch, go to church, and grow old.

Elmira and Nilla were friends before Little Bit left and she saw what the librarian was trying to do. Elmira realized Nilla couldn't do everything by herself. When she asked Nilla if she could help, the answer was a resounding yes. The two realized there were a couple of under-utilized rooms in the old depot (how Nilla got the depot in a minute). Next thing everyone knew classes taught people to play bridge, spades, bunco and hearts. There were even rumors of low stake poker games held there. Next, Elmira began teaching flower arranging. Before long, others in the community suggested and helped with classes like exercise, needlework, and the basics of fly-fishing. Most of all, the people got together and talked. Someone suggested a potluck lunch once a week followed by a songfest. Shoot, every once in a while, everyone walked over to the old folks' home and sang.

The library had success stories about the community activities there. It's been rumored that Burtus Bible even refused to move to where his kids lived after his wife died. This decision ticked off his daughter until she came to visit him. She realized the old goat was too busy to leave Hogshooter.

Sadly, we lost Little Bit a couple of years ago. She was happy all those years she helped at the library. Things are slowing down some without her. A bunch of us are determined to keep things going. We have created a new "corps" of volunteers to help with anything or anyone that needs assistance. There sure seems to be more people than ever in need of help.

I know one thing for sure. Miss Nilla missed Elmira a lot. I think you have figured out the resemblance of these two friends' lives.

Over the years, Nilla categorized the books according to the Dewey Decimal system. When the Library Congress system came along it took her twenty-years to convert. She figured if a book was in the library she knew where it was no matter what the system was used.

As I told you before, the railroad at one time in Sensible County was a viable entity. The hope was it would insure the area with sustainable growth. You will remember that didn't happen. The last passenger service disappeared and the depot build by the line stood empty. The building had a distinctive southwestern look to it and possessed several rooms. The longer it sat, the more Nilla coveted it. You have guessed by now what happened because I mentioned it above.

Before Nilla acted, she thought out her campaign to secure the depot and marshaled her minions. The library board must have known something was up when the meeting room was full for the first time in years. When asked for her report, Miss Nilla gave it to them. Not only did she ask for the old depot (which the board had no control over) but somehow she already had plans drawn up on the configuration of the remodel for the building. The prepared resolution was signed on the spot. The members felt like this act would buy them some time before anything else occurred.

They underestimated Miss Nilla but that shouldn't have come as any surprise. You see, she contacted the railroad and it agreed to deed the depot over to the library board. That wasn't all she had done. Nilla reached the proper governmental authorities and the station declared a place of special historical significance for Sensible County. The railroad picked up on this and donated historical railroad memorabilia for a special Ottawa and Northern room. The logo was prominent on the outside of the depot and remained there. Some how, Nilla persuaded the railroad to foot most of the remodel bill to make the station into the library. Pretty good, huh? Nilla got her new library, the railroad got rid of the old depot and a bunch of old junk, took a significant tax write off for protecting and remodeling a historically significant building.

Credit where credit is due, I am beginning to think this woman could have been governor of the state if she wanted to. If Nilla ever got her teeth into someone's rear, she wasn't letting go.

The dedication took place during the annual summer carnival called the picnic. She tried to get the governor to come but had to settle for the secretary of state. It still turned out to be a big deal. The depot looked great and Nilla began to work on filling the new library with materials.

Do you really think she couldn't?

Before long, the story of the new library in the old depot was all over the place. Burl (the truth) once again did his part in trying to get Nilla's story out. The state tourism magazine did a short blurb on it. A historical publication also trumpeted its revival. There was always a subtle request for support contained in these articles. While not surprising, money came into the library and its materials began to grow. Miss Nilla kept an eye out for small grant opportunities from mostly local companies. Some of them even became regular contributors. Several had a shelf with their name engraved on a small plate attached to the front of it.

Now, to big libraries this was chicken feed. But to the Hogshooter/Sensible County library, the money was valuable. The money received from these sources was gravy that added to what the library received from public taxes.

In the years following the move to the depot, the library enjoyed full support. Nilla developed a strong relationship with the community to such an extent she had all kinds of volunteers helping her. This allowed her to extend the services of the library.

An incident took place that almost changed that. Hogshooter and Sensible County were never what one would call a bastion of liberal values. There were reasons for this including the strong set of religious attitudes in the community. This heritage saw the community become isolated. In one election, Sensible was the only county in the state that the sitting governor did not carry. Even though the party in power denied it vehemently, the area received little money for roads or economic development.

This undercurrent harbored some interesting remnants of bygone ideas and philosophies. The Women's Christian Temperance Union remained active well after it had died nationally. Sensible County remained the only dry county in the state in spite of the fact alcohol flowed freely not 10 miles away and at 18 years of age in another state only twenty miles away.

Miss Nilla always tried to present a cross section of books that were popular in the country and thought provoking. She tried to keep out and out smut from the shelves of the library. But to no avail.

A group of old biddies suddenly began to stir up trouble concerning what they believed was pornography on the library shelves. I can't be sure but I have a feeling someone was feeding information to them because most were so dense you had to knock on their skulls twice before they would answer. Their concern was for the youngsters who went to the library to read this evil stuff. That argument was crazy because most of them in this rural area learned early about sex anyway and the back seats of cars were local entertainment for them.

To complicate matters, many of these ladies now raising objections to the material had been ardent supporters of Miss Nilla in some of her earlier endeavors. They felt the librarian was simply naïve in the ways of the world and she didn't realize what was contained in some of these books.

The de facto leader of the group of moral hypocrites was Ammie Ula Wintermole. AU as she was called was not exactly an intellectual giant. She was born and raised in Sensible County. Now, I don't want to spread rumors, but I have been told about the only place she was successful was finding her way home after school. She decided to leave Hogshooter and go make her fortune in the only good-sized city close to Sensible County. She did not pass the shorthand test for secretarial school. The only job she got was in a commercial laundry. Her boyfriend, Burdick (Bird) Wintermole, got lonely without her, rescued her from evil, and brought her back home. AU told everyone her decision to return home was a difficult one but her love for Bird conquered all.

Bird inherited a decent sized farm and with oil and gas royalties provided AU with a nice life. She, on the other hand, viewed herself as the leader of the social set in the area. With too much time on her hands, she began to listen to radio and television evangelists. The use of the television media by these people was relatively new. I don't want to condemn all of these people because I have listened and admired some of them. AU especially liked those who condemned anything or anyone they didn't agree with. Her message soon spread to like-minded ladies who had entirely too much time on their hands.

To Bird's credit, he was smart enough to stay out of this deal.

Now AU volunteered at the library. She got her a list of these evil writings and while Nilla was away began to check to see if any of them were on the shelves. And, yes there were a few.

Unannounced at the next library board meeting, AU came accompanied by her band of old biddies and demanded to speak. Never known for either brevity or brains, she began to drone on about the content of the books and the undermining of the children and families of Hogshooter. All of this was rather remarkable because AU and Bird never had any children.

Those who were watching Nilla realized that something was getting ready to happen and it wasn't going to be pretty. You see, when she got mad, Nilla's skin became red and splotchy beginning at the bottom of her neck and moving up. The brilliant hue had already reached Miss Nilla's chin.

After AU had moaned on for what seemed like forever, the librarian smiled and raised her hand.

"Mrs. Wintermole, have you read any of the books on your list and if you have, will you tell us what parts you object to."

"Well, I haven't actually read them myself."

"Who told you then that our library shouldn't have them on our shelves for us to read?"

"Why, Brother Hinderance, the television preacher."

"Has he read them?"

"I assume so."

"But you don't know, do you?"

"I trust him."

"Let me read you something from another book in the library and give me your opinion if I should remove it or not. Will you?"

"Sure."

"This is poetry. 'Let him kiss me with the kisses of his mouth: for thy love is better than wine. Because of the savour of they good ointments they name is an ointment poured forth, therefore do the virgins love thee...Thy navel is like a round goblet which wanteth no liquor; thy belly is like an heap of wheat set about with lilies. The two breasts are like two young roes that are twins...' AU, what do you think about this? I can read you more if you want."

"It would seem to me that your poetry is highly suggestive. To be on the safe side, I think that shouldn't be in our library."

Nilla smiled first at the audience and then to the library board. "I will be happy to remove that book if you want me to." No one said anything because the members knew full well that the other shoe was getting ready to drop.

"You see, I just read to you from the Bible. And, I didn't even have a chance to get to the begats. Why don't you let me decide what should be on the shelves of our library. Don't forget we fought a war for independence from England so we could basically believe what we wanted to believe. I would add, read what we want to read. Please rest assured, AU, that I will not let a book that doesn't have some value to be available for you to read."

Mrs. Wintermole was stunned. She was whipped up on about the head and shoulders and didn't even know it. The board members looked relieved because they did not have to make a tough decision.

Miss Nilla wasn't through. "Just a minute AU, there is one book I do want you to read." The room was like a funeral. The librarian went over to the wall and briefly searched for a book fingering several of them as she went. She uttered a "aha" and proceeded back to her adversary.

"This book is called *Fahrenheit 451*. You see, 451 is the temperature at which books catch fire. The story is about a government that decides to destroy all the books of the land. You might find it interesting."

Miss Nilla turned around and retreated to her seat. AU's mouth was agape. The chair immediately adjourned the meeting. No doubt, Nilla made both friends and a lot of enemies that day. But, one lesson was learned—there was no doubt who was in charge of the library of Hogshooter and Sensible County.

I have to assume things quieted down for several years after that little episode. Don't know for sure. You see, I hadn't returned back to Hogshooter and Sensible County yet so I can't say for sure.

When I did finally move back, I expected everything to be about the same as it was forty years before. Oh, I came back for a reunion of some sort or the other but not for an extended period of time. All the people I did know had gotten a lot grayer. Even though I deny it, I don't really think I have gotten that much older.

The one person I did see had aged a lot was Miss Nilla. She still possessed the spunk I remembered before but her body began to suffer. In a way, she seemed to be shrinking and stooped a little bit. The first time I visited with her I discovered her mind was not shrinking. That woman amazed me when she began to talk about my dad as a teacher and what she remembered about me.

The old depot didn't look quite as vibrant as it once had. I began to ask around and found the answer. The current mayor is a long-time resident who I went to school with, Aloy (Al) Scott. Al confirmed what I saw by looking at what was left of Hogshooter. It was disappearing. I asked about Miss Nilla and the library. He just shook his head. Every year for as long as he could remember, both Hogshooter and Sensible County had reduced the amount of money it could give the library. Now, there just wasn't much left. Then Al told me something that stunned me. Miss Nilla hadn't been paid in years.

After I heard this, I went to see Burl (the truth) and was surprised to find him awake. I asked him about what Al told me. He dropped his head and confirmed the matter. Almost with a tear in his eye, Burl (the truth) said that Nilla refused to let the library close. She quit taking a salary and redirected what little she got to the library. Nilla's reasoned she had enough money to live on so the rest could to the library. She worked for nothing.

Those in the town who knew about what she was doing were both appreciative and saddened. She caught one member welling up after a meeting when the board couldn't give her what she wanted. "Look, the library has to stay open because the kids won't have anywhere else to go for school support."

That might not be something she or any of us have to worry about anymore. The local school district lost most of its students. There is now a strong possibility the Hogshooter School might close and the kids transferred somewhere else. I don't know, maybe its time.

Miss Nilla had to fight one more battle about this same time and it wore her out. Over the years, she was able to get enough to keep the library technologically relevant. But lately, with the explosion of computer use it became a chore to stay current. Nilla knew what was coming and began to plan for it. She secured a small grant to get a digital connection to the old depot. Somehow, someway, she was able to get some computer equipment. Rumor had it that she might have brought the stuff with her own money. Securing it was a big deal not only for the library but for Hogshooter in particular.

Nilla took time to hold classes for anyone who wanted to learn about the use of the machines. She was amazed at the number of Hogshooter's senior citizens who began to use the internet. The schools had some computers set up but most of the people didn't have computers at home. Many kids came to the library to use them.

Nilla did everything she could to keep an eye on the students to make sure they weren't used for anything other than their intended purpose. She even bought some software to block objectionable material.

One day while she was away, a high school senior girl and her boyfriend got into the library and viewed what they wanted to. Well, the story goes they brought up some pornographic sites and well one thing led to another and the girl got pregnant. What they supposedly watched was available on his or her home computer when mom or dad wasn't watching.

The rumor spread like wildfire through the high school and then the community. Once again, the old biddies united and came after the librarian. This time Miss Nilla couldn't deflect the criticism. All the discussions took place behind closed doors but everyone in Sensible County knew what was happening. The decision was that unless a designated individual was present, no one could use the internet. That included the adults as well as the kids.

Nilla was crushed. She was mad someone in Hogshooter would even accuse her of making this stuff available. This time, the controversy took its toll on her and the community.

The girl left town and went to live with a relative in Kansas City.

Some months later, the girl's mother brought her to see Miss Nilla. She apologized for what she had done. It seems the young lady wasn't pregnant at all. She wanted to get out of Sensible County and made up the story.

The truth never got around. I hate to admit it but we humans seem to love the racy and sordid. No one wanted to hear the story was a lie about the library's internet. As far as I know, nobody in the community made the effort to go talk to Miss Nilla. Knowing her, she probably wouldn't have told them anything anyway. You see, she wanted to protect the lass. Miss Prunilla Jacobs didn't give a flip about what people thought of her. Sad part of the whole deal is that there were several of us in town that do and we didn't say any thing either.

I hadn't seen Miss Nilla for a while. A couple of times I stopped by the library just to visit with her. She wasn't there. Then one afternoon I came by to return a book, Nilla was behind the desk in a wheelchair. Nilla looked worn and I stooped to talk to her and asked how she was. Looking me straight in the eyes, she answered me, "a little tired."

Burl (the truth) wouldn't give me a straight answer for a while but he figured out I knew something was wrong.

"Nilla has cancer and won't be around long."

That statement hit me right between the eyes like a 2x4 on a jackass' head. This woman had been in Hogshooter all my life. The whole community was her family. The library was her legacy and now it would probably have to close. I searched my own soul and asked myself if there wasn't more to life than this. I knew that Miss Nilla wouldn't mirror what I was thinking.

Miss Nilla fought that cancer with the same zest that signified her life. Half the people in the state came and visited her. She told every one of them they better support her library after she was gone because if they didn't Nilla and Aunt Bessie would come back and haunt all of them. You know what, I believe her.

After Nilla died, her body lay in state at the depot. An old farm wagon pulled by two draft horses took her casket to the cemetery. Some say it was one of the largest funerals in this part of the country since Ma Barker and her outlaw sons were buried years ago in Welch, Oklahoma.

Nilla specifically instructed who was to do what at the service and it was not to be sad. My assignment was to read the opening paragraph to *A Tale of Two Cities*. You know, the one that starts out "...it was the best of times; it was the worst of times..." There was a lot of laughter and a lot of crying that afternoon.

To no one's surprise, Nilla left everything she had to the library. While significant, no one really knew how long the old depot could remain open. I and a bunch of others are going to try. There is now a plaque above the depot's door. It simply says, "Miss Nilla's Library."

I can't help but think of the O'Henry short story that Miss Nilla read to me so many years ago. He told about a sickly young girl who said she would die when the last flower died outside her window. A painter in the middle of a blizzard gave his life to paint a flower that never died so the little girl would never give up hope.

Hogshooter is dying. How long the flower we call Miss Nilla's library will last I don't know. I'm afraid it too will fade away with time...

MAIN STREET

The other day I did something people think is stupid. I started at one end of Hogshooter's main street and walked down to the other. In most towns, a person would be putting his/her life in danger to do so. That might have been the case at one time but not now. I can still remember when people drove their horse drawn wagons to town on Saturday. That was over a half a century ago now.

The yellow pages of the hysterical society spent a bit of time describing Hogshooter's businesses and what Main Street once looked like. You gathered from my ramblings these records haven't been updated for dang near as long as wagons used to be driven to town.

I wanted to start at one end of the street and walk to the other to visualize what the area must have been like. Unfortunately, I will have to walk back to relate what still exists on Main Street today.

As I indicated earlier, Pierre Something started the first store. It was located on a high spot above the creek so it wouldn't flood and was the first building on what became Main Street. The general store was crude but served the community well. Pierre took in trade goods from the settlers and the Indians in the area. He tried to stock most things they needed from durable goods to selected food stocks to equipment. Pierre soon learned his little one room wasn't near large enough to provide everything the growing community needed.

He brought in a carpenter to build a new structure. He had a bank or at least a vault there as well. The new building was an ambitious undertaking and reflective of the dreams Pierre had for Hogshooter. For some reason, the Frenchman became antsy and wanted to move on from Sensible County. The yellow notes aren't clear on why so I have searched other sources to try and find out. Couldn't locate hide nor hair of a reason. I decided to make up one. I figure it is as good as anyone else's guess.

You remember after Pierre came to the area, he soon began involved with a number of the ladies. Little people began to appear with some regularity and many of them looked like the Frenchman. My hypothesis is that Pierre's neglect to keep his pants up caused him all sorts of problems. One reason could have been pressure from one of the ladies to make an honest woman out of her. The most likely scenario was somebody, maybe a father, brother or even a husband, decided ol' Pierre needed a lesson in shotgun diplomacy. The story goes that the Frenchman simply disappeared one day.

I know for a fact the disappearance was by design. My guess is it was planned for some time. The reason for the conclusion was someone showed up the day after he left with a deed to the store. And, the clerk who worked for Pierre was told a new owner would be there that day.

No one ever heard of Pierre after his disappearance. That probably ain't right either. Seems one of the cute and very young darlins' the Frenchman was supposed to be involved with left sometimes after Pierre. The rumor has it he sent for her but the girl's mother never confirmed this. Years later, a woman did come through Hogshooter and visited with some town people. I have it on good authority it was the same girl and she became a very well to do woman. She had a gaggle of children so I can assume there was one thing Pierre never changed.

Back to the story of the store--The new buyer was Dode Phipps. He ran into Pierre somewhere, the two got to talking and Dode learned about the store being for sale. Pierre was honest about everything and suggested good price. There was only slight problem. The Frenchman didn't own the land. Later on, the new storekeeper got that problem taken care of. The particulars of how remains a mystery.

One thing was for sure, Phipps had some money. After he saw the plans for the new store, he tweaked them and gave the construction go ahead. The prevailing wood of the area, black walnut, was used. Today, that wood is like gold. Years later after the store was vacant for a long time, the owner of the local lumberyard figured out what the wood was. Grif (knothead) Dozer bought the building under the guise of clearing an eyesore. Grif is the brother of Flip (nailhead) Dozer who I wrote about earlier. He is also related to Joe (flathead) Randle. There are other 'heads' out there and I will talk about them in due time. Back to the story--Knothead made a lot of money tearing down that old store and recycling the black walnut lumber.

The new edifice was magnificent. Counters went around most of the store and it possessed separate areas for dry goods, feed, food and the like. Shelves went clear to the ceiling and a ladder slid on rollers to where needed. Dode stocked catalogs for items like seeds and clothes.

He owned this store for over fifty years.

Every Saturday, wagons surrounded the store and shoppers bought goods and visited with neighbors as well. Dode was an entrepreneur and bought eggs and milk that he in turn took to Violet and sold. He hired some of the local kids to put together crates used to take the eggs to market. These were precut and he paid the youngsters a few cents per crate to put them together. He'd candle the eggs before he put them in the crates. For you uneducated folks, this is when you hold the egg up to a candle or light to see if it is good or not.

A couple of times a week, Dode hitched up his team of horses, got the milk, cream or eggs and took them to Violet. If someone needed to take a calf or chickens or whatever there, he'd take them with him as well.

Before school started every year, families came in and to either buy or order shoes and clothes the kids needed. Dode worked with them perhaps bartering a hog or grain for what they needed. He'd even extent credit to them if requested.

He married a local girl named Maude. She turned out to be the boss of the two when it came to business. Maude ran a tight ship with credit and such. Still, Dode helped those out who needed it and sometimes Maude got all upset. They never had any kids of their own so the rascals of Hogshooter became what they didn't have.

In many ways, Phipps had a monopoly. When oil came, a lot of this changed and competition sprang up. Dode didn't care because he had all the money he ever needed. Besides, the old residents never forgot what he had done for them and he still had a good business.

I remember dad telling me about the store after electricity came to it. Dode and Maude added an ice cream freezer. It contained three big tubs, chocolate, vanilla and strawberry. If you wanted a cone, you got it from Dode. He always rounded up the cone. Maude never did that.

The store had an ice chest full of cold pop. Ice became a common luxury when it could be made locally. Many places had icehouses where the commodity was stored until it was used or melted. The chest was filled with bottles and covered with ice. If you took a bottle, you had to leave a deposit. The kids scoured the roads for empties. When they had enough, they'd redeem them for either money or merchandise.

Dad told me that Dode's store served as the post office as well. In those days, the post office was a political appointment. Whichever party was in power controlled it. With oil and Hogshooter's growth, he didn't always have it. He bought animal pelts as well. That included skunks. A hunter had to be careful and not get sprayed. In a closed area like a schoolroom, the smell could be a problem. Skunks carried rabies and there was no treatment for that. If someone got bit, he probably was going to die.

There wasn't any government regulation of in those days. Maude from time to time bought fresh rabbits or squirrels to resell. If ice was available, meat was more likely to be sold because it kept longer.

Dode was the first person in Sensible County to have a car. He always owned a big one and got a new model on a regular basis. In those early days, there weren't many around. If an emergency occurred, Dode loaded the person in the car and drove them where they needed to go.

You will remember Pierre had a safe and acted as the bank for Hogshooter. Dode did the same but saw an opportunity to make some money without working too hard. He sold the safe to the father of the Remarkable brothers and then subleased a corner of the store to him for a bank. The business remained there until the oil boom when the banker built his own building.

About the time the usefulness of the general store began to fade, so did Dode. He was a big man and ate mountains of rich food especially pork. Dode probably had a heart attack and lingered for some time. He never ran the store again. When he passed away, Maude sold the store and moved to Violet. She lived there for the rest of her life. Maude had enough money and never worried about anything.

I got hold of an old map of where many of the old buildings on main street used to be. The problem is most, if not all, were wooden and were later replaced by brick ones. Some of the old brick buildings have dates on them so I can kind of figure out what went where.

As I walk up the hill from the river (remember the original store was on a little bluff overlooking Hogshooter), I can pretty much visualize the stores. Next to where Phipps original store was a blacksmith shop. For a while, it served as a livery stable.

Owners of some early cars in town stored them there. That makes sense because no one had garages in those days. The Star

Hotel sat next to it. Hotel as we know it now might not fit its description. Probably a boarding house was more accurate. People stayed there by the day, week or month. The money they paid included a couple of meals a day. There was no indoor plumbing. Rumor has it that some other business activities took place there from time to time. I have not confirmed that fact. If those things didn't take place, I maintain they should have to make a good story.

Other early businesses sprang up including a doctor's office and drug store, a café, a dress shop, a lumberyard, the Plenty Meat Market and a barbershop. The barbershop did a brisk business because many of the men of the village stopped by for shaves every morning. Most had their own mugs for the lather and the warm towel often helped with the "sinus headache" from the night before. It was also a wonderful place to lie. You know tell stories, lie.

Oh, I forgot one building that existed on and off next to the creek for a number of years was the mill. The millers built a dam across Hogshooter Creek to get a sustainable water supply to run it. People brought their grain and it was ground for a fee or for a portion of the meal. A problem turned out to be an inconsistent water supply. After the second time the mill burned down, the owners didn't rebuild. Instead, a feed store opened and served the same purpose as the mill. It handled all kinds of seeds, veterinary supplies and even baby chicks plus rabbits. During my lifetime, I remember going in and seeing stacks of feed sacks made out of cloth. Mother told me about buying the feed and checking out the patterns on the sacks. When empty, mom washed the sacks and made them into dresses for the girls. I remember seeing my grandmother sew up a hole in a sock using a light bulb to hold it in position. Families did what was needed to meet the necessities of life.

One of the local families opened up a café in town. It operated from early in the morning for breakfast and closed right after supper. The food was good down home fixin's and nothing fancy. For a long time, it employed one of the widows in town to bake pies. The meringue stood up four inches. She came in early every morning and started all of the baked goods. These included biscuits for breakfast along with giant cinnamon rolls. For lunch and supper, she made yeast dinner rolls. Lord a mercy, I am getting hungrier by the minute just reading what the yellow pages say about her baking. She supported her kids for years after her husband died.

Another business during the early days of Hogshooter was the doctor's office and included a pharmacy. His name was Luke Indicot but everyone called him Doc. He was actually from the area and somehow ended up a doctor. I am not sure how much schooling doctors had in those days. He apparently practiced somewhere else but came back to the Hogshooter area. The yellow notes do indicate he came from a rather large family. He had four brothers, Matthew, Mark, John and Judas. Believe it or not, Judas turned out to be the black sheep in the family. I ain't making this up, I swear. He had several sisters including Mary, Martha, Ruth and Jezebel. Jez met an untimely death of some kind or another.

Folks came in to see Doc and he mixed up the medicine right there from the chemicals he kept. Patients paid him with whatever they could. If the tab got high enough, he might take a hog or barter for something else in payment. Business got so good he took on a young apprentice, Bevel Beard. Doc never married and actually lived with a local family. I am not sure if he owned the house or he rented from them. He made house calls anytime anyone needed him. That included in the middle of the night. In the wintertime when illnesses ran rampant, Doc might be out all night. Someone from the family he lived with drove the buggy and he slept between the visits.

Compared to today, his skills and medicines were primitive but he did what he could. All Doc might do was to make up an asafetida bag to put around the neck of those with colds or the flu. These stunk (that is when they really stink) to high heaven and included about anything people believed might help. Camphor was usually included to help breathing.

Doc could set a broken arm and sew up cuts but not much beyond that. A lot of people died from what today we would call ordinary ailments. I lost an uncle to lock bowels (appendicitis). Other common ailments during this time included flux, consumption, scald, dysentery, typhoid fever and hooping cough.

If you stop and think about it, kind of makes you wonder how people lived as long as they did.

Another office opened on the main street about this time as well. It was Ludie (airhead) Something's law office. Ludie was extremely smart but didn't have a lick of common sense. Ask him a question and it might take him a week to answer it and then only after reminding him ten times what you wanted. Ludie didn't go to any law school to become a lawyer. He "read" for it. This was kind of like doing an internship in the law to get the background. In his case, he spent time with Judge Perkins for a particular amount of time. Can't find any record of how long that was. Once he had "read" enough law he was able to take a test to demonstrate his competence. Ludie did all that and got his license.

Don't anyone cast a skeptical glance at this process. I know a bunch of paralegals and legal assistants now days that do most of the practicing of law in their offices. Attorneys couldn't function without them. Besides, many of them are smarter than the lawyers.

Ludie was no one's fool. Lack of common sense didn't make him a bad lawyer. He represented the folks of Sensible County for a lot of years. Pervis, his son, went on to be a lawyer as well. The kid had common sense, got involved in the oil business and enjoyed a good living from that.

I have decided I will take a little break from the businesses on the main drag. I don't want you to get concerned that the people of Hogshooter were a heathen lot because they weren't. Intersecting with Main Street was Church Street. All the places of worship were situated there. I will come back to these institutions in detail later. Their stories are some of the more interesting ones that took place in Hogshooter and Sensible County.

Let me tie up some loose ends about Main Street.

For years, the street was simply dirt. You can imagine what it got like when it rained. As the number of businesses expanded, getting from place to place in the mud was a chore. If the porches were close enough, one could navigate without getting too dirty. Remember most of the women wore long dresses in those days. Finally, the city fathers attempted to aid them and their walking. They plopped down wooden planks for the women to walk on. Trying to keep their balance and their dresses out of the mud was nigh impossible. There was another habit that disgusted the ladies as they navigated the streets. Most of the men folks chewed tobacco. A lot of the buildings had spittoons but some men just stuck their heads out the door and let fly. Not only did the women folk have to deal with the mud but now they had tobacco juice to worry about as well.

That reminds me of a story. My dad chewed Beechnut and Red Man tobacco for years. In the days before air conditioning in cars, when we went on a trip you always wanted to sit on the passenger's side in the back seat. Why? You can figure that out on your own.

Another story comes to mind. My wife has a friend whose father used to be a professional football coach. One perk was they were furnished automobiles in the team's colors. You could tell which one was Papa Henry's car because it was the one with the tobacco stains down the side. Yipe, he chewed a wee bit.

I do wish you guys would quit getting me off the subject.

Anyway, the ladies went to the town fathers and complained about the tobacco juice on their clothes. They passed an ordinance designed to keep the men from spitting in the street. Nothing in the yellow notes of the hysterical society indicates if the new ordinance was successful or not. I do hope the men who chewed were not required to swallow the spit. Now that can make you sick! That is one way, I guess, to quit using tobacco.

After the turn of the century (19th to 20th), Hogshooter made a dramatic movement into the modern world. The money the small community made in revenue from the oil boom had something to do with it. The city fathers decided a muddy street just wouldn't do for Hogshooter anymore. The village was growing and needed to demonstrate its future by doing something to Main Street besides grading it. Putting in real sidewalks was the solution. The ladies were rumored to being the driving force behind this action.

The question of what type of material used on the street caused a lot of angst during this time. Many locals wanted to build on the oil business and suggested a mixture of tar and gravel. A downside argument was the messiness of the mixture. Until the tar and gravel 'set' it was gooey and got on everything. During the summer, the tar would begin to seep as the temperature began to rise.

One person pushed another argument big time. His name was Rupert (brickhead) Shalepit. You can figure out by the name, brickhead, he came from an Indian background. His ancestors knew of substantial shale deposits in the Sensible County area. They mined the material for use in building materials. Rupert secured the mineral rights to the shale just like you would oil. He started a small but thriving business making bricks for the construction industry. If you look closely at the old buildings on Main Street, you will see they bear the mark of brickhead's company.

Rupert lobbied long and hard for Hogshooter to use his bricks to pave the main drag. He answered the argument about supporting the oil industry by saying he could buy natural gas from the wells to power his kilns. In those days there weren't any gathering systems in place and the natural gas was a nuisance and flared off. That means it was just burned with no attempt to capture and use it.

Brickhead was successful and his brick business became a viable addition to the community. When the railroad came, he used it to market his product to the rest of the area. The problem was there were lots of shalepits around and a lot of places began to make and sell the same product. The final death knell came when the railroad quit serving Hogshooter on a regular basis.

Now don't feel sorry for ol' brickhead. He was no dummy. Not only did he make a lot of money during those days but he also had an artistic side. Rupert knew the brick business wouldn't last forever and he experimented with other uses for the shale clay. He discovered it made a good grade of pottery as well. He refocused his efforts into a small but lucrative niche of making souvenirs. His product was good quality and easy to sell. The company still exists today.

You got me off the subject again.

Like I said, brickhead got the contract to put down a brick street through Hogshooter. Some of the locals argued long and hard that such a material would make the street extremely rough. Rupert answered by saying the cost in the long run would be minimal when compared to the long-term benefit.

Both were right but the cost savings argument won out. Probably all of those local leaders who made that decision have been dead for at least fifty years. Know what? That brick street is still in use and probably will be for at least another half a century. And yes, it is rough. Many other towns in the vicinity have now paved over their brick streets but not Hogshooter. About the only maintenance needed is to replace a cracked brick once in a while. Another benefit emerged. People come by the town to see the street and drive over it. Hogshooter ain't exactly a tourist center but a few people come to experience the brick street. The few shops left indicate these visitors drop a few bucks as well.

The café acquired a little notoriety as well. Some regional magazine identified its chicken fried steak as one of the ten best in this part of the country. It is pretty good. The dang thing covers most of a plate in addition to the mashed potatoes and gravy. Yipe, they still make those pies.

Got me hungry again...

Back to our discussion of Main Street...

Replacing the mud with bricks and sidewalks came just in time. The oil boom descended on Hogshooter like a May tornado. The workers flowed into the town on weekends like locust. Everyone used the new brick street and avoided the others since they remained unimproved. You had horses, wagons, buggies, cars and trucks all vying for the same space. The area could be a madhouse. By this time, electricity had come to the area and a few other amenities as well.

One of the local bigwigs visited a couple of near by cities and noted an improvement instituted in those communities. By the time he did this, the peak of the oil boom crested and workers had already started their migrations to other areas. There was a lot of money made but not for the ordinary person. That didn't make any difference. He decided Hogshooter needed a stop light.

The hysterical society notes describe the momentous day when the leaders of the community stood in the middle of the street at the intersection of Main and Church visualizing the benefits of that hanging light. They were right in realizing that the automobile was not a passing fancy and it would cause all kinds of changes to society. Now whether Hogshooter ever have a problem with the machine still has not been answered to this day.

The meeting almost ended in disaster and what happened was the impetus of the decision to put in the light. Bill (bad breath) Burpee came down the street in his new Ford roadster. Bill was supposed to be at the meeting but forgot about it. Instead, he had gone over the county line to have lunch and a nip of the nectar. That county was wet and a person could get a sip of the juice there. Bad breath had a little more than one nip when he remembered the important meeting at the intersection of Main and Church to discuss the stop light. He had trouble staying awake and he nodded off just as he approached the quorum in the street. Bill jerked back to reality just in time to swerve and miss the crowd. He did clip the Baptist preacher's overcoat and tore it beyond repair. The preacher forgave Bill and said he would say a prayer for his driving.

Bad breath's action cemented the need for the stop light in Hogshooter even though it would not have made any difference with Bill's ruining the preacher's overcoat.

The town purchased one light with an option on several more. No more were ever purchased.

The local paper gave grand coverage of the ceremony turning on the light for the first time. The school kids all came to the intersection with small flags to wave. The Baptist preacher gave the invocation; the Catholic priest dedicated the light; and the

Methodist minister gave the benediction. The Presbyterian preacher was left out. Some in Hogshooter say that was the beginning of religious intolerance in the area. Others maintain that wasn't the case and nothing like that occurred until someone brought a snake to a service. That was never been substantiated. That is a story for another time.

The light was activated after speeches and prayers. Everyone in Hogshooter realized their little town had now reached a special level of significance with that light.

Almost immediately, an undercurrent of discontent began to arise concerning the new fixture. As more and more people began to visit other places with lights the reason became clear. You see, the populace realized their light was difference. Hogshooter contracted with a new firm to make their fixture. In fact, it was the first one the company built. When turned on, green was on top, yellow in the middle and red was on the bottom. The new stop light was the opposite of the fixtures in just about every other place in the world.

It took a while for people to figure out we were different. One group called for a county grand jury investigation to see if anything suspicious took place. Another faction demanded the company replace the light with the right sequence of colors. By this time, the maker had ceased business and the owners absconded from the state.

The issue was a serious one for the community. There was a recall election and one of the city fathers was removed from office. The fact the election cost more than the stop light never entered the minds of these intellectual giants.

One positive thing happened. It opened the lines of communication between the citizens and their leaders. Everyone debated long and hard if the town should keep its special light or purchase a new one to replace it. Because of the cost, the anti-tax faction won and the old light stayed.

Over a period of time, the upside-down light became kind of an attraction. Visitors just looked at it and shook their heads. One unintended benefit did arise in that the light became a revenue source. More than one stranger to town got confused, ran the light and got a ticket. We even had a couple of colorblind individuals ticketed.

When these dastardly criminals pleaded their case in municipal court, they received no mercy. Good thing it wasn't a hanging offense.

My favorite story about the stop light took place when I was in high school. I wasn't old enough to drive but there was always someone to catch a ride with. On one Saturday night I rode with a senior, Herman (hefty) Simile. As you can imagine from his name, he was a big lad. He owned a new car. Anyway, we were cruising Main Street when we stopped at the light. On our right Rodney (ears) McElroy pulled up in his Oldsmobile. Rodney came by his nickname, ears, honestly. If the wind started blowing hard, Rodney had trouble walking. I think the ears may have given someone the idea for hang gliding.

Anyway, there wasn't anyone in town who was a better mechanic than ears. He tuned his Olds to perfection. When Rodney pulled up on the right that meant he wanted to drag race Hefty because there Main Street was only one lane either way. Hefty concurred and indicated the race would be on the count of three. The motors revved; the fingers began to count down; and when the last one went down, Rodney flew through the intersection.

We didn't move. You see the light was still red.

Rodney gave us the middle finger salute when we went by him. Seems the officer on duty saw what happened and ears got a ticket.

Years later, I heard ears had mental problems or ran afoul of the law and got put away. Don't know if that is true but I bet it all stems from the failed drag race at our upside-down stop light.

At least it makes a good story.

The light is gone now. In fact, it has been gone for several years. What happened is interesting. One year for homecoming (the high school still had enough students for a football team in those days), the senior class decided to have a rooster for the theme of their float. Being the oldest class at school, they also decided to make it a giant rooster to show they were the best. The motto on the float said: "The Senior Class: Crowing for a Victory." I remember the float was one of the better ones that homecoming.

During the parade, the judges picked the rooster as the best float and occupied a special place in the line up right after Mrs. Garboe's first grade class. The seniors knew the rooster was tall and the plan was to make just a little zig to the right to clear the stop light. Elmer (bimbam) Burgess was driving that day. He in all seriousness asked if during the homecoming parade he had to stop if the light turned red. The principal assured Elmer he did not.

As he approached the light, disaster struck. The front tire of the tractor pulling the rooster hit a pile of fresh horse droppings the pooper-scoopers missed and Elmer had the steering wheel jump out of this hands. The rooster veered directly into the light, the comb caught and down came the light. A piece of rebar reinforced the comb and it hooked the light. The wire holding the light was rotten and rusted out.

The falling of the light made the front page of the paper with first person interviews describing the disaster. "The light hung like a moth over the flames of hell before it broke loose narrowly missing several onlookers. But, its impetus caused the beacon to smash into the wall of Jasper's Secondhand store causing it to disintegrate and veer into the front window of the butcher shop." With language like that, you wonder why people loved Burl's (the truth) writings. There was talk of a statewide reporting award for best local story. Miss Nilla squashed any hope for an award when she pointed out the language was from the old Puritan Preacher's, Cotton Mather famous sermon, "Sinners in the Hands of an Angry God." Burl (the truth) said he knew that but wanted to see if anyone else remembered it.

Elmer sprang his thumb when the steering wheel whipped out of his hand. The damage was limited to the front window of the butcher shop. A rumor circulated around Hogshooter that that the rooster had real chickens inside it and the butcher shop kept them to pay for the damages.

Anyway, the headline in the Violet paper read: "Rooster lays an egg in Hogshooter." Burl (the truth) wrote an editorial against this headline pointing out that roosters don't lay eggs. I tell you what, that man never misses a thing.

There was discussion the next Monday at the café concerned whether a grand jury should be called to investigate the incident. The discussion died when no one offered to buy a second cup of coffee.

Elmer went on to be a success story. He joined the Army and became a heavy machinery operator. After he got out of the service, Elmer came back to Sensible County and bought a bulldozer plus a backhoe. He served the community well over the years. With that backhoe, Elmer could dig the best graves around. Let's face it every community needs someone like him. I saw him here while back and he told me his thumb still hurts when the weather gets damp and raw.

There has been talk over the years that the rooster debacle was the basis of the finale of the movie, *Animal House.* You will remember the Deltas interrupting the homecoming parade at Faber College. As far as I can tell, that is just a rumor and not based on fact. Makes a good story though.

All this reminds me when I was going to school over at the non-denominational Bible junior college (I will discuss this remarkable institution in some detail later). When I didn't attend the meeting for the election of sophomore class officers, my friends elected me president. One of my duties was to oversee the building of the basketball homecoming float. We always borrowed a hay wagon from a local farmer and used it to build the float on. Being a rural community, there was never a problem getting one. The class built this magnificent something and placed it in the parade. Because of the proximity to Thanksgiving, a local student agreed to return the wagon after the float was stripped. I went home knowing everything had been taken care of.

The student government sponsor was an old codger who wouldn't let us do anything without checking with the administration. What a jerk. Anyway, when I came back on Sunday, there was a letter waiting for me. It seems I had been charged with negligence (the other guy forgot to take the wagon back) and the sponsor wanted me kicked out of school. He was trying to save his rear because he messed up big time. Seems diphead (yipe) hooked the wagon up to his black Chevy (no extras of course) to return it. He misjudged a turn and broke the tongue off the wagon. I got blamed for diphead's mistake.

I was hot. I went over to the VP for Student Affairs' office and he just shook his head and laughed. Nothing happened but diphead and I don't get along to this day.

Oh, by the way, the city never replaced the stop light. The town put one of those 4-way stop signs in the middle of the intersection. Still there today and the foreboding doom for the lack of a stop light never materialized.

Fun Stuff

I 'm tired talking about Main Street. There is more stuff in the mystical yellow notes about it. Maybe I will come back later. The hysterical society does have information about fun things of Hogshooter. I even remember some of them myself. Most are gone now and that is a shame. What I liked most were harmless and didn't cost a whole lot.

Here while back I was digging through some old stuff of my dad's and I came across a picture of the Hogshooter baseball team. The picture I saw was from 1907, the year my father was born. My grandfather was in the picture. The field was over at the school and was the same one the kids still use. All of the little towns had teams and they took turns going over to the others' place. I bet they had some good disagreements over the umpire's calls. The players didn't have matching uniforms. Some had on ball pants while some just wore overalls. Rather than ball caps, two of the players had on bowlers. One guy even had on a tie. The ball gloves just barely covered their hands and the team only had two bats. I am not sure but they may have been carved out of a limb.

Later on, dad played on a team. They were apparently good because they had uniforms. Across the front were the letters 'WOW.' That stood for Woodmen of the World, an insurance company. Dad must have been quite a player because the St. Louis Cardinals talked to him about playing minor league baseball. In those days, there were minor league teams all over the place. Now, there is only a fraction of that number. What made dad unique was he batted cross handed. I saw him play softball later in life and he could hit. I don't know how he kept from breaking his wrists.

My father was a religious man and while he smoked Lucky Strikes for a lot of his life, I never saw them take a drink. He admitted he did before he died. One time the team was playing a double header. Between games, a few of the boys decided to have a nip or two and they talked dad into trying the hooch. He did not know how to drink and had a little too much. The rotgut made him sicker than a dog. Dad never drank again.

In the early days of Hogshooter's summer, the only place you could cool off was at the creek. The most popular area was around the low water dam. I came across a picture of a bunch of people taking advantage of the water. I thought most of these people were kids but that was not the case. While there were some teenagers, most were adults. Ain't no speedos there. The men wore full swimsuits including tee shirts with trunks ending above the knees. The womenfolk wore what looks like full-length dresses and leggings. I know it was swimming gear because the ladies had on bathing caps.

Below the dam were outcroppings of rocks. These extended quite a ways down the creek. Some deep pools remained full of water all of the time. During the early days of Hogshooter, this area became the site of another fishing sport—noodling for catfish. I only tried this one time and decided I wanted no part of the sport when I actually touched a fish.

What you do is feel around under the ledges or in holes until you find a catfish. Then you try to get your hand in the catfish's mouth and pull him out. For those of you who don't know about such things, their teeth are like sandpaper and can take off a layer or two of skin in a second. Below the dam, noodling ain't too bad. There are guys now who go into deep water of lakes and river to get the fish. I am talking about 50 to 75 pounders. I read in the paper recently where one man drowned while fishing this way. There are even tournaments for noodlers. More power to these people. I guess fun is in the eye of the beholder.

I read somewhere or maybe I made it up I don't remember, that these noodlers actually caught enough fish to have a community fish fry in Hogshooter. I think it was in conjunction with July 4th. Afterwards, the town put on a fireworks display.

Late in the summer every year, a carnival came to Hogshooter. One of the service clubs sponsored it and used the profits to support its community projects. You can imagine what type of a carnival would come to our little burg. Still, nobody cared. Many former residents came back every summer. It functioned kind of like a homecoming. When I was little, grandma and mom packed a lunch and we spent the whole day. For a kid it was great fun. The community band and singers put on a concert and there was local entertainment. I'll come back to the local bands later. It wasn't like the county fair because there wasn't any livestock. That event took place in the fall.

As a kid, I looked for the spicier side of life. My big brothers told me the lady carnies did other things to earn money. I looked in awe at these "unique" women and wondered what they did once it got dark: Nothing probably.

We called the event the picnic and broke up the monotony of a Hogshooter summer.

I mentioned already the pool hall. It possessed the reputation of being an unsavory place. Mom told me not go there. The older kids snuck (that is when you really sneak) off and headed there. I finally got in and was disappointed. As I mentioned before, Ol' Slim Smith and his two-piece pool cue ran the place. He made a little money hustling locals but strangers occasionally taught him a lesson. Slim made his money just keeping the place clean and taking everyone's money to use the tables.

There were both pool and snooker tables. Snooker is a more sophisticated game with smaller pockets. The pool hall did not have air conditioning. You picked the cue you wanted from a rack on the wall. Above each table was a string of beads to keep score.

The best thing about the pool hall was its mystique. I don't ever remember a girl there. Some of the tougher guys came in just to bully people around. Slim sold cigarettes to anyone within reason. There were no age restrictions in those days. Me and my buddies bought a pack and smoked all of them before we left. There was one of those pop chests where you put ice on top of the bottles like Dode Phipps used to have in his store. I always bought a double cola. Never drank a double cola anywhere else. I guess it was the pool hall drink. Slim didn't serve alcohol because Sensible County was a dry county.

Several domino tables sat in one corner. The old men came and played for hours. I used to think dominos was a simple game with little or no skill. I smarted off to one of these old farts and he invited me to sit down and play a game. He gave me a new appreciation for dominos. Spittoons sat around the tables because most of the old men chewed. Many of them didn't have any teeth anyway. This area of the pool hall always smelled bad because they missed the spittoons about half the time. The old codgers didn't help because they always passed a lot of gas. As I may have mentioned before, I believe we could feed old men beans and then harass the gas so there would be no energy shortage in this country.

Like so many things in downtown Hogshooter, the pool hall began to fall in disrepair. The old men died and the younger ones found something else to do. I don't know how many of you have seen the great movie, *The Last Picture Show*. If you have, you will remember how run-down Sam the Lion's pool hall got. Well, that is what the one in Hogshooter became. Finally, it shut its doors like so many other businesses on Main Street. I can still visualize the establishment as if it was yesterday.

Hogshooter had a bowling alley. What made ours unique was that it shared the same building as the skating rink. I asked around and found out they appeared during the oil boom. The owner, Charlie (pinhead) Stryker (I ain't kidding) realized the roughnecks and needed something to do and somewhere to spend their money. The quickest and the fastest way to do this was the combination of the two forms of recreation.

I remember them before they burned down about fifty years ago. Dang, sure seems like a lot of things burned down in Hogshooter. Remember as I said before, the motto of the volunteer fire department is 'we have never lost a lot.' Since I am now a member of that group, I can comment on it. Seriously, we try our best and everyone in town knows it.

Pinhead's bowling alley only had four lanes but they were busy all the time during those early years. There weren't any automatic pinsetters. Some poor smuck manually set the pins in the machines and lowered them onto the lane. Then he cleared the knocked down pins and put the bowling ball back into the return. They worked two lanes at once and it was hot work because there wasn't any air conditioning. The balls weighed sixteen pounds and the repetition took its toll. My brother worked there for a while one summer and I went to help him. Didn't take me long to figure out that manual labor wasn't for me. I was going to college. In just the short time, I was sweaty and smelled like a horse.

When the lanes first opened, there weren't many laws about the selling of alcohol. I know, I know, for a while there was prohibition. The reality was during this time at the bowling alley you could get about anything you wanted and that included booze. The serving of alcohol was about the least of the problems law enforcement faced. I mean the above statement. I was told by some of the old guys that for a price the local loquacious beauties let a fellow play with their pins.

A couple of notorious events in Hogshooter's history took place at the bowling alley. One is humorous and the other isn't. Someone who was actually there told me the funny one. The event didn't make into Burl's (the truth) newspaper probably because he was involved. It happened when he was very young man and trying to impress the ladies (don't know if Nilla was one of them or not).

After a considerable amount of liquid refreshments, several of the horny youngsters in town began to show off like bull elk attempting to attract Bambi's mother. None of them had success. Things began to get more and more flamboyant as more booze flowed. Finally, one of the idiots bet the others that he could knock down more pins with his head then they could. Don't take much imagination to figure out what came next. The boys took off their shoes and took turns running as fast as they could down the alley diving headfirst into the pins. Despite the whooping and hollering, management didn't figure out what was going on until it was too late. One of the honor roll graduates hit the head pin straight on and split his noggin wide open. Blood was everywhere. So here is this guy laying on the lane dead drunk and laughing with red spurting everywhere. One of the other geniuses picked up a bowling ball and tossed it down the alley. The poor drunken sucker was spread eagle and that ball hit him right in the family jewels. Not only did he have to his head stitched up but had to wear a truss for support. About a week later, the swelling went down and he could wear pants again.

The other incident was not funny because it involved a shooting. In retrospect, maybe it was a little funny. Seems a townie (someone who lived in Hogshooter) was bowling. Since there were only four lanes, people often had to share one. A cowboy from a local ranch came in town on a Saturday night with his girl friend. The proprietor put him on the same lane as the townie. From time to time, there was tension between the two groups anyway. As the evening progressed and the booze flowed, the two began to dig at each other. The townie also began to eye the cowboy's date. She was a looker.

The cowboy finally told the townie that if he didn't quit drooling he was going to knock his teeth out so he'd have more room for the spit. It was the townie turn to bowl and during his swing the ball flew backwards and landed on the cowboy's foot. The cowboy swore the townie threw the ball on purpose. He got his pistol from his date's bag and shot at the townie. It hit in the left arm. When the police got there to sort out what happened, the cowboy said he was provoked and in fear of his life because of the possibility of another bowling ball being hurled in his direction. Does that sound like his attorney talking or what?

The townie said the ball just slipped out of his hand. He had a little difficulty explaining how it flew ten feet in the air before hitting the cowboy's foot. Both men ended up doing time in jail. The cowboy's boss was a big landowner who bailed him out.

After that incident, alcohol wasn't served at the alley and most problems stopped. Hogshooter did have one famous bowler. His name was Brutus (the thumb) Thomas. He made it all the way to the state finals one year. The army drafted him and he spent his two years in special services bowling for his base. The thumb never returned to Hogshooter. Some say he read Tom Robbins cult classic, *Even Cowgirls Get the Blues,* about a girl with extraordinary sized thumbs and Brutus decided to try to cash in on his strength. No one heard from him again.

When the bowling alley became outdated and pinhead decided he wasn't going to put in automatic pinsetters, he made that part of the building into an arcade and a snack bar. That move was a good complement to the skating rink on the other side.

During the oil boom and before pinhead bought it out, the skating rink doubled as a boarding house. I am not kidding. The owner bought a bunch of surplus cots and when the rink closed at night, he rented out the cots for a buck a night and made a killing. The town did not have anywhere for the roughnecks so this arrangement worked well for the workers.

By the time pinhead got it, the boom days were over. Was not much of anything to do because television wasn't around or people couldn't afford to buy one. The skating rink did a good business even though it was open only two or three days a week. Man, do I remember doing the hokey pokey plus girls' choice and spotlight skates. I witnessed one of the most painful things I ever saw at the rink. There was a little guy about eight or nine-years-old skating. He went into the bathroom. After he finished, he stepped back and fell down. Another kid came skating by and ran over his tally whacker. I never had as much sympathy for anyone in my life as I did him. There he sat on the front steps of the rink with his legs apart and crying as he waited for his mother. Everyone felt sorry for him.

I never was good enough to have my own skates. They cost more than my family could afford. I was envious of the kids owned theirs. The girls' skates were usually white with tassels or fuzzy balls on them. These kids usually didn't play sports or do much of anything. They flew around the rink during the races. They were good. As I think back on it, they usually took a break and went out to have a smoke. I am glad I didn't have my own skates.

As television and other distractions came along, fewer people went skating. You will remember me saying fire destroyed the building. The fire department never bothered to find out what caused it because no one cared if an old building burnt down in Hogshooter. If it had happened in a large town, there would have been an investigation.

Pinhead said all the right words about rebuilding. Nobody in town took him seriously. Everyone heard the promise to rebuild before. When he bought a new Cadillac with the insurance money that closed the history of the bowling alley and the skating rink.

We had a theater for years. After I left home, it closed. Just another indication that Hogshooter was dying I guess. The yellow notes say quite a bit about the Theatorium. Strange name. Originally, the place showed movies where the whole community could gather. The early pictures of it are stunning. It had an art deco look about it. The inside was beautiful when it first opened. The early movies were silent and an accompanist played a piano or organ with the movie.

The most ornate movie theater I ever saw was in El Paso, Texas. When stationed there in the army, a group of us would catch a bus downtown. I cannot remember the name of the theater but every Sunday evening a sneak prevue showed. The ceiling looked like the stars were out when the lights would dim. Between movies, a man playing an organ rose out of the orchestra pit. I have never seen anything like it. During the era of silent movies, I can imagine the theaters in larger cities having something like this. Several years later, I returned and the theater was showing Spanish language movies. I have often wondered if that organ still came up out of the floor. I doubt it.

My first memories of the Theatorium were the Saturday afternoon movies. At least three movies and maybe a serial or two showed then. Of course, there was the news and a cartoon. I got my first indoctrination to Hopalong Cassidy there. Later, when we finally got a television, he was on some nights at 6:30. Hoppy was my hero and I have some of his movies even today. There was just something genuine about Hoppy. His horse's name was Topper. When he died, William Boyd, who played Hoppy, never rode another horse. That is loyalty. Some of the other heroes I remember were Bob Steele, Wild Bill Elliott, Lash LaRue, and Eddie Dean (the singing cowboy). Kids packed the place.

The rest of the week, the movies were a little more sophisticated. I remember going to see *Pony Express* for 14 cents. One day, school was called off for snow. I went and saw *Calamity Jane* with Doris Day. In those days, no one made you leave between shows so I stayed and saw it three times. I remember going to see *Davy Crockett*. Gosh, I sure wanted to have a coonskin cap to wear but we couldn't afford it.

When I got a little older, I went to the movies in the evening. I rode my bike downtown. No one was going to bother you in Hogshooter. We never even thought about locking up our bikes. If someone stole it, we would go find it and gang up on whoever took it. I always wanted to sit in the balcony. To do that you had to have a date. So, that had to wait a while. Must say I was disappointed with what didn't take place up there. The mystical place wasn't that special.

Fewer and fewer people went to the movie in Hogshooter. Many families moved to survive. The owner tried to stay in business with the theater only open in the evenings and finally only on the weekends.

The old façade of the Theatorium was magnificent. There was

talk a few years ago of trying to restore it or have it declared a historical building. The hysterical society looked into the process but took no action. As hard as it was to admit, a small dying town with no money simply cannot save itself.

Now it sits empty but full of memories. I thought about going down there and seeing if I could get in somehow. If there were still seats, maybe I would sit there and think about those old movies and the people who used to watch them. I might even bring a six-pack to help me.

It's time to be honest here. One reason the movie theater wasn't nearly as popular as it used to be, especially in a small town during the summer, was the opening of the local drive in. All of us hot blooded high school kids preferred going there during the summer. The name of our local drive in was the Night Owl. The locals just called it "the pit." In the days before improved contraception, ol' Doc Needle used to say more children were conceived at the pit than in the beds of Hogshooter. I know one thing Mae Reba was a popular person on Wednesday evenings.

Wednesday was dollar night at the Night Owl. As many people as you could pack into a car got in for a dollar. There were times when there was nowhere to park and watch (?) the movie. People from all of Sensible County congregated there. Every once in a while, a few fights broke out. If the weather was wet or cold, some of the windows of the autos fogged up. I wonder what was going on behind the opaqueness?

Some of the older kids brought booze in. When the weather was nice, no one stayed in the cars anyway unless a serious conversation was taking place behind those windows. You heard the distinctive "ping" of a beer can hitting the ground every few minutes. An empty beer bottle breaking might echo in the parking area as well. I knew of more than one tire suffering being a cut from a broken beer bottle. At times there was so much latex on the ground car tires couldn't get friction and they spun until they got some traction.

Daylight savings time really dug into attendance at the Owl. The weekends were still okay. That was when people hid in the trunk or in the floor to sneak in. The kids selling or taking the tickets didn't care because it was a wee bit suspicious when a guy pulled up alone in his car.

One could also just sneak in. That wasn't hard but you might not have a place to sit. Benches surrounded the concession stand so sitting there was an option. Most of the time, we hunted for a friend's car with unfogged windows.

Chester Something (yes, another one) wanted to go to the Owl one weekend but his parents told him to baby sit his little brother Simple. He threw a fit but his parents said he could take him if he wanted to go. Chester didn't have any money so he decided to sneak in the back way. In order to get there, he walked over a raised railroad track cutting across the local stockyards. Chester told his little brother if a train came by he would hang down until it passed. While he was hanging there, be sure and watch out for the bulls in the stockyard because they had recently gored two kids dangling there waiting for the train to pass.

Chester was cruel, wasn't he?

He was an ornery sucker. Chester went to see the original movie of *The Thing*. You know the one where James Arness played the monster. I have to admit, that movie kept me from sleeping a few nights. Anyway, the Somethings lived out in the country and had a bunch of dogs. One evening when Chester was alone with Simple the dogs started barking like there was no tomorrow. Chester told Simple that meant the monster was coming to their house. He proceeded to throw his screaming little brother out the door. Chester was laughing so hard he almost peed his pants. Simple did. It got deathly quiet in a few minutes and Chester began to get worried. He slowly opened the door but didn't see his little brother.

To make a long story short, Simple ran into the woods to get away from the monster. Chester found him thirty minutes later. Not only had Simple wet his pants but a skunk sprayed him. Chester wasn't out much the rest of the summer. Seemed he earned the right to stay at home.

Chester left home right after he graduated from high school. He didn't get drafted because Simple bit off his trigger finger in another fight. You have to have a trigger finger to fire a rifle. Rumor has it that Chester headed to California and opened a string of hamburger stands. I heard he experimented with topless servers. The yellow notes do not elaborate on that. Something else I heard about Chester was he became a sanitation worker. He was so successful that he bought several trucks and got some lucrative routes. Chester originally put "flaming maggot wagon" on his trucks. Someone complained and he removed it. After he changed his motto to "ain't no flies on my trucks." That motto still graces the trucks today. I recently heard he had started mining old dumps for natural gas.

Oh, I guess I strayed a little a field again. I need to mention some of Sensible County's successful citizens.

Brother Dooby of the Apostolic Brethren Church of the Holy Spirit attempted to get the pit closed down as part of his sermon series called "the sins of Sensible County." The only problem was his sermon series touched on about every thing and everyone. He included the schools, the sheriff, the pool hall, Miss Nilla's library and the other churches in Hogshooter. That all changed when Burl (the truth) ran the story on Brother Dooby's sordid background at Bible college. That is another story.

Like other things in Hogshooter, the drive in just went away on its own. Violet opened a new concept in movies. The cars parked in a circle about a central building. Each car had its own screen on which the movie was projected. I never did like it. The idea never had the same effect on me as the pit. I know it was gone before I returned to Sensible County. Now that I think about it, many things disappeared from Hogshooter by the time I returned home.

The final days of the Night Owl came from Mother Nature. I guess Brother Dooby said God took care of it. Anyway, a tornado or maybe just a strong wind came through one night and knocked down the screen. Like everything else that went away during these years, there was no reason to rebuild it.

Main Street (Again)

I know, I know, you are probably thinking how in the world a person can squeeze anything else out of this topic. Hogshooter has so much on Main Street and most of it is downright boring. I dang near agreed with you but as the Lee Marvin character in *Paint Your Wagon* told Partner (Clint Eastwood) "sometimes I get melancholy." Well, a fit of melancholy hit me and I realized the story of Hogshooter would not be complete without more.

Some stuff I will go into didn't make it into the hysterical notes. That doesn't mean it ain't important. Besides, I needed to find a place to introduce you to some of the unforgettable characters of our community.

Way back earlier, I mentioned the Remarkable brothers, Jimmie and James, and their bank. I need to review some pertinent facts concerning the bank. You remember their father, Jimmie James Remarkable (no lie), bought the original business from Dode Phipps. For the early part of its existence, the bank occupied a corner of the general store. JJ (I will call the elder this to avoid confusion), had his eye on his own building. After a few years, the germ began to grow into fruition (dang that is good). A corner lot was available so he snapped it up.

JJ talked with brickhead and he agreed to produce a special dye to color the building material. The color would only be used for the bank. He took a rough set of plans out of a banking magazine and convinced nailhead Dozer's father, hammerhead, to erect the edifice.

The progress of the structure was the main entertainment on Main Street for months. People studied and discussed everything including the next step in the construction. The café provided a good view of the site. When the weather was nice, the balcony over the café was available for viewing. The old men's coffee club spent many an hour there watching the bank's progress. The café instituted a minimum requirement to sit up there. One had to buy at least two cups of coffee and one cinnamon roll to qualify for the view. There was even talk of adding a reservation service for the prime seats.

The use of the terrace almost ended when Ol' Buzz Wintermole (bird's uncle) waited too long to go down the stairs after three cups of coffee. Buzz never had strong kidneys and while watching an intricate piece of carpentry work suddenly felt Mother Nature working. As he hurried down the steps from the terrace, Buzz tripped and went head over heels. According to bird, Buzz got scraped up pretty bad but only broke his little finger. He did lose control and it took a while for the smell to clear.

There was talk of lawsuits by both parties but that ebbed when Buzz agreed to not go back to the terrace and limit his coffee intake to two cups. The café agreed to reserve a front table on the first floor for Buzz with a twenty-four-hour notice. But a two-hour limit applied.

Bird always loved the Olympics. Years later, he recounted the incident to Burl (the truth) for the yellow notes of the hysterical society. Bird said looking back on the tumble he could only give his uncle a 7.2 because he didn't land with his feet together when he hit the bottom of the stairs. This comment elicited some discussion about the incident's inclusion in the annuals. Bird's description remained in chronicles even though they noted he suffered from bouts of dementia during this part of his life.

Back to the bank building--JJ's idea for his bank was sound.

The Tuesday his vault arrived was a special day. The grade school kids viewed the installation and watched as it came down Main Street. The company that made the vault supervised its installation. Even though it took more than two hours, Buzz stayed the whole time and watched from his front table seat in the café. Everyone agreed that the Remarkable Bank would truly be a remarkable bank.

The color of the brick generated some discussion. You will remember that brickhead devised a special color dye for the bank's bricks. The actual hue was not quite as it appeared before it was mixed with the clay and fired in the kiln. A special mason laid the brick. Terry (trowelhead) Something was sort of a legend in Sensible County. He laid brick on projects as far away as Louisville. Trowelhead was good. After about ten rows of bricks, the crowd began to murmur and someone went and got JJ. The color was unique. He did not know what to think. Then Sweetness Remarkable (JJ's wife) whispered into his ear that she liked the color. That settled any possible controversy and the unusual color for the bank stayed. Sweetness was overhead telling her gaggle of friends the pink bank would attract customers. I don't know about attracting depositors but it sure did draw a lot of comments. The Violet newspaper once again cast aspersions on its smaller neighbor brandishing the pink bank as an attempt of a dying community to attract attention. Lord knows what it would have said had the editor come over and saw the pink marble from Carthage, Missouri, that graced the inside of the lobby. Sweetness picked the marble in case you had not figured that out. Some say that was the basis of her sons' shortcomings.

Ah, Jimmie and James—now there were a pair of remarkable individuals (pun intended). JJ groomed them to take over the Remarkable Bank. They were different from birth. Sweetness always dressed them like little gentlemen and they never mixed with the common kids of Sensible County. Every time one of the local ruffians caught either one, the boys got the snot beat out of them. By the time they started school, Sweetness retreated to St. Louis where they remained until they finished college. Once in a while they returned home for a visit but that was about it.

JJ didn't really seem to mind that his wife and kids were not around. Seems he made other arrangements for female companionship during this time. Sweetness didn't care because it allowed her to "expose" James and Jimmie to the proper environment. JJ once commented that he was not sure the boys belonged to him because of their "sissyfied" appearance and expression.

When the old man died, the boys returned to Hogshooter and the bank. Sweetness did not move back because she felt her place was in proper society. JJ was smart and set everything up in trust. The boys could either return to Sensible County and run the bank or be cut off. The trust was very specific as to what happened to the money if James and Jimmie didn't run the Remarkable Bank.

They settled down and became leading citizens of Hogshooter and Sensible County. No one ever saw the boys with female companionship. The rumor mill said it each had a companion "around" but no one ever saw them. I use the term companion on purpose because the nature of James and Jimmie's sexuality remained unsolved until they died. The rumor persisted they were hermaphrodites. That meant the boys possessed sets of both male and female sex organs. I don't know if that is true or not but it sure makes for great small-town gossip.

JJ built the most exquisite house in town. Lush rose gardens surrounded it and the house was the centerpiece of Sensible County. Apparently, the trust called for the boys to live in the house. As they grew older, other rumors circulated they could not agree on anything. Don't get me wrong, they were pillars of the community and supported all the noble causes. You remember me telling you earlier about Miss Nilla working at the bank and being able to get just about anything she wanted.

This leads to another conspiracy theory that both were in love with Nilla and she played James and Jimmie against each other. I heard stories of her leaving their house in the middle of the night. I tried to confirm this with Burl (the truth) but was not able to do so.

Anyway, the boys just could not get along as they grew older. Nailhead says he contracted to redo the house and the brothers could not agree on that. Jimmie drew up his plans and James drew up his. Nailhead executed both the way the brothers wanted. The division became evident to the whole community. James wanted his outside brick painted but Jimmie wanted his cleaned. Completed, the outside of the house had two different finishes with a demilitarized zone (DMZ) of sorts going right down the middle of the house. When the final brother died some years ago, the community got a look at the inside. It was bizarre to say the least. For example, the kitchen was divided into two parts with each side having the same appliances but in different styles. James and Jimmie deeded the old house to the hysterical society for its county museum.

In searching the yellow notes, there is only one bank robbery mentioned. Maybe thieves were too overcome with the pink bricks and marble to rob it. The lone recorded crime took place about twenty or twenty-five years ago. Hogshooter still had a police officer in those days. Granted he didn't work much but he left his squad car parked in front of the bank.

The dastardly deed took place on a cold February day. The local officer was on funeral duty escorting the cortege to a small cemetery about ten miles out of town. Snow started spitting early in the morning. By the afternoon, it was a regular blizzard. Most all the businesses and the local schools closed early but not the Remarkable Bank. Jimmie was home sick that day so James and one teller stayed in the bank.

The door opened and in came a rather large man wearing a ski mask and overalls neither of which was unusual this time of the year. He walked over to James and told him it was a robbery and for him to fork over all the bills. The conversation went something like this:

James: "I ain't going to give you any money."

Robber: "I got a gun and you better give me all your bills or someone is going to get hurt."

James: "No."

Robber: "Now dammit, James, give your money or I am going to shoot you."

James reconsidered given the fact the robber knew him by name, turned over all the bills. The robber thanked him and disappeared into the blizzard. By the time some sort of peace officer got there, the culprit was long gone. The description was no help because half the county wore overalls. Snow covered up all the tracks. The robbery remains a mystery until today. One of the boys at the café thought it might make a good television movie called "the mystery of the overalls bandit." The incident didn't seem to catch anyone's attention in Hollywood.

Another theory sprouted later in the community. It centered on the brothers robbing their own bank. Ammie Ula (AU) Wintermole on her annual expedition to spend Bird's money swore she saw Jimmie on the beach in Hawaii after James had died. He had both a sweet young lady and boy with him. No one could confirm this sighting or the bank robbery connection but it might explain the validity of his sexual orientation.

I do have to give the boys credit. They saw the community dying so they unloaded the bank. The Feds closed the bank several years after the boys sold it. There was talk of fraud on the part of James and Jimmie but no investigation followed. When they died, the boys had spent about all their money and the rest went to several county organizations. As I mentioned before, their unusual house was the biggest asset and it went to the hysterical society.

A couple of people tried to reopen a business in the old bank building but nothing stuck. Finally, the local beauty and barbershop bought it for almost nothing and moved into it. It remains there today and is making a go of it.

Emma Lou and Lou Emma are the present owners of the establishment. The girls are the second generation of the prominent hairdressing family, the Curlers (I ain't lying). Their mother, Curly

Sue Curler, always wanted to be a hairdresser. She attended the Senatobia College of Hairdressing and Fingernail Care. Her diploma proudly hangs on the wall of the Cinderella Salon and Beauty Factory in the old bank building.

Curly Sue's business wasn't always located there but was first next to the old library building straddling the county line. Over the years, she became quite a legend in the area for her coiffures. Once a week, she went over to the nursing home and did hair there. Curly Sue viewed this as her community duty making sure anyone who wanted pretty hair had it. Later, she convinced her sister, Nellie (rednails) Curler to join her and do finger plus toenails. Her nickname (rednails) came from the fact she always wore bright red polish. Her motto was "if you got it, flaunt it." Nellie was self-taught but had the nicest stroke in Sensible County when she applied the polish.

Curly Sue became involved with Slick (scissorhead) Savage not soon after she came to Hogshooter. Slick of course was a barber. He was bald as a cucumber. Their mutual occupations just brought them together so to speak. The two hair professionals soon married and the twins, Emma Lou and Lou Emma, were born. With this genetic stuff flowing in their veins, no one doubted what occupation the girls would follow.

They chose to shun their mother's alma mater and instead went to the Silver Spur Institute of Beauty and Cosmetology. Given their genes, the girls shared the valedictorian award for the second quarter of that year. Their rewarded was a new pair of scissors and a dye kit.

By this time, Cinderella moved into the old bank building. What a beautiful palace. With the pink brick and marble, Curley Sue continued the color scheme on the inside. Everything was pink. Everyone who worked there had pink outfits. Well, not everyone because Slick would have none of it (the barbershop also moved to the pink palace).

After the girls returned, Curley Sue and Slick slowly began to turn over their businesses to them. They looked back in pride at what they accomplished. Curley took full credit for inventing that reddish/pink tint that all the little old ladies at the nursing home had. Slick took pride that the pink palace gave the best mullet in Sensible County.

Emma Lou and Lou Emma built on this heritage and added things like sparkling dust to the girls' make up and hair for the local high school proms. They volunteered to give hairdos and haircuts once a month at the county jail. The girls felt good hair was the secret to keeping people from repeating their criminal activities. Lou Emma became proficient in doing corpses and she was in demand by funeral parlors in the surrounding country. She made a corpse's hair look downright alive. Emma Lou would have none of that but learned how to give a decent mullet. That talent came from her daddy.

The twins are both married and have kids of their own. They have both girls and boys. It's already rumored the girls have their hearts set on following their mothers and grandmother into the hair business. One is already learning eyebrow threading to earn a little extra money while she is in high school.

While Hogshooter for the most part is slowly dying, that isn't true for the beauty salon business. A good hairdo never goes out of style. In Sensible County, bigger truly is better.

One incident did take place at the pink palace that one might say threatened the serenity of the hair business. Peebles Overlook spent all of her life in Sensible County. Rocky, as she was called by the boys, married a local man and had a small but vigorous family. Peebles always had a rather strange streak in her. Some attributed that to the rumor her mother was raped as a teenager and her uncle was really her father. This was never substantiated but for some reason was left in the yellow notes.

Rocky always had her hair done at the pink palace. Like most of the women in Hogshooter, she possessed a standing appointment. Peebles went through an extended period when she was a blonde. I don't want to start any rumors either but I always wondered if the longer a person (yeah, men do to) used peroxide to bleach his or her hair effected their brains and altered their behavior. This hypothesis is something some righteous young scholar might want to study.

There was a time when Peebles' hair was as tall as any woman's in the county. It was truly a work of art. Several years ago, there was even a discussion for a new prize category at the county fair. The thought was to encourage the hard-working hairdressers of Sensible County to create masterpieces. The judging was on height, novelty and use of hair spray to support the do. Burl (the truth) in an unsober comment even suggested contacting one of those cable channels to gauge interest in a reality series based on the premise. After all, if the Tulsa State Fair got national coverage for its cake making there was no reason the Sensible County Fair's great coiffure festival couldn't to the same.

Nothing came of the idea after Burl (the truth) sobered up. Anyway, there was no doubt Peebles hair would have been right in the middle of the contest. Curley Sue always said Rocky's hair was special and its body was especially formidable. To prove it, Curly Sue created a special Empire State Building look. That tower of hair was the pride of Hogshooter and Burl (the truth) featured the 'do' the next week in the newspaper. Others picked up the photo nationally and it appeared all over the county. The hair was so tall Peebles couldn't get into her car and she drove the family tractor until her next appointment.

The point of this is to show the pride that woman had in her hair. You will remember that Peebles acted a wee bit weird as well. You can imagine the uproar at the pink palace when Rocky came in for her appointment and announced she wanted all of her hair cut off. Lou Emma called over Emma Lou and the sisters quizzed Rocky about her wish. She replied she was sure so Lou Emma cut off those magnificent tresses. Supposedly, there was four inches of hair around the chair when the cut was finished.

At her next appointment, Peebles came in breathing fire. She wanted to know why her beautiful hair was gone. Lou Emma called Emma Lou over and the girls explained to Rocky what happened. She refused to believe their explanation and as with most controversies in Sensible County she threatened a grand jury investigation plus a lawsuit. The threat was serious and the pink palace sought guidance from the local barrister.

Nothing ever came of the controversy except that Peebles disappeared for a while. There was much speculation in the community as to why but no one was sure of the reason. Suddenly, one day she was back in town and acting as if nothing had happened.

The truth finally did come out. Peebles suffered from schizophrenia eliciting two personalities. One personality didn't like her hair and wanted it cut. The other one loved her hair and became agitated when the girls cut it. This diagnosis explained the fact that during this timeframe Rocky was observed walking down the street arguing with herself. While this behavior was not out of place in Hogshooter, it did seem unusual for Peebles.

Her return to normalcy is due to her medication. As long as she takes it, Peebles is her old self. Every so often, she wants a mean streak so she quits taking the medicine. This is a rumor.

I need to mention the Dairy Dilly. Technically, it is not really on Main Street. It has special status since the Dilly is still in existence with a good base of customers. The business gives the café downtown a run for its money. The Dairy Dilly features more of a fast-food clientele one might say. A lot of kids go there but it has regulars as well. Growing up, I remember during the summer visiting it several times a week. We went after church on Sunday and Wednesday evenings. This was kind of a bribe my parents used to get us to church without complaining or saying we were sick.

I had two favorites during the summer. The first was a hot fudge sundae with pecans on top. I always tried to get extra hot fudge because there ain't too many things better than the chocolate as it turns chewy with the ice cream. Don't get me wrong because I can still take a half gallon of good chocolate ice cream from the supermarket and a with a spoon put a major dent in the carton while watching television. Peanut butter and chocolate ice cream is not too bad either. Okay, okay, I admit it. There aren't very many types of the frozen dessert I don't like.

My other favorite ice cream from the Dairy Dilly is a soft cone dipped in warm chocolate syrup forming a crust on the outside. The eater needs to be careful because the crust breaks off and you might lose a chunk. I got the chocolate mess on my good clothes.

One non-ice cream item on the menu always grabbed me. That was its foot long chili cheese dog. Add an order of curly fries and wow what a totally useless meal. That chili left a mean stain on your clothes though. Mom never had any doubt where I had been when I came home with a big ol' greasy spot on my shirt. Add in a stain from your fresh squeezed cherry limeade and a pretty good meal was displayed. We'd sneak off from high school during lunch to eat the drippings. You kept it from falling on your clothes or it was off to the principal's office for a lie to cover your tracks. "You see, my grandmother is not well so I decided I would go to the nursing home for a few minutes at lunch. Who knows how much longer granny will live. She loves for me to bring her a snack and doesn't like to eat alone. A little of the food much have soiled my shirt." Now if you had some real guts you might add something like: "I was holding my food in one hand and was reading from the Bible. That little bit of chili must have slid off the bun and hit my shirt."

They knew I was lying. I got a too cocky one time and I over did the Bible bit. The high school office called my mom and she told them the truth. Not only did I get in trouble at school but at home also. She made me go to the nursing home every day for a week to see granny. I was a little more careful in what I said after that. While visiting, I told granny one day I was Jesus and wanted to find out her preference for lodging and food when she got to heaven. Another day I told her I was Abe Lincoln and I had forgotten my stovepipe hat. Granny saw it down the hall in her friend, Bertha's, room. A third day I stopped by with my girlfriend and introduced her as Cleopatra. No, granny had not seen my girlfriend's asp. I guess you figured out she had a little trouble with reality at the time. Don't get me wrong, I loved that woman dearly. She had a great sense of humor and Granny would have enjoyed what I was doing. I will discuss the nursing home situation in Hogshooter a little later.

A serious controversy developed during the 1950's and threatened the culinary options of Sensible County and Hogshooter. The Dairy Dilly made a killer hamburger during those days. Newspaper articles as far away as fifty miles mentioned the sandwich. People flocked to the eating establishment to sample the masterpieces. Maybe flocking to the Dairy Dilly is a little exaggeration. Perhaps a better way to put it is a lot of people traveling through Hogshooter stopped for a burger. Reminds me of the Burger Hut at Reminiscing Hills but our curly fries are better.

Anyway, there was something special about the meat's taste. The reason for the difference was the meat was a special mixture of both beef and horsemeat. I thought it was good until someone told me what it was and then all I thought of was my little pony, Chuckie. The Dairy Dilly could not to sell hamburgers until the health department cleared the matter up. The ice cream business continued though. Finally, the owner sold it and left the county in lieu of criminal charges. The burgers have never been the same.

Originally, the Dairy Dilly did not have a dining room. At the insistence of the residents on that side of town, it added a small area. The business was especially good during the morning hours. I do have to give credit where credit is due. The establishment made a killer concoction of biscuits and sausage gravy. Quite a core of folks came in every morning for coffee and fixins'. Most stayed for a while and solved many of the world's pressing problems.

This leads me to a discussion of Red "the terror" Rinehart. Now Red liked to sip the suds a wee bit. Never hurt anybody but the police stopped him on a regular basis because his breath threatened to explode. Finally, the city fathers convinced first his wife and then his daughter to take away his car keys. Hogshooter was definitely a safer place with Red off the streets.

But, Red didn't stay off the streets. For the next several years, "the terror" drove his riding lawnmower to the Dairy Dilly each morning. You drove past there and all the pickups were lined up with Red's mower. Occasionally, a John Deere tractor might be there if someone's pickup was in the shop. Everyone thought Red's driving of the mower was cute at least for a while. The old boy was a crackerjack mechanic and souped that sucker up. He'd came flying down the street and damn near run over someone. Hence, the name "the terror" was added. After repeated warnings for speeding through the school zone and almost giving the crossing guard a heart attack, the city banned Red and his lawn mower from the streets.

One would think that would be the end of it, right? No. Red crossed the other side of eighty years and got himself a motorized wheelchair. He couldn't go as fast as he used to but Red went right down the middle of the street. You honked at him but he couldn't hear and it wouldn't have made any difference. "The terror" finally had to go to the nursing home. I don't know if there is any truth to the rumor that he and some of his buddies set up a grand prix for wheelchair racing in the dining room.

Two of my favorite characters from Hogshooter were Smiley and Junior. I think most towns have residents like them. Some people are scared of them because they are different but those who know them realize what good people they are. If you have read the great classic, *To Kill a Mockingbird,* you remember Boo. He was different and people were afraid of him. Then, Boo saves Scout's life and she genuinely loves him I believe. Well, that is kind of like Smiley and Junior.

Smiley always wore overalls and walked with a bounce. Kids made fun of him but he always kept a smile on his face. He might come to church and sit there with that big grin. I have no doubt God had a special place for him in heaven. Now Smiley liked the women but never did anything. I once saw him walking, stopped and asked if he wanted a ride. He just grinned at me and said, "Nope, I'm in a hurry."

I wondered what it was like in his place and what his thinking processes were. As I grow older, I sometimes think this naïve approach to life might not be that bad. Things were simple for him and I doubt if he worried about a whole lot. You know life wouldn't be the same without people like Smiley. They complete our society. I can't believe the Nazis murdered these people because they soiled the perfect world they tried to build. Christ said something to the effect that if you do something to the least then you have done it to him. What would we have missed if society killed people with imperfect physical and mental abilities? Society is all things and people.

When Smiley died, I heard he accumulated a considerable amount of money. That makes him a lot smarter than some people I know.

Junior on the other hand had full mental abilities. He just had some trouble with his body. He rode a three-wheeled bike with flags on it. You'd see him coming from a ways off. Junior always said hello. Anytime something was going on at the high school, he was there. He especially loved the athletic events. The kids knew Junior and accepted him in the student section. There were always a couple of jerks but for the most realized how much he loved the school. One class even had him in their class picture.

Let's be honest, Junior could survive and thrive in a place like Hogshooter. That probably wouldn't be true in a larger town. From my perspective, I came back for that reason. Who knows, there but by the grace of God go I.

We don't get a whole lot of lawsuits in Sensible County. We had a big one a few years ago. I need to qualify that by saying it was big for us. And, it involved a business on Main Street.

I need to furnish a little background for this. Hemp grows wild in this part of the country. It was originally planted to provide material for ropes during one or the other wars. But it escaped and began growing all over the place. Now for you potheads out there, hemp can be marijuana. Don't everyone pack up and head for Sensible County because the stuff we have around here isn't any good to smoke.

Burl (the truth) caught wind (no pun intended) of this and thought it would make a good story. He did his research and sure enough there was hemp growing right on Main Street in Hogshooter. Burl (the truth) wrote an informative article for the Disappointment including a picture of one of the plants.

This picture led to the lawsuit.

I have tried to paint an accurate picture of Burl (the truth). He is a good guy. That doesn't mean he is friends with everyone because he isn't. One person he hasn't gotten along with for years is Dilts (the stilt) Shorts. He owns the local shoe repair shop. As you can see by his name, Dilts is rather tall. I heard the story that when tried out for the junior high basketball team the coach cried because he had to cut him. Dilts was already 6'5" and couldn't hit a basket standing underneath the rim. He didn't get much better as he grew older. He would forget about his height and continually bump into door jams. Dilts always had a bump on his forehead it seemed. Part of his problem was his feet. Here is this giant of a man who wore a size 7 shoe. His feet simply didn't fit his body.

Something happened between Dilts and Burl (the truth). I am not sure what but I heard it had something to do with a girl or an ad stilts placed in the Daily Disappointment.

Anyway, for his story Burl (the truth) took a picture of the hemp plant on Main Street. It happened to be growing in front of Dilts' store. Stilt sued for libel alleging the picture insinuated he grew pot. Any who knew Burl (the truth) realized he wasn't nearly so sharp as to think up this kind of a scheme. The judge agreed and threw out the suit. You know what, this goings on sure liven things up for a while in Hogshooter. There was talk of a grand jury to examine both sides of the situation. As usual, nothing came out of the grand jury talk.

For a while about twenty or thirty years ago, we had a car dealership in town. During the oil boom, several new car lots sprang up but quickly faded as the money left town. One entrepreneur decided there might still be enough business here to make a go of it. His name was Joe Joseph (really). He called himself "High Dollar Joe" because he gave the most for trades (or so he said). Joe took the town by storm. Before long, he was a deacon at the Baptist church.

His wife was just a wisp of a thing and they had two young kids. Joe always gave money to the school or the church for something.

Across the street from "High Dollar Joe's" car lot was a junk store. Most towns have a junk store. The place was a total eyesore. Yet, a person could go in and literally spend an hour or two. Its arrangement was chaos. If a person looked for a specific thing, then you better ask Joe. That is right. His name was also Joe. To this day, I don't know his last name. He was in the same location for years and still is. I guess he makes enough of a living to keep the place open.

I was actually going somewhere with this before I got a little sidetracked. When "High Dollar Joe" opened up the car lot across from the junk store, the other Joe saw an opportunity. He got a piece of Masonite, which I am sure he had been saving for twenty year, plus some white paint and made a sign. Ol' Joe put it right out in front of his store for everyone to see: "Low Dollar Joe's Going Out of Business Sale."

Now, "High Dollar Joe" went to the town fathers and asked them to do something. They told the car dealer that "Low Dollar Joe" had as much a right to put up that sign as he did. The battle started. "High Dollar" put up balloons and so did "Low Dollar." "High Dollar" did live radio spots from a Violet station. The station's competitor couldn't pass up the opportunity and came over to the junk store and did a remote for free. The car dealer had the Violet BBQ café offer free samples. The junk man cooked up some of his famous homemade chili and trumped his competition once again.

These games went on for a while and everyone in town got a real kick out of it. Then one morning there was a closed sign on the car dealership. Everyone wondered what happened. Speculation ran rampant about "Low Dollar Joe" running "High Dollar Joe" of business. The next Sunday at church, everyone found out. "High Dollar Joe" came up during the invitation and asked for the church's prayers. Seems the government indicted him for tax evasion. His closing had nothing to do with the junkman. I am sorry it didn't. That made a whole lot better story. I wonder what happened to him after that. I especially felt sorry for his wife and young kids.

"Low Dollar Joe"—well he enjoyed so much notoriety from the whole deal that he still calls himself that. I can't guess how old he is now. The junk store is still a fun place to go when looking for something special or unusual. One of these days I expect something from there to show up on *Antiques Roadshow* (more about our local spinoff later). By the way, all these years later Joe is still having a going out of business sale.

I thought I would be done with Main Street a long time ago but I keep thinking of things to tell you. To be honest, there really isn't much else to Hogshooter. We do have a park. As I was growing up, I used to think it was gigantic. Now I realize how small it is. All the ball fields are out by the high school so nothing like that is in the park. There are pecan trees so the place gets busy about the time of the first good frost or freeze. I bought a nutcracker and nailed it to a board. After I have scrounged a bunch of nuts and the weather is nice, I sit in the backyard and break the shells. Later while I watch television, I actually pick the meats out. Most get put in the freezer but a lot of them only make it to my mouth. Eat pretzels with your pecans if you want something good.

Got sidetracked again.

There is a bandstand or gazebo or whatever you want to call it in the park. It is round and sits about three or four feet off the ground. The structure hasn't been used much in the last few years. Two or three of us went and took a close look at it and the termites started taking it down. We decided we couldn't lose something this important to Hogshooter's history. Burl (the truth) ran a nice story about the disrepair. The readers actually sent in about fifty or seventy-five dollars. The gang down at the coffee shop challenged those from the Dairy Dilly and raised some more. We bought some treated lumber and replaced a bunch of the rotten wood. I bought a couple of gallons of paint and went to work. That old bandstand doesn't look too bad. It should last until way after I pass from this world.

When it was built about sixty or seventy years ago, it got a lot of use. You have to remember there was only radio then. Television came late to Sensible County because of its location away from any towns big enough to support a station.

Summer was always a busy time for the bandstand. We had a small community band that played every once in a while. Other towns sent their bands over as well. The local churches sponsored gospel sings a couple of times a summer. It wasn't unusual for these hymn sings to have a visiting quartet or two. I can remember a fourth of July oratorical contest one year. Families rented it out for reunions. The shell was surrounded by benches or you could bring you own chairs if you wanted to. I guess these gatherings were as much about being sociable as anything else.

Me and my buddies discovered you could actually sneak in under the bandstand. We found it a great place to take a girl before we could drive. In the night, no one could see in there unless he came right up to it and stuck a flashlight under it. We did a lot of romancing under there. The space was a good place to hide from our cop. Yes, that is singular. When I was growing up, we only had one on duty at night. His name was Billy (buffalo) Burns.

As you can figure out from his name, Billy was a rather large man. He didn't like to get out of his police car. I expect buffalo would have a heart attack if he ever went on a foot chase. Billy spends a lot of time out at the Dairy Dilly. I don't ever remember when he didn't have a spot on his shirt. Buffalo was a lady's man as well. He had quite a harem and he used his duty hours for things other than patrolling. If we could find where he parked, we liked to sneak up on him and watch the proceeding in hope of getting an education. If we ever got spotted, by the time Billy came after us we had settled under the bandstand for safety.

One incident did take place that almost got us in big trouble. Tommy (tremors) Thomas' cousin came to visit one summer. I can't remember his name but he was from a big place like Dallas or

Kansas City. About four of us decided to go and find where buffalo parked. We found him in the long driveway of the Remarkable brothers' house. The lane was tree covered and we actually climbed up a few branches for a better view.

Now the sweet thing Billy was with mirrored him in size and the front seat was just so big. The weather was hot so the windows were down. We had trouble not laughing at what took place not that we knew that much. Next thing we saw, a figure came creeping around the car. It took a minute but we realized it was Tommy's cousin and he had something in his hand. We watched in horror as he reached into the car, pulled the back of buffalo's boxers open and poured his cup of ice and coke into the space. Man, we were out of there in no time and we heard Billy cussing for two blocks. We disappeared under the bandstand and stayed there most of the night. Billy patrolled Hogshooter like never before. He gave me dirty looks for months after that and I pretended to ignore him. Buffalo couldn't really say anything because of what he was doing was during duty time.

Hogshooter can't support any officers anymore. We rely on the sheriff's department and the highway patrol for protection now. Realistically, we aren't exactly a den of sin and vice (except to the preachers).

There was a noble attempt some thirty or so years ago (or at least that is what the yellow notes called it) to revive interest in the downtown area by creating an event using the bandstand. We had a chamber of commerce in those days and they decided to have a "battle of the bands" to get people involved. In its purest sense, the idea was a noble one but in reality it turned out to be a disaster.

An entry fee generated money and booth space rented. To buy food or anything you had to have a ticket and the chamber controlled the sales plus took a cut. That part of it worked out pretty well. No one could sell alcohol since Sensible remained a dry county. Nothing kept people from bringing their own booze and they did.

Another crucial mistake was defining what types of bands could enter. There existed a certain naiveté in the people of Hogshooter. They figured a few local bands would show up. No. The entries included rock and roll (too long ago for heavy metal), country and western, polka and some bands whose music was unrecognizable. The judges for the event included the local high school music teacher, a minister, the president of the chamber and a guest judge from Violet.

The contest started well enough. As the evening progressed, the music got worse and the booze flowed more. The audience turned out to be from all over the area and not what one would say were sterling citizens. Our one cop, buffalo, was on duty so there was no crowd control. Most law-abiding citizens high tailed it out of there pretty early because they were smart enough to see what was going to happen. The kids wanted more rock and roll. The drinkers wanted more country and western and the locals loved the polka music. Empty beer bottles started flying the later it got.

When the judges announced Marvelous Marvin and his Wistful Fingers Polka Band as the winner, all hell broke loose. The drinkers thought that Tanya and her all-girl country and western band should have won. All they saw were the girls' short skirts and overlooked the fact that their music was horrible. The kids just complained to be complaining.

The area got tore up a little and was on the verge of a full riot when a sheriff's car and a police cruiser from Violet showed. Everyone disappeared in a matter of minutes except the ones under the bandstand who thought it was great.

What money the chamber earned went to pay the winners and clean up the mess left behind.

Burl (the truth) ran an editorial the next week and really laid the issues out. A lot of people thought he made good points on some things like lack of planning. Interestingly enough, he neglected to mention the fact that the Disappointment actually pushed for the event.

The boys down at the café hashed over the event for quite a

while. As usual, there was a discussion of a grand jury. No one wanted to be the person to start the petition. Apathy struck again.

Strangely enough, about six months later a discussion started whether there should be a second annual battle of the bands. In fact, inquiries from people outside the area came in who wanted to not only attend but enter a band. Several wanted booth space as well.

Afraid the event might become the Woodstock of Sensible County, the chamber declined to consider a second one.

A larger town about fifty miles away took up the idea and the event was a tremendous success. That community was better organized to host. One lesson learned was that Hogshooter really was a progressive community with good ideas.

I don't care what the yellow notes of the hysterical society say. That conclusion just ain't true. Hogshooter just fell on its face.

Hope they don't take away the yellow notes from me...

The park does have an item of significance and I am not being sarcastic. One corner of it is honors our young men who have given their all for freedom. After the First World War I, a monument honored a couple of local youngsters killed in France. The area Hogshooter grew, the monument expanded to those who gave their lives during WWII. You know, Tom Brokaw calls these men the greatest generation. I think he is right. It truly is sad to watch the paper and see how many of these heroes are going on into the nearer presence of God. It won't be long until they are gone and forgotten.

The Korean War left our community alone but not Vietnam. That is my group and several of my friends died during this conflict. The community added their names to the monument. Sounds funny to call Vietnam a conflict. Technically it is. A war can only take place when Congress declares it. They haven't done so since WWII. When you hear idiots taking about the war in Iraq or wherever, correct them. People in the United States are actually forgetting our history and what it means. Boy that is a surprise. Not!

Don't get me wrong here when I say the conflicts aren't technically wars. Young men and women die or get maimed just as badly from these non-wars as well as the declared ones. Our veterans should be honored everyday and get all the benefits they deserve and need.

There is one name on the monument who was my good buddy. Griff Griffin and I were friends all of our lives. We went to school together, played sports on the same teams and even dated sisters. When we graduated from high school, I didn't have any money for college so I decided to get drafted. I used the GI Bill to go to college after my two years. Griff decided to join because he wanted some kind of training or another. That was important to him.

Anyway, we went in together and through basic training in the same company. After that, we split with him heading to his advanced training. I had hurt a shoulder in basic and ended up staying stateside for my two years. After his training, the Army assigned Griff to Ft. Leonard Wood, Missouri, then to Nam. I took some leave to be home with him before he headed over.

After the Army discharged me, I returned home to wait for the next semester to start. One morning, a friend of ours came and told me to get over to Griff's parents' house because he was killed. I spent all day every day there until we buried him. I cried every waking moment during that time. The day of his funeral was the longest one I ever had. Whoever says that men shouldn't cry is an absolute idiot. Griff was my best friend and I still miss him.

I go to his grave on a regular basis and talk to him. The talking is for me I suppose. His parents have died and I put flowers on his grave on Memorial Day and greenery there for Christmas.

My parents used to call Memorial Day Decoration Day. We made a special trip to my grandparents' graves and 'decorate' them. That ritual seems to be dying out. That is a shame. This time is so special for me. Cremate me. My church built an area called a columbarium. I figure my ashes being there is sufficient.

During Vietnam, someone bought and put up a metal figure of a soldier kneeling before the memorial in the park. Yeah, that seems appropriate. I noticed a bird had crapped on it and left streaks. I got some soap and water to wash it off. I stood there for the longest time debating whether to scrub it off or not. To me the streaks looked like tears. It made perfect sense to me that the kneeling soldier cried for his fallen comrades. Maybe I should leave them alone. Finally, I went ahead and washed the crap off.

The kneeling soldier started to rust. I bought some good exterior black paint and redid him. Then I wondered who would do this once I am gone. I guess that is why we go to the kids with the yellow notes hoping they will remember. Damn, it is very hard writing this.

KIDS AND STUFF

The yellow notes spend a lot of time on schools and they are significant but kids are more important. I suspect most of the adults in Hogshooter went to school here. With no sustainable industry around other than farming and ranching not a whole lot of people are moving in. Many are like me returning to Sensible County to retire after spending their adult lives in other places.

Earlier I said a little bit about the schools. There used to be several small ones enrolling students from grades one through eight. None was big in the county and they were really neighborhood schools. The kids walked together to school. In fact, in the early 1900s many rode horses.

As the number of kids decreased, schools disappeared. With better roads and school buses, centralized systems took over. There isn't anything wrong with this because the students probably get a better education.

Around here, Hogshooter became the central location as these dependent systems vanished. The state took over the funding and control of schools. I am convinced teaching in rural schools is a true calling. Teachers do not get rich doing it. Many are from around here and family is very important. Several have farms and other businesses to help them get by. Teachers were the most important people in my life other than my parents. We had a B-Team basketball and the baseball coach I respected more than almost any person I knew. I could be a handful from time to time. For example the A-Team basketball coach was a jerk and played favorites. I always tried to show him up. Coach Beale told me when things got bad to play harder and make the old man recognize me. He was right. The old man had great players but couldn't win state. The second year after Coach Beale took over the Gorillas (that's our name) his team won state. He left Hogshooter, went on to get his doctorate, and became a college professor.

Did I mention he threw me out of his car coming back from a baseball game? I deserved it because I smarted off and out I went. He came back to get me. Another time I was dogging it in warmups before a basketball game and Coach Beale made us run line drills. I deserved it.

Basketball—I did love it. Our football team was horrible. We were so small we had trouble getting enough players to form a team. That was evident when all 120 pounds of me played. Besides, it hurt when those big old dudes knocked the snot out of me.

Basketball—the Gorillas were always tough.

My parents went to school in Hogshooter during the 1920s. In those days, the school didn't have an indoor gym. The teams played outside. I have a picture of mom's team. They played in dresses. Their game was six on six with three guards and three forwards. Oklahoma and Iowa didn't do away with this style until a few years ago.

The boy's team was good. Dad told about driving fifty miles away and playing indoors for the first time. The picture of the high school team is a scream. One guy wore a hair net. The picture reminds me of George Clooney in *Oh Brother Where Art Thou?* A couple more of the team members had their socks held up by garters. I would have liked to see them play.

Things were not always peachy when I played. I remember

going to a gym that did not have showers. That was an interesting ride home. My least favorite place to play was at Coodys Bluff Consolidated. Their home floor was an old community center. One time we went there in February, they forgot to turn on the heat. The gym was so cold that the basketballs wouldn't bounce until it warmed up. I really remember the floor. It was made up of blocks of wood like Boston Garden where the Celtics play. The resemblance was all that was in common. The floor had a bump in it. The bump was big enough that you could not dribble around it. If you did, the ball would bounce in some odd direction. The bump was never in the same place. Coodys Bluff's team always knew where it was and tailored their defenses accordingly. They were tough in addition to playing that bump.

We almost had a bad racial incident there. Coodys Bluff's population was not an enlightened bunch. We used to say there were only two last names in their whole school system. Hogshooter was one of the first integrated schools in its area of the state. One black family lived in the community and we grew up with their kids. The oldest son, Ronnie, could play. The Gorillas had no problems until we went to Coodys Bluff. I was still on the B-Team at the time. Also on the B-Team was an older kid who played basketball to keep in shape for football. He was a big dude. In fact, we called him big dude.

Our A-Team beat Coodys Bluff and its bump. Ronnie had a tremendous game. As soon as the Gorillas headed toward the locker room, we spied a couple of local apes (pun intended) following them. These two yelled at Ronnie all night long. Big dude immediately fell right in behind them. When they turned to go into the locker room, he put his hand on their shoulders and asked where they were going. Big dude towered over them. They stammered and stuttered something about telling Ronnie what a great game he played but they never got the chance. Big dude escorted them away and we had no trouble.

Playing in a small town was great. Everyone came to the games.

All the people recognized and called you by name. There was a lot of school spirit for the Gorillas. The cheerleaders always made a banner to run through with cute little saying on the back. One I will never forget said, "I found my thrill under Bill." Everyone knew who Bill's girlfriend was and we had some fun with the saying. They married right out of high school. They also got divorced out of high school. I suspect our graduating class was the only one in the state led into the auditorium by a pregnant student. You have got to love small towns.

One thing that wasn't fun was riding an old school bus to games. The trips seemed awful long. When it got cold, you might lay your head against the window to try and get some sleep on the way home. More than once, I woke up with my head frozen to the window. I wore a burr haircut so that was tough to do.

The cafeteria ladies made us sandwiches for the return trip. They consisted of two kinds of meat: ham and mystery meat. The mystery meat was actually roast beef. By the time we got the sandwiches, they were dry and hardly edible. I always tried to get one with ham. The roast beef sometimes turned various colors.

For the most part, these trips seemed long. I do remember one of the more interesting one. We won a big game and the coaches let us make all the noise we wanted. What they didn't know was that big dude had 'kidnapped' one of the student managers and put him in the back of the bus. The singing covered up his attempts to get the coaches attention. Someone pulled his pants off and sprayed something called 'tough skin' on his family jewels. You fellows out there who used 'tough skin' know how sticky it is. In addition to that, they took a roll of tape and covered the 'tough skin.' By the time he got the tape off, I am not sure he had any skin or hair left. We are lucky he didn't go after someone. Of course, you have to be able to walk to do that. I still feel pain when I think about it.

I had interesting teachers at Hogshooter High. I mentioned some already because I admired a few of them. Teaching is hard and even tougher in a small town. Sensible County was their home either by birth or by choice. I heard people say if they can't get any other job then they became teachers. What a joke. Teaching is as much a calling as it is a job. Many I know are passionate about what they do. Now, don't be mistaken into believing all are good teachers because they are not. Still, several ones from Hogshooter High stand out for various reasons and not all of them are good.

I remember one social studies teacher because he was bald. Before you get in an uproar, let me finish. He was an average instructor but a nice man. What I recall had nothing to do with the classroom. A couple of times a day he honkered up a goober and spit it into his handkerchief. What is wrong with that? Nothing if he stopped there. He then took the hanky and wiped it across his baldhead. His noggin had the strangest sheen to it. I always wondered what was special about that snot.

One night I dreamed I was in chemistry class getting ready for an experiment. Mr. Social Studies handkerchief and his shiny baldhead gave the instructions. I was to identify the chemicals contained in the hanky to determine what makes his head so shinny. Now that is what I call a nightmare.

Chemistry class didn't make much of an impression on me. I do remember dropping pennies in silver nitrate (I think) and then running to the cafeteria to spend them as dimes before the chemical rubbed off. That is a successful use of chemicals. I do recall someone blowing up something during the class because we waited in the hall until the vapors cleared out. That guy went on to be a chemical engineer.

Biology was a different story. I especially liked the fetal pig with the red and blue latex in its veins. Boy do I remember Zoology in college. I had that class at 7:30 in the morning and the lab about gagged me. Sorry, I wandered again. Earl the squirrel was our high school teacher. The rumor was he was a little light in the loafers. Squirrel was a good teacher and went on to teach college. He was weird. After he gave a test back, he distributed the right answers. If you challenged him on an answer, he began counting and continued until you stopped. What he was doing was taking points off as long as you argued. One of the brighter girls in class got into it with him over a test. She wouldn't give up and if I remember right she was correct. I think Earl gave her a zero. He probably changed it because I think her dad was a doctor. I bet he didn't try that crap with a college student.

We went to high school for six class periods a day unless you worked. Being an athlete, I got out the last hour for practice. My senior year I had almost no classes to take because I had all of my credits to graduate. Still, I had to come for all of those hours. I got stuck in study hall for my non-class time. Mine was in the library with the librarian, One-eye Ply. She was kind of a mean old biddy but I learned early to take advantage of her handicap. If you got on the side of her glass eye, you did anything you wanted. One-eye was always on me anyway because my nickname was toothpick. I had one in my mouth most of the time until she took it away from me. I had plenty so I really didn't care. I'd buy a small vial of cinnamon oil and soak toothpicks in it. Sometimes my lips burned. A bunch of my friends wanted them also. I loved to eat fruit chewies in study hall as a snack before lunch. I tracked One-eye as she moved around the room and sneak a bite. She never got the best of me on that one.

One of the most interesting teachers I had was the principal, fire-head. We called him that because his hair was bright red or at least who hair he had left. Our algebra teacher had surgery during the school year and fire-head took over teaching her classes. There were protractors and all kinds of gadgets to help our instructor teach geometry. He didn't use that stuff. He pulled out a lace from his shoes and tied a piece of chalk on the end. It was amazing how fire-head made perfect circles or arcs. He wasn't a bad teacher either. His jovial appearance was deceiving. Fire-head warmed your butt if you needed it.

In those days, if you did something wrong, you expected a swat or two. A teacher took you into the hall, got another teacher to witness, and POW! I know one thing, we paid attention and I expect there was a lot less problems then than with students now.

Paddling discipline worked. Two old maids taught at Hogshooter High and had for most of their lives. One of them wore her white hair in a tight bun usually with a pencil in it. She was a great teacher but if she got mad it was out in the hall and you felt it when she hit you. I'm naturally a chicken and don't like pain so I can only remember getting one pop. That was enough for me.

I learned a few things at Hogshooter High. I can still recite a speech from *Julius Cesar.* Don't remember any math though. Actually, I found out I was well prepared for college.

I think all of our coaches taught. In a small town that's the way it is. If a school got one competent in science or math it was lucky. I had Coach Football for American History. Overall, he wasn't too bad. Our classroom was in the stadium. Class time was usually short because he came in late and left early. At some time in his life and my guess playing football he broke his index finger and it was permanently straight. Coach came wandering into class picking chewing tobacco out of his teeth with that finger. I remember one time he was telling us about Ethan Allen attacking the British. Coach said the Green Mountain Boys "snuck" up on the Red Coats. About that time Blissy the brain shot her hand up and said, "Don't you mean he sneaked up?" Blissy was smart but a wee bit short on common sense. Coach Football never missed a beat and answered, "Nope, snuck is when you really sneak up on them." Remember, I used that line earlier and will a bunch later. We were about rolling in the aisles. Coach had a wry smile and I have no idea how he kept from breaking up. I am not sure Blissy has figured it out yet.

Hogshooter High was not that big but we were lucky enough to have someone capable of teaching "fizzicks" one year. Oh, I know how to spell it. Slow John, the teacher, only taught one class of the stuff and the rest of his teaching load was math. A few of us had the guts to take the course and we were immediately overwhelmed. That is when we started handing in papers with "fizzicks" on them rather than physics. The center on the basketball team was failing the course big time and it threatened his eligibility. Suddenly, he made a perfect score on a test. After that, everyone's grades improved markedly. Somehow, the center got a copy of the answer book. I often wondered about that but never asked. Slow John didn't seem to care. He only stayed through the end of the year and got a good job with an oil company. None of us remembered anything about "fizzicks" but we made it through with a good grade.

You know, teachers can be funny at times. I had a chemistry teacher in college that once reviewed a test while a couple members of the basketball team were taking it as a make up on the back row. I am not sure they ever figured out what was going on. One of my buddies who went to law school had a professor who insisted you come to class. One student came in, lay down behind the back row, and went to sleep at least a couple of times a week. That was okay because the student made the effort to come to class. The same professor gave one test a semester, a final. If you got the question right, you got one point. If not, he assumed you guessed and it was two points off. No one ever made above zero on his tests.

The toughest thing I remember about high school was burying my classmates. I suppose every school has kids that die while there. I can remember three times our little community gathered in the high school gym to say good by to a student. I mentioned before that Sensible County was a dry county. The state line was only a few miles away and a kid could buy beer at eighteen in the next state. A couple of bars there served anyone who looked like they might be that age. Especially during the summer, kids piled into cars and headed up there. The road was 'bloody 13' because it was so bad. Seemed to me someone was always having a wreck on that highway. Alcohol was the direct cause of some of the wrecks.

The shock of hearing a friend or classmate dying still stings me. I saw those caskets at the front of the gym and realized I would never see those people again. I lost a brother when I was twenty-six years old. Ever since, I have trouble going funerals. Just seeing people grieve is tough for me. One young lady's boyfriend was killed in a wreck my senior year of high school. At the funeral, she did not sit with the family. The impact on her was devastating crying through the service. Three years later, another boyfriend was coming home from college one Friday afternoon. He was thrown from his car and killed. I cannot imagine what that loss did to her. We didn't have grief counselors in those days that came to school to help us get through these times. Most of us went to church and I guess faith was where we looked for help.

Over the years, things change but many remain the same. I haven't always returned to my class reunions but the older I get the more I try. As we age, dying comes often and we realize it's part of life. During the reunions, we devote a time to remember those who died since we last met. Seems to me more and more of my schoolmates are gone now. The fellow who led the service last time has now died.

I used to make fun of old people as I listened to them retell the same stories. I don't do that anymore. Those remembrances are now part of my life and mean so much especially when you think of your lost friends.

Forgive me. None of this is in the yellow notes of the hysterical society. Maybe it should be.

Now it's time to get back to the more important stuff. Oops, most of this is not in the hysterical society notes either. Tough.

I think we were typical kids. Most of us worked during the summer or the school year or both. Many of our families needed our help so we gave it. I mentioned already about some of the things we did. Here is a good place to work in a few more.

I talked about riding with Herman (hefty) Simile racing ears McElroy. While I was away at the Bible junior college, I ran into hefty. He drove over to watch a basketball game with his new girlfriend, Sugar. She moved to town and Herman was smart enough to grab onto her. He and Sugar got caught parking in the Hogshooter cemetery. That location is one place I never parked. The next time I was in Hogshooter, Sugar and he took me to the cemetery. We three we laughing and having a good time when a red light started flashing. It was buffalo. He came up to the car serious like because he knew it was hefty's car and this was the second time buffalo caught him. He just looked and saw me, laughed, and said something about a threesome. Buffalo told us to leave and not to park in the cemetery anymore. As we left, I realized we were in buffalo's parking place.

We still laugh about that today.

Halloween in a small town is interesting. Every kid in the world, young and old was out that night. As I mentioned before, outhouse tipping was a big sport in the early days. Later it was mischief like throwing eggs and toilet papering trees and houses. One year, buffalo made a big deal about cracking down for Halloween. His warning was in the Disappointment and announced at school. He even told us the sheriff had a new police dog and it would be in town that night.

That really scared us. Not! A group of kids gathered at the high school. Buffalo came up in his police car and told us to break it up which we immediately ignored. He pulled his squad car into the crowd. When it emerged out the other side, toilet paper completely covered the car. That made him mad.

Next thing we know the sheriff pulled up with his new police dog. Seems someone also tossed eggs at buffalo's car. I didn't do it but did I ever tell you I could toss an egg over a car doing thirty miles an hour and hit the windshield of a parked car every time? You never know when such a skill will come in handy. Anyway, back to the story. Most all the kids took the hint and broke up the mob but a couple of the older guys sassed the cops and began to run. Here comes the dog after them. They hurtled a chain link fence and the poor dog never saw it. The collision knocked that poor puppy cold. He was okay when he woke up. The sheriff and his dog limited themselves to real crimes after that.

Buffalo was mad. He threatened to call for a grand jury to investigate the goings on that Halloween. And, as with most other grand juries mentioned in Sensible County, nothing came out of it.

That Halloween was about the same time as the great victory bell incident at the high school. Someone got the wild idea

Hogshooter High needed a victory bell. It would only be used during seasons other than football (that's because we never won any games). When a sports team won, the bell rang. At first, the bell sat in front of the high school. I have to give whoever thought of the bell some credit because it did have a nice sound to it. Then for some reason, the bell became the repeated target of vandals painting rather provocative sayings on it. The bell had to go. Someone had the idea of putting it on top of the high school. Access was controlled and it couldn't be vandalized.

Right. The team was playing someone worse than them one football homecoming. At a small school you have more than one homecoming. The team Hogshooter played was so bad the victory bell would finally be rung after a football game. The Gorillas won and the bell sounded. It never did. Unbeknownst to all but a very few, agile Andy scaled the side of the high school and cut the clapper out of the victory bell. Agile didn't like football and this was his protest. He went on to be a green beret. The victory bell never rang again. All Hogshooter High had after that was a girl dressed up like a gorilla. We blamed the incident on the high school we played that night. They professed innocence and they were.

Agile was kind of character in his own right. I remember going out with him a few times before we were able to drive. You realize that in a small town everyone knows almost everyone else. There weren't a lot of doors locked in those days. We went looking for something to do and Andy had a strange desire that could have gotten us in trouble. Agile found a house with no one home, went in, and moved the furniture around. I never had the guts to go in. I will admit that I flipped a few breakers on houses where the boxes were available. No telling what might have happened to us if buffalo caught us. He might have tried to lynch us.

There was a pecking system at the high school about certain things. The one I remember was where you sat in the cafeteria. To state it another way, only seniors sat in a particular area. I remembered going through my freshman, sophomore and junior years envying the seniors sitting in that special alcove. We were hot stuff when it came our turn.

A critical challenge to our authority happened one day when an underclassman sat in the alcove. I do not really remember the reason but a bunch of the seniors got mad. They challenged the junior class to fight. More specifically, there was to be three fights. There would be a small guy, a middle guy and big guys fights. No, I wasn't one of them. I always considered myself a lover and I did not like pain. Anyway, one day after school we all headed out to Cadillac Road for the skirmishes. I don't remember much except the juniors won all three. Nothing got hurt except our pride. The juniors didn't start sitting in our alcove or anything. Everyone was friends after that. You pretty much had to be in a small town like Hogshooter.

It's interesting or sad now to see or hear the news about teachers being charged with molesting their students. A young teacher coming to Hogshooter and always dated his students. Several of them ended up marrying local girls and having families. I'm sure statutory rape statutes were on the books but I don't ever remember a case involving that law. Half of the guys in town dated younger girls. I guess ignorance is bliss. Several the guys I knew from Sensible County could have been put away for a long time.

This makes one wonder what stuff did take place we never knew about. I am sure there were molestations. There weren't a lot of tolerances when I was growing up. If a young lady got pregnant, there was a wedding. I don't remember any discussion about that. You committed the act so you paid the price. I never heard the word abortion until long after I left Hogshooter.

A lot of this has to do with media coverage today. It seems like anything of interest happening locally is on the national wire. These services love strange or bizarre events. I am sure these same types of happenings took place when I was a kid. The media simply did not have the capacity in those days to make it news. I like that---make it the news. Half of what takes place today was not newsworthy back then. I cannot believe we actually pay attention to some of the things that happen today.

Let me take a stab at this. I am going to put something that happened when I was a kid into today's media circus terms.

"This is Morris Mouth of International Cable Connection Reaction of Little Value News reporting from rural Sensible County. I have learned about a significant news event of little value that is happening right now.

I am standing in front of the outhouse of Purvis Peeler waiting for him to emerge to visit with us.

Here he is now. Mr. Peeler, I learned from an anonymous tip that you will no longer be using this facility after today. Any comment?

Wait a second until I get my bib hooked back on my overalls. What do you want?

Is it true that you won't or can't be using this facility after today?

You mean this outhouse?

Yes, sir.

If we can, Mr. Mouth, I would like to move a little further away from the door. It gets a mite rank this time of year so close to the hole.

Come on Purvis, you can tell me why you have to move? It's all of the liberals putting environmental requirements, isn't it? The American people want to know all about it.

Well, I hadn't really thought about that.

Be honest, you and your family are harassed by the EPA because it said you had to do an environment impact statement before you could dig a new hole. Isn't that right sir?

Not that I know of.

Purvis, isn't it true you still have a thunder mug in the house that you use at night so you don't have to come outside?

Yes. The kids use it more than my wife and I.

You were threatened by the government because you are soiling this fertile land by tossing its contents on the pasture?

Not that I know of.

Purvis, haven't you been contacted by the government concerning this matter?

Yes.

Haven't you also been contacted by the conservative think tank, People's Poop Rights Against Government Interference, to take your case?

Yes.

Well, Mr. Peeler, did you tell them someone is interfering with your Constitutional rights?

No.

Well, what did you tell them?

I told them we were shutting down the two-holer because we ran out of catalogs.

So, the government is now interfering with you mail?

Not that I know of.

What are you going to do?

Well, for right now, I sent the misses to town to the grocery store to buy an eight pack of toilet paper.

How are you going to deal with the government over this issue of interference with your bodily function rights?

I am telling them to go ahead and run the new sewer line down here because we want hooked up.

They are forcing you to take part in a governmental subsidy program to build onto your house?

Nope. My wife told me that she is tired of going out in all kinds of weather and she wants to stay inside where it is warm.

Is it true someone offered you a reality television series for next fall chronicling your run ins with the government?

What is reality television?

There you have it ladies and gentlemen, another sad story of government interference in the every day lives of American citizens. Tomorrow I will be reporting on another example of excessive nonsense of something that has no value whatsoever but I have to because the people are so desperate for the media to makeup something to report on.

From rural Sensible County, this is Morris Mouth of International Cable Connection Reaction of Little Value News."

Dang I am good. This may open up a whole new area for the media. Yes, remember you heard it here first. I suggested a cable channel depicting the trials and tribulations of bodily functions in Sensible County. This can't be any worse than some of the stuff shown now on the cable channels. I better not add the above to the yellow notes of the hysterical society.

For the longest time, Hogshooter High School couldn't have a prom. The ministerial alliance declared dancing was the devil's work. The Catholics voted against the resolution and the Presbyterians said they did not care because they would do it anyway. Caught in the middle was the school board. As long as the conservative element held forth the high school kids were caught in limbo (not the dance). There were dances in town all the time but not sanctioned ones.

Personally, I was so riddled with guilt while growing up that I still can't dance today. My wife disagrees and says it's because I have a total lack of rhythm. I dispute that. I think the real reason is because I didn't want to hurt my parents. They grew up during the depression when religion was one of the few things people depended on. To them there were simply some things you didn't do and dancing was one of them.

We got our first television because of a prom. Mom and dad told my older brother they would buy a TV if he wouldn't go to the prom. Sounded like a great deal to him so he didn't go.

Television--I wasn't exactly the darling of the neighborhood. One time the lady in the house across the street told me if I was good I could watch her family's favorite show with them. I did it. I hadn't seen many shows yet so I was thrilled. The program was Liberace. I stayed about five minutes and left. It wasn't worth it to me to be good so that I *could* watch him.

Back to the prom...Now Violet, you know the town a few miles away that has Wal-Mart, wasn't quite as conservative as Hogshooter. The high school kids got wind of our situation. We knew most of the students from there. In fact, a lot of them were our cousins or teammates. Violet held its junior/senior prom at a big barn on private property. My cousin from Violet, Richie, called me with an idea. He talked with a bunch of the kids and their prom was on a Friday night. Would we be interested in using the barn on Saturday night? They would leave the decorations up and host us for the dance if we wanted.

I quietly talked with a bunch of our students and we thought it was a great idea. We let in sympathetic parents to help chaperon (and pay for) the dance. We included Miss Nilla. I figured if anyone started bitching about the evils of dancing, she would take care of them. I was right. Plus, with her chaperoning the event a lot of kids got to go. Many later got in trouble because they failed to mention the event was a dance.

Anyway, the prom was a great success. The kids from the two towns got along well. To be honest, the students from Violet didn't have to do host that dance. We returned the favor later. Our event just happened to be at a lake and involved booze. We did not let Miss Nilla know about that one. Buffalo found out about it and nearly got the whole county in trouble.

I do remember in the 1950's when Hogshooter made the national news. It started out as a bad thing but worked out in the end. I remember the incident because I tried to help a little.

The time was late autumn. No one had any air conditioning so the houses stayed open a lot of the time. The days were crisp and the evenings were nippy. A local family had a little girl about two years old. One afternoon, mom and the girl went down for a nap. Sometime later, the child woke up and noticed her mother was still asleep. She saw the family's two dogs outside and decided she wanted to go and play with them. By the way, I am writing what everyone believed took place. No one knew for sure.

The mother woke up from her nap and realized her daughter took a chair, unhooked the screen door and went outside. Initially there was thought someone broke into the house but that changed later. Not being able to find the child, mom panicked. The family lived in a rural area with clumps of forest and water all over the place. The under growth was especially thick.

She called the sheriff and soon it seemed everyone in Sensible County descended on the area to search for the child. There was urgency to find the little girl for a couple of reasons. Several years before a child disappeared and he was never found. Currently, the little girl only had a diaper on and the temperature was to be chilly that night.

I went with my father and helped look for the child. By the time everyone got organized, the sun was already going down and the temperature was plunging. In those days, we didn't have daylight savings time so it got dark early. I remember people and news media from all over descended on the area. Today it would really been a zoo.

Anyway, we looked all night. Because of the temperature, there was a genuine concern for the little tyke. The mother was devastated. The whole county worked together providing food plus coffee. A place to rest was established and the searchers rotated to take a break.

The morning broke and a light covering of frost lay on the ground. About thirty minutes after sunup, the news started to filter in she was found. A doctor and an ambulance stood by waiting for the worst. Soon after, a group crashed through the brush carrying her limp body wrapped in a blanket. As they got closer to the house, her family ran to meet them and the girl raised her head. The doctor and ambulance moved toward them and off to the hospital they all went.

Turned out the little girl was fine. She followed her dogs into the woods after they took off after some scent. After it got dark, the youngster laid down on some leaves next to a stream. As she went to sleep, her two dogs surrounded her with their bodies and she slept warmly that night. To the puppies, that baby was part of their family and nothing was going to happen to her.

Those dogs lived a number of years after that and a special bond always existed between them and the little girl. Sensible County made the newsreel at the movie the next week. I remember seeing a picture of the baby and her puppies.

To this day, I have no patience with anyone who abuses a pet. If someone hurts one of God's pets, I think they should have the same done to them as what they did to that animal.

Don't forget, God spelled backwards is doG.

Ah, such is life in Sensible County.

CHURCHES

I thought about this subject for a long time. The history of churches in Hogshooter and Sensible County is included in the yellow notes. In my way of thinking, they don't tell the whole story. They talk about the "brush arbor" revivals in Hogshooter and some of the early tent ones as well. As I point out later when I talk about the Bible College, I come from conservative stock. I still have those basic values today but I just approach them from a little different point of view.

In the early days with no radio and television, church was an important deal and rightfully so. With tough times and more unexplained happenings than today, spiritual aid was important. What comfort could a family have but God when their babies died with a cough or a belly ache? My mom told about selling a calf so a minister could come and preach at a brush arbor built by her family. As a child, I remember going to a tent revival to hear some great evangelist preach. This fellow wearing a white suit with a bright red tie and slicked back hair got up and yelled a lot. Inside that tent, the temperature soared to above 100 degrees. The audience members were passing out like flies. The altar call seemed to last forever. The preacher kept saying God was telling him to keep the invitation open for just a little longer. My simple faith as a kid was God telling me to close it. I wanted my hot fudge sundae from the Dairy Dilly.

I do remember Brother Testament asking hammerhead Dozer to share with the audience a vision he told the preacher. Hammerhead was a piece of work. He began telling about the spirit coming into him as he stood on the banks of the Jordan River. He saw a figure beckoning him to come across. Next thing he knew, someone baptized him and he felt like a new man with a clean soul. The vision moved Brother Testament.

My Uncle Cletus was not impressed. He knew hammerhead all his life and his rendition of what happened on the way home was different. Cletus almost laughed during the testimony. He saw hammerhead with Roscoe (dandy) Beam a couple of hours before the service. Seems Roscoe Beam's still produced a remarkably smooth run of corn sippins' and he offered hammerhead a nip in hopes of selling some elixir. Hammerhead agreed and purchased a jar from which he liberally partook before Brother Testament's preaching.

This is where my Uncle Cletus comes into the story. He happened by just as hammerhead fell into Pickle Creek. He and a couple of other fellows pulled hammerhead out. Though sopping wet, the old boy seemed changed. He also smelled like a bar. Cletus had no doubt hammerhead saw a vision and then fell into the creek fully believing it was the Jordan River. That batch of Roscoe's elixir must have been smooth.

Something good came of this event. To his dying breath, hammerhead believed what he testified to that night. He turned into a God-fearing man who never took another drink. Yes, I believe that God does work in mysterious ways and hammerhead is a prime example.

By the way, over the years, I heard hammerhead tell this story many times. I think it improved a lot with age.

Before I was born, dad told an interesting story of something that happened at a brush arbor meeting. For those of you who do not know what a brush arbor is, it is a structure constructed out of doors to give some protection from the elements during a revival service. It is built of rough materials and only offers protection by means of a makeshift roof.

These meetings were common during the summer months. They usually lasted for a week with services every night and sometimes twice a day on the weekends. An evangelist from outside the area preached although someone local could minister. Sometimes all the churches got together to sponsor it but often just one church did. The preacher received a "love offering" collected during each service.

Most preachers came from other churches but there were full time traveling evangelists. A local family or families provided a place for him to stay and often he divided his meals with others in the community. The evangelist spent the days visiting attempting to get people to come to the evening services. The success of these meetings depended on the number of people "saved."

During one meeting Tiny Murphy was converted. Now Tiny wasn't (tiny, that is). In fact, he was one of the largest people in the community. No revival was complete without a baptism. In the Hogshooter area, there was a relatively calm place next to the old ford on the river. The local baptisms often took place there.

The visiting evangelist was a slender man who probably did not weigh more than 120 pounds. Tiny was more than twice that. The minister wasn't daunted and was determined to carry out God's work. He leaned over to Tiny and said, "I'll get into the water but you are on your own getting out."

Successfully baptized, Tiny became a pillar of the community. The minister recovered from his back injury in a couple of weeks.

Church Street in Hogshooter got its name because there are churches on it. Duh! I am sure there are other streets in the country named that and I have been to Church Street in Burlington, Vermont. Most churches have been in Hogshooter for years and are what we might consider established. There hasn't been much church building going on for quite a while. In fact, the Christian

Church folded and sold their building to another group I will talk about shortly.

Pierre Something helped start the Catholic Church not long after he sort of founded Hogshooter. While we have discussed some about Pierre coming to the area, unanswered questions simmered just below the surface on what really happened. You will remember old Pierre just showed up and there is considerable speculation if Something was really his last name. There was no doubt from his French background he was a Catholic. When priests came to the area and ministered to the Indians as well as to the little community on the banks of the creek, some tension seemed to exist between the two. There is no record either way of whether Pierre actually attended mass or not. Maybe the reason for all of this was he was a priest himself and had to leave the priesthood. There might be some validity to this rumor given the fact he appreciated the ladies the way he did.

The Catholics always had a strong presence in Sensible County. The group is not quite as vigorous now because of the decline in population. The current priest is of Vietnamese origin and ministers to several other churches in the area. Violet's is the largest around but still not big enough to have a priest of its own. Father Lam lives in Hogshooter because that is where the parish house is located. A big nice building is located there as well. It used to be a Catholic school but closed a number of years ago. For a time, it served Native American students in the area.

The Protestants line the sides of Church Street. There are the Baptists, Methodists and the Presbyterians. The Apostolic Brethren Church of the Holy Spirit bought the old Christian Church building. I mentioned it before because of the Brother Dooby scandal. The Baptist Church is the biggest followed by the Methodist and the Presbyterians. None are very large.

Over the years, the ministers in these churches were either very young or very old. The young ones were getting started and Hogshooter was a "good place to be from." The other side was old ministers simply cannot get the types of churches they want but are not ready to retire. A place like Sensible County is where they go. This doesn't mean they aren't dedicated or good ministers. It's just the reality of the situation.

The Presbyterian Church is now so small it actually shares a minister with another congregation in a town about thirty miles away. The Presbyterians have money and a nice building. They don't want to give up their identity as a freestanding church. I am not aware of anyone under 55 years of age being a member.

My Grandmother Josefina (Josie for short) lived in a Sensible County town not as big as Hogshooter. It didn't have a school or any real business base. The town literally started to disappear. As the older population died, no one replaced them.

Grandma Josie went to a little church there all of her life. I can remember going to it in the summer and the windows were open when it was hot. The pews were not pews at all but slats of wood nailed together and painted. Oh, they were so hard you couldn't help but squirm. It had no nursery so all the members of the family sat together. If a kid started crying, someone got up and took the child outside. Originally, the church had an outdoor privy. In later years, I remember going to church with her and she proudly showed me the newly added indoor bathroom.

For most of my life, the preacher there was her cousin, Ralph. The only way he afforded being a minister was because he also taught school in the little town before the school closed. While that little church's building was crude, I don't ever think I felt as much love anywhere else as I did there. I always felt at home.

Ralph died and most everyone moved away. Granny and her friends refused to quit going to that church. It was theirs since they were kids. I remember a picture of the congregation one Sunday and there were just three old ladies. Hymnals in hand, they made a joyful noise unto the Lord. In the background, you could see the Sunday School attendance board. A lot of you will remember these. You changed the numbers to reflect the attendance and the offering amount. That Sunday the attendance was 3 and the offering was $1.00.

I went back by there in the last year. The building is boarded up. Its memories will remain.

Surrounding the building (it is not the church, the people were the church) is a cemetery. Most of those little churches had them. This particular one sits on a hill. I thought what a wonderful place to be after you die because of the view. One set of my grandparents are buried are there.

I still remember Grandma Josie's funeral. She wrote it out ahead of time. The idea was for Ralph to preach it but he died before her. The old preacher who performed the service knew her for a while. He followed along with what she wrote down. I never will forget coming to the closing hymn. The old man looked over his glasses at the audience and said, "Josie says you are to sing 'When the Roll is Called Up Yonder I'll be There.' By the way, she adds that you are to sing it like you mean it!"

Now, that is my Grandma!

I should tell you about Brother Dooby of the Apostolic Brethren Church of the Holy Spirit. I have teased you with it a couple of times already.

You will remember, I indicated the Christian Church didn't exist in Hogshooter any more. A group bought the building for the Apostolic Church. It was a non-denominational group of charismatic Christians. To their credit and considering the population of the area, they do pretty well. The reason why has been the subject of national and international inquiry for a number of years.

Anyway, Tyrus Dooby was the church's minister with his wife, Zelda. They had a son and a daughter. Neither were lookers but the few times I visited with Brother Dooby he seemed nice enough. He possessed a seriousness about him when it came to religion. The family fit quite nicely into the community. He advocated a very narrow perspective when it came to morals and raising children. Brother Dooby often appeared before the school board for one reason or another. None of this bothered most people because he took an interest in what was going on in the schools.

Then something happened at the church. For several weeks, there were meetings and special prayer sessions. Only members were privy to the happenings. Then suddenly, a small article appeared in the Disappointment from the board of deacons stating after prayerful consideration Brother Tyrus Dooby decided to pursue another opportunity.

That seemed strange to me but it wasn't any of my business. Later, I found out what happened. Tyrus came out of the Army and went to a religious college. There he met Zelda. These types of colleges observed very strict rules in those days. The girls had to be in the dorms early every evening. Well, Tyrus and Zelda missed the hours several times. Finally, the dean called them into his office and asked why they were late. Tyrus replied they started praying and simply lost track of the time. The excuse was accepted with the proviso that it didn't happen again.

Well, it did and Tyrus and Zelda prayed so hard she got pregnant. The college expelled them.

Someone in Hogshooter found out about this incident. Tyrus and Zelda never lied about what happened. They loved their kids and when asked in Sensible County about it, they told the truth.

You know, I find it a paradox that a religion based on forgiveness would not forgive Tyrus and Zelda. I hope they find what they are looking for in life. I am just sorry we didn't have the capacity to let them stay in Hogshooter.

For the most part, all of the churches get along pretty well. There is tension from time to time but the disagreements are civil. A few years back, a full-fledged feud broke out between the Catholics and the Baptists. Now before anyone gets their panties in a wad, everyone in this part of the country knew about it and thought it was the stupidest thing that happened in Sensible County that year. During my lifetime, every population and every church, for that matter, have people who lose total consciousness when it comes to reality. To them, everything is black or white. There are no shades of gray. If you do not agree with them, then you are wrong. The worst abusers of reality are politicians. They are always right no matter what their positions are.

Anyway, I may add a section on politicians later. The yellow notes of the hysterical society probably can't take this much stress.

The controversy erupted on the signs outside the churches. Putting the times of services and special announcements are fine. It's those idiotic little sayings that drive me absolutely nuts. There are actual places you can buy these if you aren't smart enough to think them up yourself. Anyway, the feud broke out on the signs. I think that Burl (the truth) egged the situation on by running a picture of the signs each time they were changed. He called it news. We talked about the whole deal and we both agreed how stupid the situation was. Burl (the truth) admitted he encouraged the two sides to disagree. When I looked at it from that perspective, maybe it wasn't too bad after all. By encouraging the two parties, the feud demonstrated how stupid they could be. A faction in each church immediately jumped to the defense of their congregation and the sign battle became a struggle between good and evil.

The marquees went something like this:

Catholic: "Next Saturday at 10 AM Father Lam will hold the annual blessing of the animals in the parish hall."

Baptist: "We pray for the souls of people because animals don't have souls."

Catholic: "We pray for all God's creatures and including heathens who don't like dogs."

Baptist: "Pets don't go to heaven."

Catholic: "All of God's creatures go to heaven."

Baptist: "Only humans have souls and can accept Christ."

Catholic: "So, babies don't go to heaven because they haven't accepted Christ?"

Baptist: "Babies have souls."

Catholic: "God thought so much of our pets He made them before humans."

Baptist: "Humans were made last in His image."

Catholic: "Women were made after men so they must be perfect."

Baptist: "Women were made from man's rib and the woman obeys her husband."

Catholic: "Tell your wife that she must obey you. Then duck."

Baptist: "God gave dominion over all the animals to man."

Catholic: "Since I have dominion over the animals, I want my dog to go to heaven."

Baptist: "Dogs have no more soul than a rock."

Catholic: "The streets of heaven are paved with gold. Gold is made from a rock so dogs must be in heaven."

Baptist: "May God forgive you your sins."

Catholic: "And yours. Remember, God is simply doG spelled backwards!"

Finally, all this nonsense stopped when the congregations made it stop. At the height of the controversy, a rumor started that someone in the Baptist church contacted immigration and reported that Father Lam was illegal. When Burl (the truth) reported the rumor in the Disappointment, the community finally took a good hard look at itself and put a stop to this war of words.

Ain't it amazing...

None of this is as bad as what happened in a rural community about fifty miles from Hogshooter. I am not going to name it because I might get sued or shot. In those hills, I would more than likely get shot.

There is a very small church way back in the sticks. It only has about twenty-five members and you really have to look to find it. The church actually meets in the upstairs of a small store that one of its members owns. The rumor was it took the Bible literally and the members reflected that way of thinking in their appearances. Another item that surfaced from time to time was the use of venomous snakes in its services. That belief comes from Mark 16:18. All this is rumor. From time to time, kids sneak out there and try to peek into the windows or disrupt the services in some way. That was hard to do since the church met upstairs above the store.

Some high school boys tried it again and this time they were going to get up the stairs and look in. As they approached the door, a man exited carrying a snake. The kids were so scared they got out of there as fast as they could. The story of the man carrying that snake flashed through the county like wildfire.

The next week one of the members got into a heated discussion with a church member from one of the "mainline" denominations. Things got testy and the rural member was holding his own quoting scripture. All the other man said was "well, we don't keep any snakes upstairs at our church." The rural man got the strangest look on his face and asked what he was talking about. The member told him about what the boys saw. Then, a wide smile came on the rural fellow's face and he started laughing. The boys had indeed seen a snake. Somehow, a garter snake made it upstairs and it was simply being removed.

No one believed that story. The truth simply isn't any fun. Most people wanted there to be serpents upstairs.

I for one much prefer a conspiracy theory.

As the churches in Hogshooter began to dry up, it became harder for them to raise money. A lot of them turned to special events like a Wednesday night dinner or other types of activities to help with things like youth activities. One of the most successful was the Methodist's twice-yearly bean supper. This turned out to be a big deal as a fundraiser and because the food was very good. Not only were there beans and cornbread served but homemade desserts as well.

The little church named a friend of mine as the minister. A planning session for the bean supper was after his first Sunday sermon. The woman in charge asked the minister's wife to attend and serve on the committee. Obviously, she agreed. Before the meeting started, the member told the minister's wife about Sister Bernice. She was the oldest member at the church and served on the committee. Bernice was a widow woman and didn't have much money. The committee always asked her first what she wanted to bring. Then the group proceeded to plan from there.

The meeting started well and the chairwoman asked Sister Bernice what she wanted to bring for the supper.

She replied, "I think I will bring some of those special onions this time."

"Special onions, Sister Bernice?"

"Yes, those special onions. They have some strange name. Let me see if I can remember them. Oh, yes, I will bring the Viagra onions," she proudly added.

For just a second, there was a stunned silence over the committee. The new minister's wife did not know what to do but the situation quickly moved on when everyone realized that Sister Bernice was bringing the Vidalia onions. And, that is what she brought.

Apparently, the word got out about the Viagra onions. That bean supper was the biggest success the church ever hosted. The line to get in stretched around two sides of the building. The rumor is the number of men attending the bean supper was up considerably. Maybe I should change that wording and say the number of men attending the bean supper grew. Uh, well, you know what I am trying to say.

In Hogshooter, groups of college kids come to the churches in town. It didn't make any difference what denomination groups came to the churches for various reasons. Some colleges called them revival teams and they held services on Friday and Saturday nights plus Sunday mornings. The meetings included activities intended to get the local kids to come to church. For the most part, these were successful and accomplished some good things. Other schools sent out musical groups to sing at churches and college choirs toured at various times of the year.

One of my buddies attended a small college in a neighboring state. The school's musical program was quite good. He sang in a men's quartet that went out several weekends a year to put on musical programs. Often times the churches they visited were small so the singers attended Sunday School or whatever was taking place there with the rest of the members.

At one of these small churches, the quartet sat on the front row during the church school lesson. One of the more mature ladies shared what she was supposed to say. Now, any of you that have been Sunday School teachers know you are basically presented at least an outline of what you are to teach. This particular day the lesson dealt with the significance of circumcision in the Jewish tradition. During the course of the lesson, she got confused and started talking about the requirement of castration. The young men from the college immediately caught the mistake and became uncomfortable. Remember now, these guys are sitting in the front row as this lady gets louder and louder about the necessity of castrating all the men.

I am sure some ladies in the audience agreed with the teacher about the necessity of castrating the men folks. I am just as sure that the men in the audience became quite concerned. My friend in the group reported the experience as quite new to his understanding of Jewish history. He reported as he listened to her expound on the subject, he felt a certain pseudo pain beginning to grow in his groin area.

The next year he had an opportunity to return to the church but politely refused. He didn't want to take a chance of the practice being implemented.

I have known a lot of PK's during my life. For you whose light takes some time to turn on, PK stands for "preacher's kid." This group can be an interesting lot. Many of them follow their fathers or mothers into church work. When I was growing up, there was usually a literal interpretation of the New Testament that would not allow women to do many things in the church. Thankfully, many of the main line denominations are changing and allowing women to become ministers or at least play a major role in a congregation. I don't believe for a minute that God is a chauvinist in this regard. Let's face it, women can relate much better to certain groups than men can. Enough of that...

Now don't you guys who are PK's get mad at me because you know full well that what I am going to say is absolutely true. Some of these people were the wildest human beings I knew. I guess an element of revolt was present in their lives because of their parents' expectations. For some going to college, it was the first time they were away from home. While the opportunities to rebel were few at a religious college, there were freedoms and temptations. Many took full advantages of the vices of life and enjoyed them. I remember one brother and sister whose father was a chaplain in the military. They lasted a year or two and transferred to a state university. As I looked back, I suspect their agreement with their father was to come to the Christian college first and then they could transfer.

Again, don't get the idea these kids weren't good people because they were. I suppose in a way their new freedom is similar to the Amish "rumspringa" except maybe not quite so extreme. There simply comes a point in a person's life where he/she needs to try out the world.

I remember one PK I will never forget. I was in the service with him in El Paso. His parents were missionaries in South America. As a result, he lived in a very structured environment. When he reached a certain age, it was off to a Christian high school. After that, he returned to the United States to attend a denominational college. In all ways, he was bilingual. Spanish, not Mexican, was just as much a first language to him as English.

Several of us went out a bunch times while we were in El Paso. This guy drank like few people I have ever been around. As I listened to him talk, I realized this was an act of rebellion. His life finally presented him with an opportunity to sample the palette of the real world.

I am not fluent in Spanish or any other language. Some people would even go so far as to say I'm not fluent in English. During my time I was in El Paso, I had the feeling on some occasions that the locals mocked soldiers. This happened once when I was with my friend. A group of locals said something and he turned, faced them, and let out a string of perfect Spanish. The locals looked stunned and I thought there might be trouble. We quickly left.

When we were safely away, I asked what he said. He cussed out the group using perfect Spanish not like their butchered language. And, he added some words they had never heard. I wondered what happened to this guy. Like many of the PKs I have known, he might be in religious work now. Who knows...

Church Camps...ah, they come in all sizes and types. As my kids grew, it seemed like there was one for every season and reason. When I was young, there were only a few. For my denomination, one huge camp operated for only a few weeks during the summer. I tried to avoid going. A couple of years I had to go. The size and location of your church determined which week you attended. If the congregation owned its cabin, the church picked when its kids attended. The church rented it out to other groups when not in use.

My church wasn't big or affluent enough to have a cabin. We rented one and shared it with people we did not know. It had no air conditioning and two floors. The girls stayed upstairs and the boys down. Each church was responsible for cooking the meals and chaperoning the kids. I am sure it was a nightmare for the adults.

Those attending were all junior and senior high kids so you begin to get an idea of the environment. Several thousand kids went each week. Most of the males looked for girls and vice versa. My daughter has a friend whose parents made her go every year. She said a new measure of the success of the camp was how many girls got pregnant. I hope that is not true but I wouldn't be surprised. One of my roommates in college married a young lady whose parents ran one of these camps. He'd help a lot of the time and used to go down to the sewage pond to count the number of used condoms in the sewage lagoon.

When I went to camp, I never knew about any of this. In the mornings, we were supposed to go to Bible classes. They were boring and horrible. We tried to sneak out. There were no classes relevant to real world issues. As I look back, Church seemed to be the logical place to talk about things like that. Real problems were not discussed. Some churches have now made real progress in educating kids about sex and drugs.

In Hogshooter's state, sex education is not in schools. People wonder why we have one of the highest rates of teenage pregnancies in the United States. Duh. I guess the politicians believe if you talk about sex and drugs then kids will want to do them. More likely, they will want to try them if they don't know anything.

Anyway, back to the church camp. Every evening the campers gathered in a big open-air tabernacle to worship. Groups tried to sneak off and not go. Roving "enforcers" herded these kids back to the service. In this giant building, you had several thousand kids pressed together in 90-to-100-degree temperatures. Huge fans tried to keep the air moving. In these hot times, it wasn't unusual for scores of kids to be overcome with heat. That old open-air tabernacle has been replaced with an air-conditioned one. A church was lucky if its cabin had air conditioning. Our group was never that lucky. The sides just opened and everyone hoped for a breeze.

One summer a funny and to some sad happening took place during camp. Our church hired a new minister and he was a neat man. He brought his young family with him to spend a couple of days with the kids from church. The minister was aware of what took place at camp and he "rescued" some of us for a while one day. There were some attractions nearby and he took us to see them. The group that went had a good time with his family.

On the way back, someone noted several roadside stands were selling cider. To some in our very conservative church the connotation of the word cider alone would lend it a sin. The preacher knew better, agreed to stop and let us each buy a bottle of either apple or cherry cider. A quart of apple cider is a lot so several of us took what we didn't drink back to the cabin.

In our church, we had a kid who was the orneriest person who ever lived. He came by it honestly. His mother and big sister were on him all the time. Poor Bobby could not do anything right. One or the other was always in his face. Bobby wasn't the brightest bulb on the string. I almost think he tried to do things to spite the ladies in the family.

Bobby went to camp with us but didn't go on our little side trip to town. When we returned, he asked what we carried. We told him.

Now remember, I have said Bobby's pulp was not strained from his orange juice so he immediately thought we had hard cider. He asked if he could have some. Our response was sure but it would be a little bit for some reason or the other. We took one of the almost empty bottles, put tea and alum in it and then peed to fill it up. Then we gave it to Bobby. He drank most of it and said he was getting drunk. He staggered around for the rest of the afternoon. I don't think I have laughed any harder in my life.

I wonder what ever happened to Bobby. I am sure he was drafted and that was good for him. Hopefully, Bobby stayed away from that cider!

I told you about my Grandma Josie. What a beautiful human being she was. My mother was her daughter in every way. I have never known a sweeter, kinder person than mom. I don't ever remember hearing her say a bad word about anyone. She was a seamstress and my how she could sew. Besides her family, I think she loved her God and her church almost as much. Mom sat by the hour in front of the picture window in our house reading her Bible. After she died, I went through them and compiled her comments. I found them to be interesting and astute.

To her sin was everywhere and she constantly battled it. I suspect over her lifetime mom had fights with the devil like the one written by Benet in *The Devil and Daniel Webster*. I don't think there was anything worst to her than alcohol. My guess is that nary a dram passed her lips her whole life.

Mom and Dad both loved their garden. One year there was an infestation of slugs and these rascals ate her tomatoes. She tried about everything but nothing worked. Finally, she called the local agricultural extension agent and he told her what to do. When he did, Mom was horrified. She was to buy some beer, pour it in saucers and put it into the garden. The slugs went for the beer and the tomatoes were safe.

I am certain Mom agonized about this but finally told Dad to go to the store and get a couple of cans of beer. He was to make sure no one saw him. He did and put the saucers in the garden. Mom fretted and worried about that beer in her refrigerator. I guess she was afraid God (through the minister of course) would make a surprise visit to her house and demand to see if there was any beer in the refrigerator. That is one guilty conscience. By the way, the slugs died.

There is an old joke that is on point here. "What do you do when you see a fellow Baptist in a liquor store? Ignore him and he will ignore you."

I can say that I know there are angels in this world and in my life because my mother was one.

Ignore the Yellow Notes

I started pretending I was revising the yellow notes of the hysterical society. I suspect you realized by now that idea has gone by the wayside. Besides, a lot of the interesting things don't fit nicely into any of the categories I have covered.

The older I get, the more I love elderly. My uncle says the older you get the quicker you get older. He is well into his mid-90's now. There is a lot of truth to that statement. The average age of the people left in Hogshooter rose over the last few years. I bet you can go to many rural communities these days and find this to be the norm. One growth business in Sensible County the last few years is retirement homes. We used to call them nursing homes but I guess you can't do that anymore.

My parents were an interesting self-study in what happens when you get old. Dad worked up into his eighties before he finally decided to retire. My parents were lucky because they didn't suffer from dementia or senility. In fact, there isn't a history of cancer or any serious diseases in my family. Dad drove until a few months before his death at 93. His eyes actually improved later in life after cataract surgery. Almost every evening they went to a local restaurant to eat. They discovered pizza late in life. I believe dad ate either bacon and eggs or sausage and eggs at least five or six times a week his whole lifetime. Finally killed him at 93.

When dad was about 90, mom got worried about him. His cholesterol was high and she told him to watch what he ate. I said, "Mom, he's 90 years old let him eat what he wants." After my great aunt had a stroke, my great uncle used to take her for an ice cream cone every night. He used to say it was time to go get a "dip." At their ages, I figured they earned whatever they wanted.

My parents lived full and good lives. Every time the church doors opened, they were there. Dad had a key and was often the first person to greet everyone. There wasn't a baby or kid he couldn't win over. Fridays and Saturdays were special as well. These were garage sale days. Dad got a copy of the paper and mapped out a route in Hogshooter and neighboring communities. Off they went early in the morning. Sometimes they came home with interesting stuff. I finally asked mom why she was buying what I thought was junk. She informed me she wanted to make sure they had plenty to sell when they had a yard sale.

While I shook my head at what she said, in retrospect that makes complete sense now.

Food...mom and dad lived through the depression. I am sure times were tough but they did not have to worry about that later in life. Their garden was the envy of east Hogshooter. Dad kept it rotor tilled and ready. He always added sheep manure for fertilizer. Cow or horse manure would not do. It had to be sheep. Dad knew something that is for sure.

They planted about everything you can think of from corn to green beans to squash to okra to tomatoes to cucumbers and the list seemed endless. Even though just the two of them, mom canned enough food to feed Hogshooter for a year. She even canned fish dad caught. She kept two refrigerators and one freezer full of food. Mom also kept cash in the freezer. Guess that is cold, hard cash. Sorry, I couldn't pass that one up. When anyone came to visit, he or she left with a box of food. By the way, mom also made and froze pies. Now those were to kill for I want to tell you.

As often happens, they began to slip some physically and a little mentally as well. Mom never stood up to dad in her life but she finally told him it was time to go to a nursing home (that is what she called it). That is a switch when a parent asks to go. My parents tried assisted living first and mom loved it. Dad didn't but said the reason he wanted to leave was because mom was working too hard. My brother and I did not approve of them leaving so he got people from the church to help and move them back home.

Dad got sick and passed away. For the next year, mom enjoyed the nursing home. One of her friends moved in also. That woman informed her kids this was now her home and she wasn't going back to the old house.

When I first visited mom, I felt terrified of the place. The sights and smells overwhelmed me. That all changed. The residents were good people just transitioning to another part of their lives. Everyone had a kiddie gate on his/her door. If you didn't, everyone came wandering in. There was one horny old fellow who pictured himself a ladies' man. He got caught in bed with one gal and fancied themselves as boyfriend and girlfriend.

Mom got sick and for a brief time went to another facility for rehab. Why? Don't get me started. It had something to do with government rules. Anyway, she shared a room with another lady and every evening her boyfriend came down and they started making out. That made Mom mad. After she moved back to her nursing home, I found out the couple got married.

I told you the story of the man who had wheelchair races in the nursing home. Before these places knew about dementia and the like, they were pretty wide open. As you drove by, people sat out front enjoying the sun or whatever. In those days, Burl (the truth) ran a police blotter in the Disappointment. There was an entry that buffalo was called to the alley behind the nursing home. It seems two of the residents snuck out (remember that is when you really sneak out) and fought. This event caused a sensation in the community for a while. As usual, a group wanted a grand jury investigation into the nursing home running a fighting ring for gambling purposes. There weren't enough signatures secured but some wanted to know where to place their bets.

That was the same day buffalo was called to the grade school because two amorous dogs were "hung up" and distracting the students. A bucket of cold water cured the problem. The same thing happened to one of my friend's gospel quartet. The four men sang in the front of the church and saw out the glass doors at the back. Two dogs began to do what came naturally and the men in the quartet had difficulty finishing their concert. Temptation is hell.

A married couple in Hogshooter by the names of Spiffy and Ida Albert moved to the local nursing home. The agreement with management was the couple (one or both) could come and go as they pleased during the day. Both lost some of their mental facilities. Each became convinced the other was crazy. As a result, it wasn't uncommon for one of them to be at the sheriff's office trying to get their spouse committed. The Remarkable Bank was still open during this time. Spiffy went down one day and said he needed new checks. The customer service representative secured the pertinent information. She told him the free checks were blue in color and would be ready the next day. Spiffy said he wanted green checks. Again, the nice lady told him all they had were blue. He got mad and told her that if he didn't get green ones then he would piss on the blue ones until they turned green. Spiffy was committed right full time after that.

This is also about the time an escaped disco era mental patient tried to rob the bank. He came in wearing a broad hat and six-inch high shoes. The Remarkable brothers chased him down the street and tackled him.

Crime has never been a big problem in Hogshooter.

We did have a recent incident where the city finally confiscated the driver's license of Nipper Beatty. Nipper is quite a legend in Sensible County for his service during WWII, the big one. Stationed in England for a while, he took part in the D-Day landing. According to him, Ike asked his advice often and the Allies won the war because of him.

Nipper's mind began to slip from time to time and he had a little trouble driving. He told the City Council this was London and they needed to drive on the left side of the road or someone would get hurt. He did clip Mrs. Smith's rose trellis a couple of times when he drove on the left. The council asked him about his parallel parking and Nipper replied as long as there was a car in front and back he was fine. He backed up until he hit the first car and pulled forward until he hit the second one. Then he'd split the difference. While his logic was crystal-clear, the town fathers decided he needed to surrender his license.

We used to have our own mortuary in Hogshooter. We called it the funeral home. No one is there most of the time. A bunch over at Violet bought it. The phone rings over there and then people come and open up the Hogshooter building.

From when the mortuary opened during the oil boom until it sold out, it remained in one family. The Polks were a cornerstone of the community. During most of this time, the "face" of the funeral business was Chief Polk. I never heard what his real name was because everyone called him Chief. He wore a dark suit with a wicked little smile on his face. Growing up, someone told me he went to a special doctor and the smile was surgically placed on his face. I was stupid enough to believe it.

I asked Burl (the truth) about the Polk Family funeral home and he filled me in on its history. Chief's pappy first opened the mortuary on Main Street. Apparently, Mr. Polk (everyone always called him this) was in the funeral business many years before he came to Hogshooter. He didn't have a motorized hearse in those days but one pulled by a couple of huge black horses. Whenever there was a funeral, those magnificent stallions slowly came down the street from the funeral home to the church and then the cemetery. They wore black feather plumes attached to their harnesses as they clip-clopped down the street. Mr. Polk never got in a hurry. Don't guess one should be in a hurry for a funeral.

Burl (the truth) even showed me a picture from the archives of the Disappointment taken the day the horses were retired. They were something. The wagon they pulled had glass sides so everyone could see the casket. Brass poles decorated the top. That had to be some special way to go to the cemetery.

From the time Chief could walk, he was going to be in the funeral business. His daddy gave him a little wagon and he often pulled it all over Hogshooter wailing like an ambulance. Remember, in those days the funeral homes often owned the ambulance services.

Anytime Chief heard about a dog, cat or some other animal dying, he came flying through town and picked up that poor creature. He'd bring it back to his little "workshop" behind his parent's house and prepare it for burial. I'm not sure what he did to the bodies and I ain't going to ask. The Chief possessed a little plot of ground and he'd dig a hole and bury the body. There was no doubt that boy was following his father into the "business."

Burl (the truth) told a story about Chief when he was away at mortuary school. Seemed Chief saw a cat killed and placed it in a paper sack. He put the sack in the back seat of his car with the windows down. He worked in this small town's funeral home as an intern. He noticed an elderly woman walking by his car. She glanced in and saw that sack. She studied it for a while and then went on down the street. A little while later, she passed by it again and studied the sack a little more. The lady looked around and then stepped away. Then she approached the car again, looked around, reached in and grabbed the sack.

By this time, Chief was about to die (pun intended) laughing so he slipped out and followed her down the street. She entered the local café and sat at a table in the front window. Chief decided to watch her for a while. Finally, he could tell that she was dying (pun intended) of curiosity to see what was inside the bag. Finally, after looking around again, she slowly opened the sack and let out a scream. She fainted dead (pun intended) on the spot and fell out of her chair.

Next thing Chief knew, an ambulance came screaming down the street and put her on a gurney and loaded her into the vehicle.

As they did, a waitress in the café motioned them to stop. She picked up the sack with the dead cat in it and put it on her chest. Chief said the last time he saw the woman was as they loaded her into the ambulance with that dead cat on her chest. Over the years, he often wondered if the old lady ever recovered and what happened to that cat.

Another story Chief told dealt with a friend of his who worked his way through college driving an ambulance for a smalltown mortuary. One of the benefits of the job was he used the apartment above the funeral home. Chief said this young man was a very heavy sleeper and one night got a little lit up and couldn't make it up the stairs. He stripped and crawled in an open casket and passed out. Some of his friends came by and found him. One of them concocted this great idea. They put the casket into the ambulance and took it over to a local women's college. They placed the casket in the dining room in the middle of the night. As it started to serve breakfast, one of the friends opened the casket. One can only imagine the chaos or delight that followed as the female students came in for their mandatory meal. When he finally did wake up, he couldn't get out and had to wait until rescued.

The situation turned out well because someone left three phone numbers in the casket and a red ribbon placed on a certain part of his anatomy. For several months, young ladies passed him on the street and conveyed they liked his red ribbon.

For a while, Burl (the truth) said the funeral home had a blond mortician. She lost her job over a specific incident. This whole situation sounds a little fishy to me but I'll relate it. She was in charge of two funerals of gentlemen who died the same day. The bodies were prepared for viewing and the families invited in to look at them. The first family liked what they saw but noted the other body was wearing a brown suit and indicated they wished they had used the deceased's one of the same color. The other family said they liked the blue color of the other body's suit. The next day the families returned just before the funerals. Low and behold the one body now had on a brown suit and the other a blue one. The families were very pleased but wondered how the blonde mortician was able to switch the suits on such short notice. She indicated that it really wasn't a problem. All she did was to switch the heads of the bodies to fit the right color! Got ya!

When I was growing up, I was a good basketball player. Chief and his wife only had girls and he always sponsored kids' teams of various kinds. He was a good athlete and especially had an interest in basketball. Chief took us boys to every tournament he could find. We won a bunch and somehow qualified for a YMCA tournament in Dallas. He pulled some strings and a company from Violet flew us down free of charge on their plane. When we landed, one of those big mortuary cars from a local funeral home met our plane and took us to the tournament. I bet we were the only team that ever arrived like that. Our team went on to win that competition. I never will forget that and it would never have happened without Chief's help.

The mortuary had a black fellow named Walter who worked there. I remembered him as well as Chief. He said that when business was slow, his father hunted for things to keep them busy. Walter and he hid in the caskets with the lids down to keep away from his dad. Chief also said they took naps in there. I can just visualize an Edgar Allen Poe story about someone who gets inside a casket and the lid falls and locks. It was bad enough walking down Main Street and going past the big window with an open casket on display. Imagine one yelling at you.

There was a rumor while I was growing up that the funeral home went out every Halloween and buried the bodies of the paupers it accumulated during the year. Another one said it kept all of these in a big refrigerator and on Halloween cleaned it out by selling the bodies for dog food. They stopped when they found a person in there who was actually still alive or at least that is what I heard.

I asked Chief about this and he just smiled. He worked until he was old. He'd wear a black suit and his hair was snow white and combed straight back. None of his daughters wanted to go into the business and he sold the mortuary. Chief went to live with one of the girls. I heard he had a stroke and was in bad shape. Knowing him, he has extensive instructions as to his funeral. His empty plot is next to his wife in the Hogshooter Cemetery.

Adjacent to the cemetery is Doody's Dumps Road. It is extremely hilly. We used to go over it fast and you felt your car leaving the ground. Yes, I know that is stupid. There is a story that a local kid was killed doing that very thing on the road. The legend goes he was decapitated and his head was never found. The body is buried in the Hogshooter Cemetery and when the weather is just right the body comes out looking for his head.

Over the years, this phenomenon became the ghost light of Sensible County. I can remember as a kid going on a church outing and waiting for the head to come out. I never saw it and don't know if anyone ever did. Chief told me there was actually methane gas there and when the weather conditions were just right you could see something.

Well, I don't know about that but my buddies and I convinced some unsuspecting young ladies to go on snipe hunts with us. The idea was to get them out in the woods under the pretense of hunting for these little birds called snipes. I never knew of anyone who actually caught one of these little boogers. Another favorite activity with the girls was going to see the submarine races. You go to a pond or lake and park. It takes an intelligent person to fall for that trick. Most of the time everyone knew what was going to happen and why the couples parked at the lake.

My favorite excuse to park was a watermelon roast. The idea was to get a date, go out in the country, build a fire and throw a watermelon in the fire. The sphere would explode and then you went out in the dark and got a piece. Can't you just visualize a bunch of teenagers laughing at this?

When someone died in Hogshooter and cremated, I figured Chief buried the ashes in the cemetery. I found out differently a few years ago at one of our high school reunions. Sally Blue came up and started talking with me about the time her friend Nancy and I broke one of her mother's antique chairs. I remembered it but high tailed it out and she took the heat. Anyway, Sally asked if I noticed there was a for sale sign up at her old house. I did. She said her mother died and her ashes were out in the car. Sally was going over later that night to spread the ashes in the flowerbeds according to her mother's wishes. Sally related how she snuck (that is when you really sneak) onto the fourteenth tee of a local golf course and put her dad's ashes there.

That got me to thinking. Cremation makes a lot of sense to me now. As I mentioned before, that is what I am going to do. I have thought about my ashes being put at the old drive-in theater or given to someone I didn't like to irritate them. An ex-wife would be an example. I will settle for a local church.

I need to talk about Crazy Cal Whippersnicker (I ain't kidding) since I have been dealing with the cemetery. We used to have a nine-hole golf course in Hogshooter. It is gone now and new assisted living center and pig farm occupy the land. The boys down at the café didn't like what happened out there and talked about a grand jury investigation. However, no one could figure out if the sale was against the law since it was private property.

The Birdie and Bogey Gold Club of Sensible County was quite the gathering place. The course hosted the Hogshooter Open and attracted the best golfers from around the area. The first prize the last year of the tournament was a gift basket of Sensible County goods and certificates. Of special note was a free mullet from the Cinderella hair salon, a lawn mower tune up, and a year's supply of homemade hemorrhoid cream from Booker's Drug in Violet. You can make all the fun of it you want but that cream is a special blend of hemorrhoid medicine and is in great demand because it shrinks those boogers right up.

The last open took place years ago. The reason for its cancellation was Red (the terror) Rinehart got drunk and drove his lawn mower (which he was using for a cart to carry his three clubs) into the pond on the golf course and dang near drowned. He threatened to sue but backed off when the sponsors showed the terror pictures of his trail. Seems he forgot, engaged the mower blade and damaged several fairways. The embarrassment to the male golfers was the real reason for the cancellation of the event. The winner the last year was ten-year old Ivy (five iron) Driver. She was a natural golfer and won by nine shots. Ivy went on to be quite the player. She got a scholarship to Wisteria Tech but got kicked out for not going to class and spending too much time playing with the boys' golf team.

Now, I better get back to Crazy Cal, the golf course and the cemetery. What I haven't told you about our golf course was it had sand greens. Some of you old timers know about these. You hit your ball onto the sand. Once you got there, you took this big heavy steel contraption and smoothed a path to the hole. Your putt was on this smooth path. If you really wanted to cheat, one could draw a little rut on the path and try to get your golf ball to stay in that crease right into the hole. Believe me it's a lot more difficult than it sounds.

When Crazy Cal played golf with me, he only got one club. It was usually a three wood. Cal played the whole course with the club. And, he ran all the time. That was good because his shots were so bad he needed to chase them down in order to stay with us.

The second hole was right next to the cemetery. I do mean right next to it. A barbed wire fence separated the two and it was no more than five feet from the tee and the fairway. There was one little bush about half way down toward the green. Crazy Cal teed off and sliced his drive into the cemetery. He took his club and climbed over the fence to play out. It was not unusual for us to play out of the cemetery. On one particular day, Chief was burying some poor smuck and Cal's golf ball lands no more than ten feet from the graveside service. Undaunted, Crazy played his next shot back to the fairway during the prayer. I thought Chief was going to kill Cal and he probably would have if he could've caught him. Remember that one little bush I mentioned before? Well, I was hiding behind it because for once in my life I was totally embarrassed. Cal wasn't.

Crazy never had many golf balls. Personally, I considered a round successful if I finished with as many balls as I started with.

They did not have to be the same ones. Cal played until he lost all of his balls. Then he would go over to the pond on the course and strip down to his shorts and dive in. He gathered as many balls as he could find, put his clothes back on and start playing again. If someone wanted to play while he was in the pond, Cal dove under the water until after the shot. If the shot went into the pond, it was his.

The Remarkables owned a mausoleum at the cemetery. Their family was all there. The lock on the gate broke so you could actually go down the steps into the crypt. In the dark, it was scary. Around Halloween one year, Crazy and I had dates with a couple of young girls from Violet. We parked in the cemetery and after a while, the four of us needed a break so we got out of the car. Crazy suggested I show the girls the mausoleum while he took care of some business. I figured he just needed to go behind a tree and relieve himself. I was acting like a big man and told some story about something that happened in the crypt. We got there and the girls were holding on to me (which I liked) as we started down the steps. The gate creaked open and as we stepped in the light caught sight of a body hanging from the top of the ceiling. Everyone thought it was a joke until it screamed. You talk about racing out of that place the three of us must have set a world's record. Then we hear then horse laugh. Crazy set the whole thing up a head of time. He had a harness with a rope and pretended to be hanging there. I could've killed him but the girls cuddled up to us afterwards.

Crazy went over to the Bible College with me for a while. The school asked him to leave. We had no air conditioning in the dorms so it got hot in the fall. We left the windows open with the screens off most of the time. In those days when a construction crew worked on the road, they didn't have battery-powered flashers to warn of the work. Instead, they had old round ball-like smudge pots full of some type of fuel. You lit the pots and the flame warned a driver of the work. They were dirty and nasty.

One night Cal got one of those and lit it. A guy he didn't like roomed right below him. Crazy straightened out several metal coat hangers and hooked them onto this lit smudge pot. He lowered it out the window and began to swing it back and forth until he got into the room and let go. I remember the black smoke pouring out the room.

As I look back on this, it's a wonder the whole place didn't burn down. Nothing happened so I guess it went out.

Every fall and spring the college hosted a high school day. The idea was to bring in kids to look the campus over and convince them to attend school there. The administration warned the college students to be on their best behavior during this time. Crazy had a special greeting for the high school students.

He had this powerful stereo set up which he strung between two rooms. Cal turned on some of his records like a train that sounded like it was moving between the rooms. That was okay but he really got in trouble later on. At the precise instant a group of visitors including a pastor walked behind the dorm Crazy ramped up the stereo as loud as he could playing the song, the stripper. Next thing you know, Crazy is in the dean of students' office in big trouble. He didn't come back the next semester.

Before he left, Cal asked if he could go with me to the local laundry. I said sure because I went the same afternoon every week. Anyway, I am studying while I wait for my clothes and I hear a noise. I look up at one of those big commercial dryers and Crazy Cal is going around and around in it. Somehow, he had got money in, crawled into the dryer and started it.

I probably remember that incident the most when I think of him. And, he seemed to enjoy it.

THE BIBLE COLLEGE

I apologize to you historical purists out there. As I indicated at the beginning of the last chapter, I abandoned the yellow notes and will continue to do so. I am going to leave Sensible County for a while. There is a connection to my beloved home because many of the people I write about are from here. Besides, this stuff is a lot more interesting than the junk taking place in Hogshooter.

A little background to set the stage for the following. Few people from Sensible County went to college before I graduated from Hogshooter High. Most males went to avoid the draft. Sensible County is poor so many graduates did not have the money to attend. Other than oil royalties for a few lucky families, most everyone worked in agriculture.

I couldn't afford college right out of high school. My parents encouraged me to attend but I decided it was not fair for them to put me through college. Rather than join, I let the army draft me to get the GI Bill. Viet Nam hadn't cranked up much in the early 1960s.

Only twenty years old when discharged. I didn't know much about college. I was smart enough to realize I wasn't ready for a major university. Hogshooter High was so small it couldn't afford a counselor to help us determine things like that. Most college recruiters weren't going to come to a hole in the road like Sensible County. I wanted to go to college but was at a loss as to where.

Once discharged, I decided to take it easy for a while. There was a young pastor at my parents' church and I soon struck up a friendship with him. He knew of my situation and told me about a small Christian college some fifty miles away. In fact, he took me there for a visit and I liked the looks of the place. The college hoped to grow and built a new men's dormitory. Surprisingly, the tuition was reasonable. The preacher told me other local kids including Crazy Cal attended.

So, I enrolled.

Things were strict during this time at lots of colleges including here. I will just call it Bible for short. That's not its real name but I am conservative and don't want to get sued. Until a few years before I arrived, the men and women couldn't ride in cars together unless chaperoned. Thankfully, that rule was relaxed by the time I arrived. Unless you stayed at home, you lived in the dorms.

Girls had specific hours. Boys didn't. The girls were in their dorms by nine o'clock on most nights. On Wednesday nights after church, they stayed out until nine-thirty. Friday nights the curfew was eleven-thirty but back to ten-thirty on Saturdays because everyone was to get up and go to church Sunday morning. While not required, most people did. There were exceptions to these rules for special reasons or events such as homecoming. Girls wore dresses everywhere unless attending casual events. The men wore pants or jeans with no shorts in public.

At all times, students demonstrated what the administration deemed Christian behavior. The school forbade alcohol use but males could smoke. Students disappeared in the middle of the semester and it usually was for breaking a rule. The year before I got there, the administration expelled a student for something (probably alcohol). As he hitchhiked home, a news reporter from a local television station picked him up. He related what happened and that evening a story appeared on the station about the expulsion. The story made Bible look bad and eventually helped in loosening of some of its stupid rules. The expelled student went to California and started a chain of very successful restaurants.

Rules did not really bother me at this point in my life. I knew nothing about college, was a church going kid and I just returned from the Army. The first "omen" occurred on my way to school for first time when I came across a car afire in the middle of the highway. Maybe it was something like the burning bush appearing to Moses. Didn't have any significance for me at the time but maybe it should have. The second clue was when my roommate did not show up. At least I knew Crazy (for what that is worth) and a couple of others. I seriously thought about turning around and going home. I stayed and everything fell into place.

Most of the kids at Bible were a couple of years younger than me because of my time in the Army. That age difference helped with the girls. Several other veterans attended Bible. Most were ministerial students and considerably older than other students. I spotted them because of their black suits and white socks. Getting an education was important so they could go on to seminary. Many were scouting for a wife. Stop and think about it, how many bachelor ministers do you know? I have already told you the saga of Brother Dooby and his wife.

Everyone attended chapel four days a week in the new college gymnasium. Not what one would say is a typical place to hold church. It shouldn't take you long to figure out the quality of our chapel speakers. Here is this little Christian college out in the middle of nowhere. As a result, most of our chapel speakers were small church preachers from surrounding communities who thrilled us with last Sunday's sermons. Yipe, they were bad.

Chapel was mandatory with assigned seats. The ministerial students took roll because I guess the administration did not trust us peons. The first year my chapel partner was a basketball player from some little town in the Bootheel of Missouri. He drove me absolutely nuts. His girlfriend (later wife) was still in high school. She came the next year and he sort of returned to normal. Each student only got so many cuts (misses) and they doubled on days before holidays. I always saved mine up, took them then and went home early.

One thing I did learn to do was sleep in chapel. I could sit down, put my head in my hands and I was out. Then I magically woke up as chapel ended. I do remember one guy going to sleep and losing a shoe. What was so bad about that you ask? Well, all of our seats were in the upper deck and it was a ten-foot drop to the gym floor where the preacher was. So right in the middle of the sermon, pow! and this shoe hits the floor. That did spice things up a bit. It was almost as good as when someone dropped a collection bucket from up there and change flew everywhere.

We endured a fall and spring revival. Bible brought in some hotshot preacher to hammer at us for a week. They spoke during chapel and every evening as well. I got to the point I cut the final morning of the revival. The pressure to go "forward" always became intense that last day. I discovered that the older I got the less I needed that. The experience became more emotional than anything else. This is one reason later in life I became a Presbyterian. I know my shortcomings and God will take care of me if I ask. The continued emotional stress and its value are no longer relevant to me.

After the revival, the administration announced how many people were saved or rededicated their lives. The purpose of the services was to keep score. Even today, I hear mainline denominations crow about how many people they baptize each year. Does anyone really believe God keeps score and grades a church by these figures? I have a feeling Christians may be in for a big surprise when they judged before Him.

Oops, I just preached.

One chapel speaker I never forgot. You remember me saying that many of our speakers were area ministers who just recycled last Sunday's sermon. Every so often, a non-minister speaker spoke in chapel.

Both my freshman and sophomore years we had such a person. He was a chicken farmer for Clinton, Missouri. I suspect he was a graduate of Bible College at some point and probably gave a little money. The school only had three or four hundred students at the time and endowment meant something about anatomy rather than how much money it had.

This guy was a piece of work. He wore a wig whose color didn't exactly match his real hair. In fact, it was not even close. His clothes never matched. He wore plaids with stripes and checks. In later years I saw nothing wrong with this until my wife began nagging, uh, excuse me, suggesting I needed to take a look at my own clothes. Anyway, we made fun of this poor smuck every time he came to campus to speak. He drove a nice convertible and we'd see him spinning around campus with someone or the other. I always wondered how he kept that hairpiece on.

About thirty years later, I got to thinking about that old-boy. This time I didn't think about his hairpiece or his clothes. I remembered his speech. What is interesting about me recalling what he said was it was pertinent to my life. Both years he spoke on Russell Conwell's famous speech, *Acres of Diamonds*. Conwell was an ordained minister who became a very successful Chautauqua speaker. For you artless heathen out there, Chautauqua is a small town in upper New York. In the 1800's it started the tradition of bringing in guest speakers during the summer for entertainment. They delivered different speeches every evening. The practice became so successful that many communities followed suit. As a result, troupes of these traveling individuals made their way across areas of Eastern and Midwest America.

Russell Conwell was one of these individuals. Someone estimated that he gave his famous *Acres of Diamonds* speech thousands of times during his life. Thirty or so years after making fun of our chapel guest, I finally remembered what he said. Kind of scary, huh? I discovered priceless ideas that changed my life.

The story goes something like this. A farmer owned land and furnished a good living for his family. One day a stranger stopped at his village and began telling of a river of diamonds. To get the jewels, someone just bent over and scooped them up by the handfuls. The farmer became enthralled with the story and believed he could find those diamonds. He sold his land, said goodbye to his family, and started his quest. For years, he wandered to all the corners of the world searching for this easy wealth. The farmer never found the river of diamonds.

Finally, he returned to his home. By this time, the farmer was a broken man. His family was gone. He went to the person who bought his land and asked if he could walk it one last time. The landowner agreed. As the farmer came to the edge after trekking all over it, he started to ford the stream. He looked down...it was full of diamonds. The man traveled all over the world searching for something he already possessed.

I took many years to learn this powerful lesson. I know one professor who had job offers from one coast to the other and never took any of them. When I told him this story, it just clicked. Sometimes the good Lord has plans for you. You don't realize it until later in your life.

Kind of like what one of my favorite singers, Joni Mitchell, wrote in her hit, *Big Yellow Taxi,* excuse the paraphrase... "Sometimes you don't know what you got until it's gone."

As mentioned, we lived in dorms. For the guys, that wasn't too bad because a new one opened for the fall semester I arrived. The rooms were suites with a bathroom in between the two rooms. Before, all the men shared one per floor.

That bathroom/shower became very important during my first year. A city of about one hundred thousand people was thirty miles from campus. When we wanted to get away from small Bible Town, we'd head up to Big Cheese. A young lady friend of mine drove her Thunderbird up there and somehow a big "yield" sign from the interstate highway ended up in her back seat. I wasn't involved in the taking of the sign but only in abetting its hiding. Anyway, the sign made it back to Bible Town that evening and into the boys' dorm. The next thing we knew the Dean of Students was going room to room searching for that sign. Somehow, it ended up in our suite. I'm no dummy and even though I was innocent there would be dire consequences for us if he found the sign it in our room. Thinking quickly, I put the sign in the shower between the two rooms. I turned up the hot water until it steamed the mirror. Then I stepped into the shower.

There was a knock on the door and the Dean of Students entered. We did not have any constitutional rights for anything at Bible College. Anyway, the Dean was hot. He cracked the door to the bathroom and called in as the steam rolled out. I told him I was in the shower and that satisfied him. Obviously, he didn't find the sign that night. I don't know what happened but it disappeared from our room as quickly as possible.

Our dorm rooms were nice except they had stone floors and no air conditioning. Those floors got chilly in the wintertime and always noisy. I ran a fan no matter what the season to cover up the hallway activities. When talking about Crazy Cal, I mentioned tossing the smudge pot in the room and it not burning down the whole place. Those stone floors were probably a good idea. Another useful item I learned that first year was aftershave lotion. In those days, there weren't counters in department stores with rows of high-priced colognes. There might be a row or two at the local drug store and that was about it. I forgot to tell you about Lilac when I described some of the characters in Hogshooter. He was a homeless person. I did not know his real name although I am sure some in town did. At the time, the whole state was dry so unless you were affluent you couldn't get real booze. Lilac was an alcoholic and he got his name because he went into the dry goods store on Main Street and bought Lilac After Shave and Cologne. It was cheap and about fifty percent alcohol. Lilac got his buzz drinking the stuff but it also ate his brain away.

We didn't drink the stuff but it was highly flammable because of its high alcohol content. Someone studied in his room and all of a sudden a blue flame flared up from under the door. It burned itself out in a second or two. Alcohol burns blue so someone came down the hall, squirted lotion under the door and tossed in a match. It was quite a sight especially with the lights out.

Looking back, it's a wonder we did not burn the whole place down. If a fire had started, the extinguishers wouldn't have worked because we emptied them on someone. One time in chemistry class, our professor let us have a fire extinguisher fight because they were dated and needed to be recharged. It was a lot of fun except for all the chemicals clinging to your clothes.

Speaking of fire extinguishers, one of the basketball players got hold of an empty one. He drove a Volkswagen. You walked down the street minding your own business when a stream of water came from Bake's car. I don't know what the range of the stream was but it was hard to hide from.

Speaking of Volkswagens, Winnie had one. I tossed a water balloon in hers and about flooded the thing out. That was over forty years ago and she reminded me of it at our last reunion. Winnie still hasn't forgiven me. Oh, well... Another time a group of us picked up a Bug and lifted it over a low pipe rail. Then we chained it to a tree in front of the dining hall. You know, the smallest things made us happy.

I mentioned we'd head up to Big Cheese to escape Bible Town. I went up there on a Friday night with Rip (roaring) Robert and two young ladies. One of them was quite a babe. Turned out she was only interested in an upper classman, Slammin' Shannon. Slammin' always wore his pants about four inches above his shoes. Her name was Cora Belle Rippatoe.

We went to Big Cheese for some fun and we stopped at a big Katz store. These were combinations of drugstores, liquor stores and about every other type of store you wanted. I went to one in Kansas City that sold pets. Anyway, Cora Belle decides to play deaf and communicate in sign language. I didn't know whether to hide in embarrassment or to take part. She'd embarrass you by grunting or making noises if you didn't play along. The evening was quite an experience and interesting. Try it sometime and you won't believe all the looks you get. I only did that one time.

I never did date her because I never had a chance. She and

Slammin' got married but it didn't last long. Cora Belle went on to be an airline stewardess. I lost track of her years ago.

A lot of the mischief taking place in the dorms dealt with water. Some of the mischievous things we did outside the dorm also dealt with water. I guess we just liked water. Each dorm had at least one "parent" assigned to it. The new men's dorm parents were Mom and Pop Rock. For some reason dorm adults were called mom or pop. They were retired from doing something else and being a dorm parent was a good deal. Each dorm had a little apartment where they lived free of charge. In essence, they rode herd on about two hundred eighteen to twenty-four-year-olds. I would have found something else to do.

Remember, Bible College was little. But, it possessed a good basketball team. Some high school players saw the school as an opportunity to demonstrate their skills. Many of them had grown up as big fish in little ponds. They'd come to Baptist and take it by storm. Many enrolled during the summer after they graduated from high school, took a course or two and got the feel of the school.

One such player was Bobby Joe Stanley. Now, Bobby Joe was a good small-town player but not a great one. He was also a wee bit ornery. His first summer at Bible he stayed in old Men's Hall because the new dorm was not open yet. The weather turned extremely hot so every window in the place was open. Water fights broke out for heat relief if nothing else.

One afternoon he looked out the window toward the center of campus and saw Pop Rock walking back to the dorm. His mischief light went on and he ran and got a couple of cups of water. Just before Pop entered the door, Bobby Joe hit him with the water. Snickering to himself, he retreated to his room to enjoy his coup. Ten or fifteen minutes later, a knock came on his door and there stood a still wet Pop Rock. The conversation went something like this.

"Bobby Joe, why did you throw water on me?"

"Pop, I didn't throw water on you."

"Let me ask you again, why did you throw water on me?"

"What makes you think I threw water on you?"

"Because you are the only person in the dorm."

"Oh."

Pop liked Bobby Joe so he didn't get into trouble. He never did make it as a basketball player at Bible. The spring of the next year, he died in a car wreck. The accident was a freak one. Bobby Joe was riding around with a couple of girls from the town. The highway had a lip and the car hit one. He went through the back window and killed.

I remember his funeral in his high school gym. Man, I hated those services. I have attended many for people who died too young...

Each wing on each floor of the dorm had a counselor. This person was of in charge of holding down the chaos. It was a thankless job and the holders of the position usually got a small scholarship. At Bible, most of these guys were ministerial students. Some were total jerks but a lot of them were just average teenagers. One good guy was Claude Mac. He was an ordained minister. He got up early and went to the little chapel in the dorm to pray. One morning he got up, opened his door and a cup of water fell on him. He looked around and every door in the whole dorm had a cup of water on it. Can you imagine how much work it took to put a cup of water on every door? If a person took as much time studying, as it did to accomplish that, the person would make straight A's.

Claude immediately solved the mystery of the guilty party and he removed most of the cups before any other feet were baptized. How did he figure it out? Claude looked for the room that didn't have a cup on its doorknob. That was the guilty person. Yipe, we had some people whose smarts resembled a turkey looking up at the rain until they drowned.

One of my roommates got the crazy idea to see how much water a condom held. So, we filled one up. It turned out huge and we decided to take it to the car. That was no easy chore. Three of us carefully maneuvered the thing until we got it into the back seat. We cruised around town until we found someone we knew and then throw it at them. That was really a stupid idea. When we finally found one of the town girls, the monster burst and flooded the floorboard in the backseat. Believe me that was the last time I tried anything like that.

Town girls...they are a dear subject to me and other male students at Bible. This little village had more than its share of beautiful young ladies. Many of them spent time cruising past the college and smiling. Several of the college men ended up dating and even marrying the young women.

There was one young lady who always said something negative to say about the college guys and especially the local girls who dated them. I found out about it and asked her for a date. To my surprise, she accepted and it went okay I guess. The key thing I accomplished was she quit bitching about us taking out the locals.

Then there was Miss Lucy...The high school invited some Bible students to the high school and review some speeches. I noted Lucy long before that. I was quite a bit older and doubted if I could get a date with her anyway. Besides, she was the cousin of the young lady I took out before.

Her speech was a demonstration of cheerleading. Lucy was tall with beautiful eyes. The school year was about over and my girlfriend was leaving so I decided to take a chance. To my absolute surprise, she went out with me and we had a very good time. I went home for the summer and I came back once to see her. That next year I returned to my girl while Lucy was a senior in high school. Same thing happened at the end of that year. I transferred the next year but right before school started I came back to see her. Lucy had a boyfriend but he left to go play football at some little college so we spent some more time together.

Lucy left for some small out of state girls' college. I lost track of her. This is a situation where you take a two by four and pound yourself right between your eyes. She sent be a copy of "The Little Prince" with a handwritten note for me. I still have the book.

There will always be a spot in my heart for town girls...

When I think of big water fights, I remember two incidents.

The first occurred when a water line on the bottom floor of the dorm burst right before chapel. There was six inches of water down there. A bunch skipped chapel to "clean up their rooms." What they meant to say was they played in the water and had a monumental water fight.

The best water fight involved my roommates and me challenging the whole campus to a battle. The spring weather was nice so we decided a water fight was in order. The event was to take place at the local park after supper one evening. However, we prepared for the event by purchasing all the round balloons in town. We easily filled and tossed them. The balloons left were long ones that were very difficult to throw. We literally had boxes of balloons already filled with water.

The park was a beautiful place (still is today) with a large rock gate at its entrance. One of my roommates stood unseen inside the gate. As the cars entered for the fight, he tossed a water balloon into the vehicle. Once everyone parked their cars, it was a free for all. Those balloons we filled did not last too long. Believe me, we got wet also. I looked up and someone brought a bucket and scooped up the water from the park's lake. After a while, it didn't really make too much difference who one threw water anyway. Everybody got wet.

On the way back to school, I drove and kept a balloon or two from the fight. I saw this car coming toward us and I told the other guy in the front seat to steer. I roll the glass down and hurl the water balloon at the car. I missed and hit the edge of the window. Got the whole inside of the car soaked. I never said I was an intellectual giant, did I?

That park was beautiful. The city built all types of games and stuff for the community. Someone decided to have a swing-jumping contest there. (Yes, it is stupid). The idea was to get the swing going as high and fast as you can and then jump out. The person with the longest jump won. Stop and think about this. The contest is a real-life application of the laws of physics. If you jump out too high in the swing you don't go very far. The secret was for the jumper to hurl himself from the seat to maximize not only height but forward thrust. In a way, the jumping was both an art and a science. How is that explanation for justifying something stupid?

I won and didn't break my ankle. I did have enough sense to wear cowboy boots to give me a little support. Yipe, this victory ranks right up there with my winning a head-butting contest in the sixth grade. The kid I out butted ended up going to prison. I do hope that my head butt didn't contribute to that. I don't think it did because he didn't use a defense of insanity during his trial. I can see his attorney's exchange before the judge now.

"Excuse me your Honor I am notifying the court that my client would like to change his plea from not guilty to not guilty by reason of insanity.

So enter into the record that counsel has appraised the court the defendant has complied with the notification of an affirmative defense as required by state law. Now counsel, what underlying facts will you present to establish this insanity?

The underlying brain damage occurred as the result of a vicious head butt in the sixth grade.

Excuse me, what did you say?

The brain damage took place during a head-butting contest between the students at Hogshooter Elementary School.

Do you have an expert witness who will testify to this and if you do what are his qualifications?

I have such an expert your Honor. His name is little Billy Bastard and he was the winner of the contest. He is the champion head butter of all of Sensible County.

Does the prosecution have any questions to challenge this expert witness' qualifications?

Yes we do. I would like to ask a couple of questions of the witness if I might.

Proceed counsel.

Thank you, your Honor. Now, Mr. Bastard, how can you prove that you are the head-butting champion of Sensible County?

It is all very simple. I have in my possession a picture of me taken right after the contest. You will note the discolored knot on my forehead. That is as the result of the head-butting contest.

Objection, Judge. This statement alone does not prove that the defendant suffered a brain injury..."

Well, I think you get the idea about what I am talking. I did consider having Bible petition the NCAA to allow both swing jumping and head butting to become intercollegiate sports. Their response to me was certain areas of the country would dominate the new sports if approved. The individuals in these places are extremely hardheaded and they jump to conclusions.

Never thought of that but Bible could recruit from these areas to remain competitive...

Bible College (2)

I didn't realize there was so much to say about Bible. Many interesting happenings took place in the dorms and didn't include water. Bible's village was rural. Many students came from small communities and farms. One such classmate was little Stevie Morgan.

Stevie wanted to go to the state university's agriculture school but his parents couldn't afford it or he wasn't smart enough. I suspect you can reach your own conclusion about which one it was. Stevie idolized his cousin, Hayseed, who was able to graduate and was a successful aggie outstanding in his field (get it?).

Anyway, Stevie bought a calf just a few months old. He decided to hide it in the dorm room until he got the poor thing home. Strange cow sounds came from the end of the hall. Stevie dismissed inquiries by saying they were animal sounds he recorded at his parents' farm. He played the sounds to keep from getting homesick. I think it is apparent not all the folks at Bible possessed all the chicks in their barnyards because his excuse worked for a few days.

His forced sale so to speak came a day later. At Bible, the administration had enough sense to hire a cleaning woman to take care of the bathrooms in the suites. Miss Clorox (I ain't lying) knocked on Stevie's door in her shrill voice and got no answer except a moo. As she entered the room, this horrendous smell came from behind a mattress leaning against the wall. She peered behind the mattress, let out a scream and passed plum out. When the rescuers found her that poor calf was licking Clorox's face trying to revive her.

The smell turned out to be the scours. For you agriculturally inhibited, that is the name given for cattle dysentery.

Stevie realized his predicament immediately, loaded the calf in the back of his convertible and headed out of town. The last time I saw that poor animal he was peering back toward Bible. By the way, the name Stevie gave the calf was lamb chop. I ain't lying. You will remember when I started writing about the incident, I stated Stevie light bulb was not screwed in all the way.

There was talk about a grand jury investigation into the calf matter. The people of the Bible's community are cousins of the people in Hogshooter. When it became unclear of the fate of the calf, the talk quickly shifted to more pressing matters such as the large crazy lady who pulled her tube top up to scratch and caused three people to faint. The old men decided to have their coffee down at the bus stop the next time she came to town.

Two enlightened students attending Bible were the Stupid cousins, Duncehead and Dunderhead. They are related to all of the "heads" you met earlier in this brilliant work. If they gave grades for lack of complete common sense, Dunce and Dunder get A's. The boys lived on the top floor of the dorm. They weren't what you would say attention getters except you didn't want to be at their table in the cafeteria. I will expand on the food subject later. Yes, I am sorry to say there is still more to come.

The robust cousins apparently did not have many activities in their lives except to think up new adventures. Somehow, they got a stick of dynamite. What happened at this point is a matter of some speculation. One thing for sure is that Dunce and Dunder's fuse wasn't lit but the dynamite's was. The boys tossed the stick on the roof of the dorm. The resulting explosion caused some damage to the room right below it. I know you can guess who lived there. The boys tossed the dynamite above their own room.

I will say the explosion caused a bit of excitement for a while. Some of us didn't know about the explosion. We had beans that day in the cafeteria and eruptions occurred naturally anyway.

The resulting investigation quickly assigned blame. We lined up down the street as the Stupid cousins were cashiered out of town like being dishonorably discharged from the military.

After serving the appropriate amount of probation for their acts, the Army drafted Duncehead and Dunderhead. Dunce quickly volunteered to become an ordnance expert. His career was exemplary until he played with a shell one day and it blew off his little toe. Dunce was medically retired and given a purple heart. Dunder had a successful career as an artillery specialist. Well, it was successful for a while anyway. Seems he played with his cannon one day and accidentally squeezed off a round. The shell landed in a cemetery destroying the graves of two local citizens sparking rumors of their freed ghosts. The army decided Dunder should return to civilian life as soon as possible.

The boys reunited after the military and got jobs at the local quarry. Dunce and Dunder blow up things up all they want. The company psychologist counseled them about taking their work home with them.

They recently returned to a homecoming event at Bible. Both gave credit for their successful lives and careers to the experience they gained at college. When they die, the cousins want to go to the big ammo dump in the sky. That is food for thought if you ask me.

There were times when entertainment was a little slow around Bible. Certain nights of the week, the local movie was open. I think it cost 35 cents to get in. A lot of the time, we simply found other things to entertain ourselves.

One such activity was "the best man on campus" contest.

Someone updated the results and posted them daily around campus. I am not sure the young women had any idea what the results meant. Only the top ten times were listed. No other explanation appeared.

The contest was who could pee the longest. Contestants followed specific rules for their time to be included on the list. First, a contestant could not use alcohol to build up pressure. This was a no brainer because Bible would throw anyone out for using alcohol. Second, there was an official timekeeper using a stopwatch to witness the event. Third, an impartial judge observed the entry and ruled on any dispute. Fourth, a break in the stream terminated the time.

It wasn't unusual in the evening to see groups of young men in obvious pain letting the pressure build before letting it fly so to speak. The event did from time to time turn into a wee bit of a circus as certain individuals performed. Being a judge was an exceptionally dangerous activity because of splatter.

No doubt, however, one undisputed king emerged. He possessed at least half of the top ten times. His name was Nogood Gooch. When he performed, the bathroom became crowded with spectators vying for positions. The man just let loose with a steady dribble. The stream went on and on. The audience was amazed at his continued set of performances. In my way of thinking, Guinness should have recognized Nogood because sports' history has rarely seen anything like this.

Longevity peeing could have put Bible on the map along with swing jumping and head butting. The world might be a better place if it took notice of the particular skills exhibited at this marvelous small college.

Gooch was known for his curl in the front of his hair. It was perfect and the same everyday. Many a night, we watched Nogood dribble with a hair curler perched on his head. No young lady who could match that curl or worked harder on her hair than Nogood. I did notice that curler was rather greasy.

A young man moved onto our floor our sophomore year who probably fell off a horse too many times growing up. Bless his heart and his family because they wanted him to get a college education.

His name was Charlie Bill DeBracy. I asked Charlie Bill where his name came from and he told me it was from English literature. While I am not a good student of this area, I remembered one of the Norman knights in *Ivanhoe* was named DeBracy. He didn't remember where the Charlie Bill came from. Maybe it came from one of the lesser-known English writers like Shakespeare's young sister, Morgana. If I remember right, she wrote some memorable works (under a pen name of course) like The Knight Who Drowned in the Avon When His Armor Rusted plus the ribald classic Lady Cynthia's Rusted Chastity Belt. There may have been a Charlie Bill in one of those masterpieces.

You will remember that Bible College was about as conservative as an evangelic school to be. Sin and Catholics were the two real common enemies everyone at the school recognized.

Several of us on the dorm floor decided we needed to convert Charlie Bill to Catholicism. Not really of course. Our group included a couple of ministerial students who wanted to join us in our quest for a good time. We began to take turns having "mass" outside Charlie Bill's door every evening. During freshman initiation, we wore little green beanies. We put on the beanies, turned our bathrobes around backwards and conducted the service. Some of us actually knew a little Latin so we threw that in.

Something totally unexpected happened. Charlie Bill got upset and went to the Dean of Students. He shook his head and told us to back off. It was time anyway because being a Catholic wasn't fun anymore. Besides, I never was a big fan of fish anytime much less on Fridays. I did like the fact they used real wine during communion. We called it the Lord's Supper. My dad was a deacon and we used grape juice served out of these shot glasses. They had this little squirt utensil with a bulb on the end that you squeezed to get the juice into the shot glasses. Dad brought it home to clean it. I filled it up with grape juice and drank by squirting it into my mouth. Next thing I know I am sick and throwing up. I thought God was mad at me for messing around with this Lord's Supper thing.

When I was in the Army during basic training, this ritual took on a new perspective for me. The military had to let you go to church. My buddy was a Catholic and I was protestant. He'd go to services with me and I'd go to Mass with him. We took grape juice during my communion and wine during his. As I look back on it, I don't think the good Lord cared about us taking it twice. We were both good Christians and I believe He'd just smile at our ingenuity.

By the way, this friend, a helicopter pilot was shot down and killed in Laos.

I need to tell you about the ballad of Sidney and Sidney. Although sharing the same name, they were nothing alike. That isn't exactly true because they had one thing in common. The two Sidneys never washed their clothes or at least not very often. They'd just toss the dirty stuff in the bottom of each's closet and leave them. I do suppose when one or the other needed something he's just dig it out and put it back on.

One walked down the hall and knew exactly where he was. I guess the smell was so bad in the room it didn't bother either one of them. Someone it did bother was big slick. He lived in the suite with them so one can only imagine how bad it stunk in his room. Big slick tried about everything to get the boys to wash their clothes. I guess once a semester was often enough. He had no luck. So, big slick began to think of ways to jar the Sidney boys into action.

He liked to fish. Big slick went and caught a good mess but instead of cleaning and eating them he put half of them in the bottom of each Sidney's closet. Then he got each aside without the other and the conversation went something like this.

"Hey, Sidney, you know how your room stinks because Sidney won't wash his clothes?

Yeah.

Well, I got a way to break him of the habit. Will you help me and we can cure him of it once and for all.

Okay.

I went out and caught some fish and I put them under the dirty stuff in Sidney's closet. No matter how bad the smell gets, don't say a word. He will finally figure it out and wash his stuff.

That is a great idea.

Now remember, Sidney, no matter how bad it gets you can't say a word to him about the smell. Okay?

Got it."

You now have the scenario big slick devised. A mess of dead fish was rotting in the bottom of both closets under the dirty clothes. Each Sidney believed the fish was under the stuff in the other's closet not knowing it was in his clothes as well. You can imagine how bad the stink got before one of them figured out what was going on.

Did it break them of not washing their clothes? I don't remember and it doesn't really make any difference. It's a great story and it really did happen.

I need to add one other smelly story here. To this day, I don't know what happened. A group of us sat in our room one afternoon and I begin to smell something. I never smelled anything that bad in my life. I got down on my hands and knees to look around. I did not find anything and I even commented on that terrible smell. After a while, it went away. One of my friends started laughing after two guys left. Everyone took off their shoes. It seems the stink came from feet. He was right because I smelled it later when I visited their room. What caused it I have no idea but I do know we didn't have bug problems in our room for some time after that. He failed his Army physical. I often wandered if it was because of his feet.

Think what smelly feet might be in war. A ticker tape parade might be held celebrating the victory caused by stinking feet. I am certain no gas mask could fully protect one from those tootsies...

There was one central dining hall at Bible. You get an idea of how small the college was because one place fed all the students at once. Everyone signed in and the food served family style. You picked people you wanted to sit with. If you were dating someone, of course you sat next to her. The clothing regulations applied for the dining room so there were no shorts or anything such as that. Actually, the food wasn't bad. Now a days most colleges contract for food services. At Bible there was a group of town ladies who cooked like they were at home.

One person, usually a ministerial student, said the blessing. The advantage to giving the prayer was you got to eat first. One night the prayer was simply "thanks for the food." He got in trouble. Another time it was "good God, good meat, yeah God, let's eat." He got in big trouble. Actually, his sentiment was the closest to what everyone thought. You gauged how hungry the prayer maker was by the length of the blessing. If he was famished, it was short and sweet. If it was long, the guy probably been snacking.

The family style seating meant if you ran out of some of the food, you just held the bowl up and a person waiting the table came and got it, refilled it and returned the dish to the table. Still, there was one individual you didn't want at your table. Big John was about 6'4" and skinny. My, that boy could eat. I have been at his table on more than one occasion and watched him get the mashed potatoes first. Big John took the spoon and emptied the whole bowl on his plate! It wasn't like we couldn't get more food it was the idea that one person did that. And, he did it at every meal. That boy put away the groceries. I hope he got a good job because he needed one to pay for his food.

Sunday lunch was good in the dining hall. Many non-students came after church to eat and sometimes the line was long. I figured out one of my professors was pastor at a small church about ten miles out of town. When he preached it was never more than fifteen minutes. I made my appearance for brownie points out there and was back to the dining hall to be first in line. My parents didn't raise any dummy.

Speaking of food, two of my best friends always went trout fishing on the first day of the spring season. One year they brought back some fish and the only place they had to cook was in their popcorn popper. You can imagine the smell. They got in trouble for doing that. I think you realize we got in trouble for a lot of things. Don't get me wrong, most of this was little stuff and nothing came of it. It wasn't like the Stupid cousins throwing dynamite on the dorm. In looking back, being dinged for this little stuff caused several people to transfer to a state school.

Probably the worst experience with food during my years at college was when one of the mothers sent back a ham for us to snack on. It was great. We kept that booger covered, came in and cut off a slice every once in a while. Remember the guys in the dorm are young and at times lacked common sense. We didn't have little refrigerators in those days and we had no idea what a microwave was. Anyway, about Thursday after the ham appeared on Sunday one of us came to slice off a piece off and it was covered with maggots. By not refrigerating the ham, we successfully completed a biological experiment on the growing of parasites in pork. I tried to get credit for it in zoology but the professor had no sense of humor. None of us got sick.

Maybe things like this were the reason we ate out a lot if we could afford it.

For a late-night snack, we all headed out to the truck stop. Its proper name was Truck Stop. Creative, wasn't it? A person got eggs, bacon and hash browns for like $1.50. The man who ran the place in the evening was a total jerk. He was always threatening to throw us out even though college students provided about half his business on some nights.

If you were dating, a ritual developed quickly for your evening's activities. After eating in the dining hall, you'd pick up you steady and head for the park. Remember that Bible's little town had a beautiful park. There was no daylight savings time and the girls had to be in early. I didn't know what a FM radio station was because everything was AM. Many of the small-town stations went off the air at sundown by FCC edict. The call letters for the local station was something like KBLUUUUR. Anyway, the last song it played before going off the air the whole time I attended Bible was the Righteous Brothers' "You've Lost that Lovin' Feelin'." To this day, that is one of my favorite songs.

Anyway, you found a nice secluded place in the park and parked. If you lost track of time, the city locked the park with you in it. Yeah, you guessed, that meant more trouble. Sometimes it was worth it.

Many couples figured out their true loves once they got to Bible. No, I am not talking about Brother Dooby again. The weddings usually started the summer after our first year and continued on a regular basis. I remember one couple got married at a small country church right after finals for the fall semester. A bunch of us stayed around because they were friends. This little sanctuary was packed. It was cold outside and the heating vents for the church were in the middle aisle. As each bridesmaid walked down toward the front, her veil puffed up. When the bride came down hers was more prominent because of its size. Isn't it funny what a person remembers? They are still married today some fifty plus years later.

I want to relate one other "love related" happening. A dating couple came to school the second year I attended Bible. They were always together and the girl wore a raincoat. That went on for most of the semester until she had a baby one night in the dorm. She successfully hid her pregnancy from everyone including her roommate. I don't know how that happened but it took a lot of work. Oh, by the way, the college asked her, her boyfriend and the baby to leave.

Classes often started with a prayer. A rather interesting individual was a long-time instructor at Bible. One day he was giving a test and he called on a friend of mine to pray. He hadn't studied for the test and he proceeded to pray for the whole class period! As far as I know, my friend didn't get into any trouble because he appeared to be genuine. Personally, I thought he should get an A for simple creatively and persistence. I could have never done that.

One of the biggest honors at Bible was to receive the Image award. This honor went to the male and female student who best represented what Bible stood for. The same instructor sent in the name of one particular student who was involved in a lot of the activities on campus. He made a good choice for the Image award. But, the student smoked. When the instructor found this out, he withdrew his name and lowered the mark he made in his class by a full letter grade. This was not a good example of Christian tolerance.

A strange thing happened to me my last semester at Bible. One of the activities prohibited was dancing. I never understood this because the Old Testament specifically tells the story of King David dancing in front of the Lord to praise him.

Anyway, one of the basketball players and I were invited to go to a dance once Saturday night. I don't dance. Miss Lucy was at this dance and I sure wanted to see her. It took place in the basement of one of the local churches. The dance was well chaperoned. We went in, stayed a while and then left. We didn't dance.

The next day, the Dean of Students got six or eight calls about us being at this dance. His high school age daughter was also at the dance and saved our rears. She came to our defense and told her father we didn't dance. Nothing ever came from the incident.

Over the years, I have thought about this and wondered just how stupid some of these rules were. The college could have thrown me out of school for such a transgression. The town students who attended Bible had the same rules. Were they prohibited from attending a dance in their hometown?

Interesting.

I hope you enjoyed my excursion into the happenings at Bible. While not in the yellow notes of the hysterical society, I gave you a better idea about this part of the country by telling about Bible. Things have changed a lot over the years and students can wear shorts and do not have to go to chapel all the time.

There is one thing I do want to make clear about my time at Bible. These days were some of my life's best. Even coming out of the military, I wasn't mature enough to survive at a state school. I needed Bible. After I left there, I went to a state college and by that time I was ready.

I met some of the best people I have known in my life there. For all the crazy rules and regulations, the people were fantastic. Many are still my friends today.

STUFF

Now that I have you all crying from that sentimental bunk at the end of Bible, I will return to Sensible County and more "stuff." Please note that I did not say it was important because that might be lying and I sure don't want to do that.

Have you ever been to a shivaree? Unless you are a little bit older, chances are not. The earliest one I remember was in a smaller community than Hogshooter. I was young. Basically, a shivaree is an initiation for a newly married couple. That first one was an eye opener for a young fellow like me. Most of the men brought their shotguns and a lot of the community went to the place where the newlyweds stayed. The men fired their shotguns and the women banged on pots and pans to wake the couple up. They did a bunch of stuff I don't remember but the couple took the activity good naturally. I suspect they took part in many of them so they knew what to expect. I can't remember for sure but I seem to think the couple got gifts from the crowd.

I do vividly remember another shivaree that took place while I was a student at Bible. Several of us became friends with Big Willy, one of the locals. He was one smart student and ended up being a science or math teacher. Anyway, he married his high school sweetheart just before the start of the fall semester one year. I told

Big Willy a bunch of us were coming over for a shivaree. He said that was fine but he would come after me.

He and his wife lived in an apartment over a store off the square. One thing I love about small towns is their squares. Most are novelties now days because you can't put a Wal-Mart on a square. That's a shame. I sometimes have a problem with squares because I can't figure out how to get around the dang things. Squares remind me of the lyrics of the old Kingston Trio song, the *MTA*. "Did he ever return? No, he never returned. His fate is not learned. He may ride forever 'neath the streets of Boston. He's the man who never returned." Please forgive me if I messed up the lyrics. Anyway, I'm afraid I wouldn't be smart enough to figure out how to get off the square and be there forever. I have the same fear of a rotary in New England.

Back to Big Willy's shivaree... He wouldn't answer the door so someone climbed up onto the second-floor porch and started beating on the window. The couple finally acknowledged the crowd and came down. Big Willy was not happy. The first thing we did was make them take turns pushing each other around the town square in a wheelbarrow. Two or three guys had to help her because Willy wasn't a small lad. After that was done, it was off to the golf course (remember I wrote about it before) to toss the happy couple into the pond.

Since I knew Willy's disposition, I decided better hang back. This strategy seemed to work as the crowd approached the pond. Then I heard Big Willy's voice boom out calling my name. "Where are you?" I simply replied, "Taking my new boots off," because I was getting wet. Sure enough, he grabbed me and a bunch of the crowd ended up going into the pond that night. I do remember the water was a little chilly.

Later, Willy was in a car wreck and almost killed. People wondered how he survived because the wreckage was all over the place. The couple got divorced. I saw him years ago at one of the reunions and he was teaching at a small high school. He found his calling and I suspect he did a really good job. Big Willy was a good man.

I was listening to the radio the other day (oldies of course) and I heard a song that reminded me of growing up. Rock and roll was just catching on when I was a kid. No one spent time trying to decide if a song was pop, hop, rap, country, rockabilly, soul, acid rock or whatever. They were all rock and roll. I think you get the idea. All we did was turn on your local station and listen. As the sun went down, a new world began to open up with the 50,000 watt AM giants drowning out anything local. As I mentioned before, many of the smaller ones simply went off the air at sunset.

Some the large stations I heard were KOMA in Oklahoma City, WLS in Chicago, KMOX in St. Louis, KAAY in Little Rock, KOA in Denver and ones in New Orleans, Cleveland plus others that faded in and out. I remember the DJ in Chicago who got in trouble when he dedicated a song to all the virgins and added "it only hurts for a little while."

In later years when I did a lot of driving at night, I liked to listen to the Mexican stations. They weren't tied to any American rules so these powerful stations literally blasted across the America's heartland to the Canadian border. There was one out of Del Rio, Texas, (actually in Ciudad Acuna, Mexico) I listened to late at night. Since there was no government regulation, I am sure their advertising rates were cheap for the coverage. Many Americans sponsored programs on the station late at night. I remember Sister somebody from Houston who would send you your fortune in exchange for money. I especially remember the evangelists. They got after it with their fire and brimstone sermons. They promised gifts for a donation. An autographed picture of Jesus Christ was one but the preacher never said who signed it. A small vial of oil for anointing was another and I never did find out if it was twenty weight or what. Many gave out prayer cloths. My favorite one was a promise to send you something to keep your hair in. I guess that was a healing gift. After all, everyone knew to put your hand on the radio and the healing power came through. I heard later you actually received a little box to put your hair in if it fell out. No, I didn't send in any money I just heard about it. The evangelist wasn't lying because you could keep your hair in that little booger. I wondered how many people actually sent their hard- earned money to these people.

Sorry for straying there. During this great period in rock and roll history, some people from Hogshooter and Sensible County thought they could make it big. A music teacher from Violet got an agent and recorded a song called "Moonlight in Vermont Twist." It never caught on so he returned to teaching. I do have to give this man credit for trying because he had a great voice.

Hoofie (the mountain) Hoofenberger was different. He possessed a little talent and a lot of ambition. Taking a clue from the Big Bopper, he changed his name to the H Man. Hoof was a large man and had a slight problem with BO. I am sure this didn't aid his attempted climb in the world of rock and roll. The cause of his problem remained a mystery.

Now the H Man formed a local band and wrote a couple of songs. Both were pretty bad. The power of PR began to take over and Hoofie was everywhere. His songs played on the local radio stations and the skating rink or sock hops featured his band. I remember going to one of his dances and he was absolutely pathetic. The younger kids went wild. The girls hung all over him. The rumor circulated he was going to be charged with statutory rape if he didn't quit messing around with the young girls.

His signature song was entitled "Your Two Moon Pied Eyes in the Sky." I ain't lying to you. Here is what I remember of the lyrics. Now, again, don't try and get me committed because I wouldn't or couldn't make these up.

"As I worked before dawn, I dreamed I saw your beautiful eyes reflecting in the stock tank,

When my horse slipped on a paddy, I remember my heart skipping a beat when I thought of you,

The whippoorwill called my love darling as the lonely coyote answered from over the hill,

My yearning for you tugged on the heartstrings of my heart like my John Deere pulling a cow out of the mud,"

And then the chorus refrained, "Wahoo, Wahoo, Wahoo, I ain't nothing without you."

I ask you do those lyrics just bring tears to your eyes?

The effect of that song was dramatic in Sensible County. Next thing anyone knew, the song climbed to number one. In those formative days of rock and roll, even our little county tabulated its favorites and awarded a number one hit. Burl (the truth) even ran a story about the H Man and his apparent road to stardom. Hoofie was the headliner that summer for several weeks at the downtown grandstand. The first week a good crowd showed up but every week after audience slowly began to fade away until only his little teenybopper harem was left. Someone said the beginning-of-the-end was when the crowd figured out he only knew a few songs. Burl (the truth) told me in confidence he believed his decline hastened when the stage gave way under Hoofie's rather hefty physique. The reason given by the singer to Burl (the truth) was termites.

Many of the leading citizens of the area just sat back and basked in Hoofie's success until the big scandal broke. Some people compared it to the Alan Freed payola scandal that shook the early foundation of rock and roll. I would not go that far. As usual, when the facts of what took place broke, the boys down at the café called for a grand jury investigation. One of the old gang said that wasn't going to happen until everyone agreed to call one to investigate the UFO's invading his house and eating his peanut butter every night.

Someone figured out that Hoofie's father owned the radio station. One of his dj's got mad at the old man and turned the table (like that?) by pointing out that he made up the top ten every week. There was actually no basis for the H Man's long run at number one. Burl (the truth) vehemently denied the rumor Hoofie's old man paid him to write those nice articles in the disappointment. When asked, Burl (the truth) kept muttering something about a legal privilege that only the news media has. He made no further comment on the rumor the newspaper secured some sorely needed new equipment about the same time. Burl (the truth) even wrote a wonderfully dull editorial outlining the sanctity of the complete freedom of the press. I am sure he felt vindicated after that editorial but everyone in town knew he was full of crap. Once again, there was talk of a grand jury to examine a misuse of the press. Fearing an editorial pointing out their folly, the boys at the Dairy Dilly backed off. Instead, they turned their ire toward their competition at the café and accused them of slander. No one is sure what for but that didn't make any difference.

The scandal soon quieted down and there were no calls for a grand jury investigation of anything for a month until the mayor accused both the guys at the Dairy Dilly and the café of trying to sabotage his car for his political views. It turned out a mechanic found the remains of a dead skunk under the hood.

Hoofie faded from view. He was convinced he should be a star and left Hogshooter and Sensible County to become one. Some say he changed his name to the Big El and became an Elvis impersonator. I do know for a while his father displayed the first royalties check Hoofie received for "Your Two Moon Pied Eyes in the Sky." It was $1.37. I still wonder today who in the world played that song.

Excuse me an emergency just occurred and as a member of the Hogshooter Volunteer Fire Department I have to report for duty. Something bad happened to call us out. I will return as fast as I can.

I'm back. I admit that was the strangest call I have ever been on. It was to the nursing home. When we get a call there, it usually means bad news. Thank goodness, that wasn't the case today. By the time we responded, most of the town was already at the nursing home. We have to report to the station first and then respond. You have to wait until enough members are there to man the truck. Our problem today was one of the firefighters was taking a dump and had to finish. That is just one of those unforeseen circumstances we work with.

The problem was with Grandma Finney. The incident played out this way. Grandma's room has a lot of stuff in it because she's been a resident there for some time. So, space is at a premium. She moved her wheelchair across the room from her couch and placed her laundry basket under it. Granny decided she needed to use the wheelchair to go down the hall. As she reached for it, she realized the wheel locks had not set and it moved. The old gal lost her balance and fell butt first into the laundry basket. The result was a ninety-three-year-old woman wedged in with her feet sticking out. Grandma Finney is a stubborn sort to say the least. She wasn't going to let this get the best of her not to mention the embarrassment she'd endure from everybody in Hogshooter. Granny realized if she scooted the basket a little, she could reach the phone. This she did and called her daughter, Eudora, to come over and help. She neglected to tell Dorie what the problem was and her daughter took a while to get to the nursing home. You have to realize Eudora doesn't come to see her mom very often. She figured since she lived close by that was good enough. That all changed one day when Dorie received a call from the home telling her that if she wanted to see her mother alive she better get over there. Naturally, the daughter came running. Dorie found her mother just fine. Granny simply wanted to see her daughter and said nothing about dying. The ruse worked perfectly and Eudora came a lot more often. On this day, someone called for us because the sight of an old lady wedged in a laundry basket had to be an emergency. By the time we got there, everyone in the room including Granny, Eudora, staff and residents were laughing so loud we heard it down the hall. The old lady was still in the basket and didn't seem in any discomfort at all.

We quickly rescued her and everything returned to normal.

Granny later told Dorie she did have one problem before anyone arrived. Old man Castro saw her in the laundry basket predicament and asked if he could join her. He suffers from a wee bit of dementia at times and always wants to come into the women's room for a "date." She told him she would slap the snot out of him if he did and he decided against it. I have no doubt Grandma Finney would have kept her word.

As I just mentioned, Mr. Castro has a tendency to float in and out of reality. I don't think that is really a bad thing because I do that more and more these days. Here while back, I was enjoying my morning coffee at the café when a friend who works for the phone company came in. He was grinning and shaking his head. When I quizzed him about what was going on, he replied he took a service call in Mr. Castro's room at the nursing home.

The old man complained his phone wasn't working and he couldn't call anyone. The repairman said he'd get a new one for him and it should work. He fiddled around the room with his back to Castro and then asked the old man to try the new one. It worked perfectly.

You see, the reason the phone wouldn't work was because he was dialing the numbers on his TV remote and that danged call just wouldn't go through. You can figure out what the repairman did.

The moral of the story is if your television remote rings go ahead and answer it because old man Castro is trying to get in touch with you!

Mr. Castro was a regular for years at the café. After the telephone man left, he decided a grand jury investigation was needed to figure out if someone was deliberately messing with his phone service. He got his Big Chief tablet and crayons out and began canvassing the residents. The head nurse convinced him she would take the signatures and get them filed at the courthouse. The old rascal had forty-two signatures. They were a significant bunch including Ronald Reagan, Franklin Roosevelt and Harry Truman. Not often do you get names like that requesting a grand jury.

Everyone got a good laugh about that one until the boys at the café found out about it. One seriously discussed calling a grand jury to investigate why the head nurse hadn't filed the petition at the courthouse.

The saddest part of this whole deal is that the old man knew more about the workings of the court system than most of the kids at the high school.

You remember a few pages back I told you about an old boy who wanted a grand jury investigation into aliens eating his peanut butter. That person is Rip (the ripper) Flamingo. The nickname comes from his high school days but I won't go into any more detail than that. He still has the same problem today.

Sensible County has quite a history with aliens. I do not want to spread rumors but all this began to make sense to me when I saw the movie, *Men in Black.* We have some scary looking people around here but I always chalked it up to genetics.

Rip swears he visits with aliens on a regular basis. I'm not too sure he doesn't. He lives out of town a ways with his wife, Florida. She is a nice lady and not a bit crazy. Florida tells stories of her husband standing out in thunderstorms hoping to get hit by lightening. I think his wishes were answered a few times. She dismisses the whole thing as too much pickle juice hitting the electrical system. Florida won't admit it but the ripper operated a still for years. All of the makings are for his consumption so at times his partaking is significant because he has to stay up with the cooking mash.

I do have to admit that over the years I became enthralled with his alien adventures. Rip swears he's been aboard spaceships on numerous occasions for breeding purposes. Florida vehemently disputes this fact but gives few details to support her position. Rip states the aliens that take him can assume various personae. They are bright and florescent colors. They breed two at a time and they paint him their two colors before they begin. If the aliens are red and yellow, then he is painted orange. I think you get the picture and it does get ugly when you begin to think of all possibilities. After these trysts, the ripper maintains he is exhausted and sleeps for days. Florida disputes this and says her husband is simply sleeping off the fruit of his squeezins.

According to the ripper, another group of aliens kidnapped him and held him for observation. This bunch told Rip they wanted to study him because his body is perfect. They wanted to replicate it so they would fit in with the populace and colonize earth. That thought is truly scary to me. If you see large numbers of people running around together with huge beer bellies, giant noses and ears that look like the flaps on a 747, then you know Rip has been cloned.

I had some concerns a couple of weeks ago he was telling the truth. On a beautiful, warm evening, I was driving with my window down enjoying the breeze. As I came upon the ripper house, I began to hear strange noises from his pasture. Oh, it was blood curdling. I began to see lights in the field coming from about where the noises echoed. I parked my pickup, got my hotshot cattle prod out and ventured into the field. As I got closer, I noticed Rip running around howling. He built a small fire and he went one direction for a while and then the reverse. Flashlights tied in the surrounding trees created an eerie aura. He did seem to be using some strange language. Every once in a while, Rip stopped and took a swig from a container on a log next to the fire. He'd shake his head, take a deep breath and start again.

By the way, the ripper was naked. I can tell you for sure from this observation it was not a pretty sight.

All of a sudden, the man gave out a scream and collapsed. I looked around to make sure there were no aliens and I was the only one. I snuck (that is when you really sneak) up to Rip to make sure he was still alive. He appeared to be but he soiled himself. I carefully gathered him up and took him to my vehicle where I tossed him into the pickup bed. The man was still out cold. Florida saw me coming and met me in the yard. She didn't seem overly concerned and told me to toss her husband into the stock tank. When I did, the ripper started to snort some. I figured it was time to get the heck out of dodge. Florida thanked me and indicated she would take it from there. I believed her.

The next morning at the café, Rip had no recollection of the night before. He did advance a new theory. The ripper indicated he was pretty sure that Florida was an alien and sent to terrorize him for the rest of his life. Yipe, I have to agree with the old boy that he is partially right at least.

Last week, Rip came in for his morning coffee with a big smile on his face. I asked him why he was so happy. He said two of his alien offspring were recently honored. That statement did pique my curiosity. When I asked him what for, he replied the honors were from the state fair. One took a blue ribbon in the Angus calf category and the other a white ribbon in the Belgian draft horse competition. I do suppose that would make a fellow proud.

I can't wait to hear next week's adventures from whatever zone the ripper is experiencing.

Hogshooter used to advertise itself as the "paradingest small town in America." Now I realize "paradingest" isn't a word but Miss Nilla blessed the idea of using it and to most people in Sensible County that made it okay. I can remember as a kid running down to Main Street to get my favorite position on the curb in front of the bank. That was the most important place in town because the parades always came by there.

The town seemed to have a parade for about everything. I already mentioned the one at homecoming and the rooster tearing down the stop light. There was the Easter Parade where the children dressed up in their best clothes the Saturday before that scared day. All the kids from Sensible County who knew about it wanted to have a part. Strutting down the street was something. The little guys were pulled in their wagons. At the end of the parade route was an egg hunt of a sort. Most of the stuff wasn't eggs but candy. Maybe the reason some many kids got in trouble the next day at church was because of excessive candy absorption.

The one atheist in town objected but he was placated when a giant bunny was added at the end of the parade. Santa Claus' Christmas float was changed with some bright colored crepe paper and no one noticed.

The 4th of July parade was another favorite of mine. We had flags and banners. Because it was the summer not a whole lot of high school bands took part. I always liked the bands because of their different colored uniforms. Some were large and some small. As I remember back, a few of the bands couldn't carry a tune. To me as a kid that didn't make any difference.

I remember the VFW marching in the 4th of July parade. I sat with my mouth gaped open as they came by in their uniforms carrying rifles. Kids never noticed the jackets being too tight because of their overhanging guts. After I came out of the service, I never wanted to march in one the parades. In fact, I went ahead and gave all my uniforms away.

A cannon adored the front of the VFW building. A bunch of us when we were high school tried to fire that thing one night. All we accomplished was a loud noise and a crack in the muzzle. Guess what? There was talk of a grand jury investigation down at the café. That died when a couple of the older guys admitted they tried firing the cannon when they were in high school.

One thing I remember about Independence Day parade was Stinky Gash throwing some kind of a firecracker to upset the horses. They in turn followed nature's calling which caused havoc to the marchers behind the horses. No one wanted to "cut their foot" so to speak in some fresh droppings. By the way, if you ever want to play a fun game try Frisbee tag in a wet pasture with new manure piles. It can be challenging and messy. In later years, the businesses on Main Street joined to pay pooper-scoopers to follow the horses.

Oh, by the way, Stinky Gash was not a kid. I reckon him about forty years old when this took place.

Veterans Day was always a big event in Hogshooter. The kids liked this parade because we got out of school to watch it. Vets from all over the county came to march. When I was young, I remembered someone from the Spanish American War but never remember anyone from the Civil War marching. There were still plenty of folks from WWI and WWII. I later figured out how important these people were to the freedom of our country. Even though I am a veteran, I have never considered myself in the same category as these folks. They were special.

When I returned a few years ago, I was shocked at how few Veterans marched. There was no one from the first war and the number from WWII decreased at a rapid pace. Even though I didn't have a uniform anymore, I have walked in the last few. I lied when I said earlier I hadn't.

When I was a kid, we stayed for the speeches. I guess they were politicians. They talked about veterans and what they meant to the country. Lately it is hard to get anyone to come to somewhere as small as Hogshooter. When they do, they spew out more hate than anything else and they are lousy speakers. Oh, well.

We used to also have a Founders Day parade but don't anymore. It went away after the centennial celebration for Hogshooter. The threat of a lawsuit did it in. Someone got the idea to put the oldest surviving citizen in town on a chuck wagon to lead the parade. Now that I think about it, I don't guess you should put the oldest dead person on there would you? Anyway, the old man chosen had been born the same year as Hogshooter was officially founded. It seemed like a good idea and the committee knew the driver was there next to him. Just to be safe, they tied a rope around his waist to make sure he didn't fall out. Well, about halfway through the parade, the old fellow nodded off and the chuck wagon hit a bump. The driver was busy trying to calm the horses after Stinky had thrown another firecracker. The old man slid sideways off the seat and precariously hung over the side. He couldn't go any further but he did get some bumps and bruises. There was talk of a lawsuit and a grand jury investigation but the old man said he hadn't had that much fun in years.

You Larry McMurtry fans will remember him writing about the old man riding a horse in his novel, *Texasville*. His story is a lot funnier than ours. Besides, we didn't have Duane's twins starting a massive egg fight. Although we did have some kids start a fight by throwing about some fresh droppings one time. It was kind of funny until Sweetness and Little Bit took a shot. Then all the kids got into trouble. The men at the café especially enjoyed it and there was no talk of any grand jury investigation.

My favorite parade is Christmas. Believe it or not, the parade is still going strong. The town is committed to continuing the tradition. Everyone in the county knows the date ahead of time and reserves it. There are no politics involved and people or groups flock from all over including Violet to take part. I asked someone in our sister city about that and he said as a kid he remembered coming over. The Hogshooter Christmas parade is just a Sensible County tradition.

Technically, a non-governmental group sponsors the parade so there is no arguing about what or who can or cannot be included. All the churches are involved and have floats. In fact, several from outside Hogshooter join with one of the local churches to help sponsor an activity. Donuts, juice and coffee are served to the participants of the event before it starts. Up on Church Street the different denominations group together to serve hot chocolate or coffee to those attending the parade.

There are probably more high school bands coming to Hogshooter than any other parade around. They even come from outside of Sensible County.

After the parade is over, everyone gathers at the grandstand for Christmas carols. Then Santa Claus sets up shop and the kids come up and whisper their lists to him. Each child gets an apple or some candy. The citizens of Hogshooter are determined to keep this tradition alive. JJ and the bank used to foot the bill but the Wal-Mart in Violet does so now.

When I was a kid, the bank in conjunction with the schools put on a Christmas party for students. We went to the high school for entertainment of both a local and national flavor. One year JJ got Homer and Jethro to come. If you don't know who these guys are look them up on the internet. One wore a yellow suit and the other a red one. I still can remember them singing their hit, *How Much is that Hound Dog in the Window.* The song was a parody of *How Much is that Doggie in the Window.* I still remember the line "I do hope that flea bag is for sale."

We also had the high school band and chorus perform. When it ended, each child got a bag of goodies and a silver dollar. I never will forget that. That tradition went by the way years ago.

Santa Claus for the Christmas parade was Morton (the mountain) Magoon. You get the idea from the name Mort was a large man. I will compare all the other Santa Clauses I see at

Christmas against this man. He'd grow this magnificent white beard and I literally expected to see him come down my chimney on Christmas Eve. The Mountain put up with a lot such as kids wetting on him but the man never complained. Even after he got cancer, Mort wouldn't neglect his duty until he simply couldn't do it anymore. I can still see him at the end of the parade bellowing out "Merry Christmas." Everyone knew he meant it.

The organizers of the parade struggled with his replacement for some time after he died. The first replacement was just too skinny and wore a false beard. I remember one little child looking up and saying, "that isn't Santa Claus." Finally, the organizers found a fellow from Violet who does a credible job. The kids accepted him and Mort was no doubt pleased as he looked down from the great workshop in the sky.

Now, the parade hasn't always been smooth and absent of controversy. Several years ago, the organizers decided to get the high school kids more involved. After a few meetings, they decided the kids would serve as Santa's helpers during the parade and afterwards. The teenagers decided themselves what to wear. No adult bothered to check with them as to their costumes. The young women showed up in very short dresses with full petticoats. They barely covered their bottoms. As they walked dirty old (and young) men called from the crowd asking them to bend over. The young men helpers didn't wear any underwear. Someone said Ammie Ula (AU) Wintermole fainted. That wasn't unusual because she fainted at everything including a stop light changing.

The week after the parade, there was a joint meeting with the boys at the café and the Dairy Dilly to discuss the incident. After a spirited discussion, they agreed to call for a grand jury to investigate into the pornographic display of the high school boys. The dirty old men saw nothing wrong with the young ladies and unanimously passed a resolution to invite them back.

Not to be out done by the men, the Ladies Auxiliary called an emergency meeting and went into executive session in violation of its bylaws. After their spirited discussion, the group called for a grand jury investigation of the pornographic display of the young women. You guessed it. They commended the boys for their costumes and requested their return.

The district attorney just shook his head. The dispute died down after a milk truck missed a curve and rolled over. Everyone thought there should be an investigation dealing the ecological disaster it caused out at Fornie Beaufort's culvert and bar ditch.

The organizing committee for the Christmas parade agreed to allow the kids to continue to serve as elves. They added a proviso that a group of PTA mothers from the high school would be in charge of the costumes. This action ended the great 'elf' controversy of Sensible County.

I have glancing over the yellow notes to see if I have missed anything. As I indicated before much of what I have been talking about really can't go in there. I reckon these days I could put about anything in and it'd get approved by the hysterical society. There simply ain't too many of us left and most can't or don't want to remember what is contained in the yellow notes anyway.

There is one entry at the end that I will have to investigate further because I don't believe it is true. Most of the stuff I have added can't be verified or is of little consequence. This one entry, well, it's too far out.

Tookie (tapehead) Babble says he invented duct tape. I am sorry but that just can't be true. Took is old enough because the stuff popped up during WWII. I decided to look all this up on the internet. I do suppose he could have because its invention, discovery or whatever you want to call it remains somewhat clouded.

His story as outlined in the yellow notes goes something like this. Tapehead says he was looking around in his barn one day before the start of WWII. One of his old cows had a problem with an open wound and he was trying to mix up a salve for it. He had various components out there he used before so Tookie decided to mix them all together. After he did, he put the mixture on a rag to place it on the wound when his wife called from the house and said he had a phone call. When he came back, the rag stuck to a bench.

To this point, I don't have a lot of trouble with what he is saying. The rest of it I do. Took says he knew he had something special and approached the government. When he demonstrated, they were excited. Out of his patriotic duty, he refused to get a patent or whatever to protect his invention.

Right. And, I found Noah's Ark up on the plateau overlooking the creek. Maybe some of this story has to do with the fact that tapehead and Rip are good buddies. I am sure they have discussed the duct tape matter with their alien friends over a cup or two of Rip's home brew.

This did get me to thinking about duct tape. I do have to say that it is a marvelous invention. Shoot, for you morons out there, the stuff helped save the Apollo 13 mission and was used on the moon. I don't reckon a farm or business functions without using the stuff at some point. We even had a girl in a town make a dress out of duct tape. That had to hurt because it would stick to certain parts of the body. When I mentioned this one morning during coffee, the waitress down at the café slapped me upside the head and called me a dirty old man. There went her tip. Noticing a number of puzzled looks from the others in earshot, she went on to explain the young lady put the tape over a dress she made out of white cotton fabric. There was a chorus of "ohs" arising at the same time. A couple of the older widowers displayed disappointed looks on their faces.

For the next several days, the focus of our earth changing discussions during our morning experience centered on the use of duct tape. Probably the most enlightening conversation centered on Si McIntosh's confessions of his family's use of the stuff. I have to admit Si provided fodder for thought. He is a third generation American. I thought he was from Scotland because of his last name and the first name he gave to his son, Angus. When I inquired about the matter, Si informed me that Angus was named after his favorite bull, Angus the Angus. I do believe that is the first time I ever knew of someone named after a bull.

There have been instances of an animal named after a person. A great uncle in my family named an old cow Bossy. When I was growing up, Bossy was a common name for a milk cow. I once asked Uncle Cordial about the moniker and he named the old cow after his wife. When I pointed out her name was Wisteria, he informed me that Wisty complained, i.e., bitched a lot so he named the cow, Bossy, after her. I was young at the time so I asked Aunt Wisty about that and she got a rather concerned look on her face. The bruise on Uncle Cordial's face didn't last but about a week and the cut didn't require any stitches. He told me that everything he told me about Wisty was a secret. I felt bad for about ten minutes after what I had done.

I better get back to Si. He confessed his family wasn't really from Scotland. Their original name was McIntoshavitchski. His great-grandfather realizing most of his children didn't carry full buckets of milk in their cranial areas, changed the name to its current spelling. On proper musing, one does have to get the old man some credit. Not only is it easier to spell but the spitting during the pronunciation is curtailed.

Angus is a plumber and a dang good one if I do say. There isn't a drip or leak that the boy can't find. His hourly fee is very reasonable and he gives pricing breaks to old people and voluptuous 'customers' as well. Such civic spirit is commendable. But, Angus has a problem. The boy is a rather large young man and he has trouble from time to time. As he bends over to work under the local sinks, his blue jeans ride down and part of his anatomy shows. Over a period of years, several prominent ladies commented on their embarrassment to either their husbands or the local authorities. They got little sympathy from either. When Angus' mother found this out, she told her son to find a solution to the situation.

The boy is no dummy and knew he couldn't be a civic embar-ass-ment if his business was to survive. Duct tape solved his problem. One strategic strip covered the area in question. Angus even bought the solution in colors so if he is working at one of the ladies' house for more than a day he changes the tape's hue. This just goes to show the ingenuity of the Hogshooter community.

Every time I hear Si comment on his son's problem it "cracks' me up. Sorry.

That man Si is a genius when it comes to duct tape. He used it extensively when it came to his car. Someone broadsided him and the perpetrator didn't have any insurance. Si used the tape to keep his door closed. He also covered the window opening with the stuff. When his daughter decided to go to fortune telling school over in Kansas, Si duct taped all of her stuff to her vehicle so she would not have to make more than one trip. The highway patrolman who stopped her said he'd never seen anything quite like it. The compliment brought a smile to his face and Si even helped pay his daughter's fine.

Si bought some goats to clear out the underbrush around the three acres south of his house. He was afraid they might run off but didn't want to put up any barbed wire down there. To solve the problem. he put up a couple fence posts and ran the duct tape between them. Si finally figured out that didn't work too well when he came down and got the goats out of the stuff. He reversed the sticky side and solved the problem that is until the old billy goat began to eat the tape. Si thought about putting up an electrical fence but decided not to when he remembered the one he put up when Angus was a youngster. Seems the boy had to pee real bad so he let go on the wire. Turned out the boy was not sterile but he did walk bowlegged for a while.

Si discovered another use for duct tape was making Christmas decorations. He had a bunch of old plywood left in the pasture when the tornado came through and blew off the church's roof a couple of miles away. He took some of the colored tape and made various decorations with it. It took a lot of tape and the lines were exactly straight but no one noticed. The McIntosh family felt especially proud because people from all over Sensible County made a special effort to come and look at their handy work. The local Christmas committee even gave Si a special award for his masterpiece if he promised to not enter a float in the local parade for five years. He is looking forward to the end of the period and has several ideas for eye-catching floats using duct tape.

A slight problem developed during the holiday season as people traveled down Si's section line to view his decorations. Ever the opportunist, Rip (the ripper) decided to set up a table in his pasture close to the McIntosh family property. He had a little "juice" left over from his holidaymakings. Rip brews some extra and gives it away to his friends in decorated jars. He adds a little cinnamon and peppermint flavor to the brew. Anyway, some people ask for an extra amount to spice up their party drinks. A significant portion of a bottle ended up in the Catholic Church's Christmas Eve refreshments after Mass one year. While the attendance was down for the Christmas Day service, the next year's Eve Mass became an interdenominational affair when the rumor started the eggnog would be a repeat of the previous year's special taste. Father Lam disavowed any knowledge of the rumor but did so with a smile on his face. Good Christian (although not Catholic) that he is, Rip felt obligated to help.

On the entrance to the section line, Rip sat up his booth. All the sign said was "Christmas Cheer." Most of the men who came to look at the decorations were commanded to do so by their wives. A brief stop at the booth improved their dispositions and the attractiveness of the duct tape figures. One man after stopping at Rip's and waiting in line for some time to move down the road, swore he saw the figure of St. Elmo in the decorations. Burl (the truth) wrote a story for the disappointment outlining the saint story. Next thing we knew, a national wire service picked up the story and people really flocked to Si's decorations. CBS sent a 60 Minutes' crew down and the story should air soon. The Vatican indicated it is sending a delegation and there may be a sainthood in this deal but we are not sure for whom.

Burl (the truth) forgot to mention in his story all of the other visions besides St. Elmo the gentleman saw that night had nothing to do with religion.

The Feds read the paper and sent a team from ATF (Alcohol,

Tobacco and Firearms) to investigate Rip's actions. By the time they got here, all of the evidence was gone. They did investigate an area of dead grass where supposedly one of the "sippers" urinated. One of the ATF investigators was able to get a sip of the Christmas brew on his own. He promised to come back next year about this time for further investigation of the alleged incident. He requested an extra bottle from Rip when he returned so he could perform "further testing."

Okay, I realize I strayed from the original subject but I am returning to it. I should mention that Si's wife, Bernice, got into the duct tape fad. She authored, with the help of the local state agricultural extension service, a series of pamphlets on some uses of the tape. The first was of course, "Christmas Decorating with Duct Tape" which was followed by "Easter Activities with Duct Tape." Others in the series include "Decorating Your Farm House with Duct Tape," "Creating Rustic Antiques with Duct Tape," "The Zen of Duct Tape," and the wildly popular "Ducting Taping for the Intellectually Illiterate." Bernice is under contract for "Scrapbooking with Duct Tape." A reality television series called "Fantasy Duct Taping" is in the early stages of development. The thrust of the program will have teams compete each week to complete a series of tasks using duct tape. The jobs will become increasingly more difficult. A panel of experts and one celebrity guest will judge the works. The public will be allowed to call in their votes. At least one team a week will be eliminated until a winner is declared.

Because of the duct tape craze sweeping the nation, several state fairs and the one in Sensible County added a duct tape category to their craft awards. There is even a pig-decorating category being considered locally. I might add that a local antique appraisal show valued a Bernice corncob and duct tape doll at $500. She is now considering a national tour of her duct tape workshops.

Si felt a little left out because of his wife's success with duct tape. He is writing a book entitled "Duct Tape Meditation and How to

Book," or "How Duct Tape Changed My Wife." Burl (the truth) is serving as a ghostwriter.

Bernice and Si's kids have "stuck" to the duct tape subject as well. Their daughter the fortuneteller (remember I introduced her a while back) has now written "Tarot Cards, Duct Tape and Other Mysteries." She is currently editing "Duct Tape Hair Removal and Feminine Beauty Tips." Angus realized the opportunity and has contracts for "Plumbing and Duct Tape Revocations Tips" plus "Confessions of a Duct Tape Addict." He is now regular on the morning show at Violet's television station. About once a week, he takes phone calls and offers advice on home improvement projects and duct tape.

A hardware store in Violet donated a case of duct tape to the elementary schools in Sensible County. The manager stated to Burl (the truth) it was never too early to introduce tomorrow's leaders to duct tape. His message was America would be a much better place if kids know how to use the stuff. One mother disagreed and showed up at the store to point out where her son had stuck the tape to his hair. Ever the opportunist, the manager complimented the youth on his ingenuity and gave his mother a free roll of the miracle product.

There just seems to be no end to the duct tape craze in Sensible County. One local church posted the sermon topic for the next Sunday on its sign. "Trust in God and not duct tape." This slogan led to a couple of days of spirited discussion down at the café. The conclusion was to give the reverend a chance.

The senior class at the high school derived their class slogan from this magical stuff. "Duct taped friends for life." Their homecoming float made use of copious amounts of the magic adhesive. After the parade, nothing was salvaged and the float burned.

Even the nursing home got involved much to the chagrin of the staff. One old fellow got hold a roll and covered the lower half of this body with the stuff. He insisted he was only putting on his pants. The doctor prescribed a strong muscle relaxant before the staff removed the tape. An interesting conspiracy theory developed while he was so relaxed. He kept mentioning Miss Renoysa Perez as trying to seduce him. When asked about it, Renoysa just smiled, kept rocking and said, "he learned his lesson." She is now a suspect in the taping of Zoe Smerkle to her chair while waiting for her shower. The result of this activity is the nursing home has barred duct tape for use by the residents. One roll for staff use only is kept locked up in the medicine cabinet with the other drugs.

The boys at the Dairy Dilly heard about it and wondered if the prohibition was a violation of the constitutional rights of the nursing home residents. They posted a sign at the bait shop for comments and to test if there was support for a grand jury investigation. Most of the comments had nothing to do with the subject matter so the boys suspected they had been sabotaged by their enemies, the café coffee drinkers.

Just think about all this. None of these great things would've happened if it had not been for Tookie (tapehead) Babble's inventing duct tape. I thought about a slogan and theme for a new television show. I'll call it "The Tape that Held American Together Through Good and Bad Times." If it's like Sensible County, there will be a lot of people lining up to tell their stories. Shoot, I think I will approach the boys at the café tomorrow morning during coffee to see if there is an interest in creating a duct tape hall of fame. Hogshooter would make an idea location for it. Si will probably be the first member.

I was going to end this masterpiece but a couple of things have riled folks up around here. We have a new mayor and city council as of the elections last month. It's not like they have a mandate or anything since only one person ran for mayor and two of the five council seats are vacate. We folks here in Hogshooter should give them credit for stirring things up. Usually the most people get upset is when the Baptists serve beans and cornbread at their Wednesday night dinner or when the Dairy Dilly has one of its Mexican mystery food nights.

The new mayor is Dewey Drum. Calling Dewey a new mayor is a misnomer because he has held the office on two other occasions. A recall election twenty years ago removed him from office. He lost the only contested election for mayor anyone can remember five years ago. Ola Olifson defeated him easily. The only votes Dewey got were from his family and there is a doubt if his wife voted for him. Seems she went home to mother about that time but cast an absentee ballot. Ola couldn't fill out his term because the electric cooperative transferred him to another part of the state. The men folk of Hogshooter hated to see him go. His grandmother recruited a bride from Sweden for him. She was a looker. The first time she came into the café, Old Islie Something's mouth gaped open and his false teeth fell clear out first on the table and then on the floor. Evoking the five-second rule, Islie picked those boogers up quickly and popped him back into place.

Now, I guess I better get back to the matter at hand. Dewey has the noble idea we need to develop some civic pride. The council is discussing two ideas. Because there are only three of them and we have an open meetings law, their attempts at discussion are somewhat hampered. They can't even have coffee together in the morning because it may be a violation of the said law. So each morning the three may sure they don't sit at the same table. We do have a nefarious element during the coffee hour who would welcome the chance to pounce on them with a grand jury investigation.

The first idea was to team up with some foreign city and create a sister city arrangement. The problem with this is not many people in Hogshooter have been out of Sensible County or the state. Multiply this with the fact our little town has no industry, a declining population and maybe no schools after this year. About our only connection with a foreign country occurred a few years ago when Nastasia (nasty) Nurenburg was an exchange student for a year. About the only thing memorable about nasty was for the senior class boys. All of them felt it was their personal responsibility to make the poor maid feel at home. Their energy levels increased when she left.

Drum Drummone had an idea for a Mexican sister city. That

made a lot of sense because of the proximity of that country to us. Drum said he spent some time in a town just across the border from Texas and thought that might make a good partnership. After several days of trying to think of the name of the town, he finally gave up. He admitted about the only thing he remembered about place was that its name was Rio something. Drum said the week's memory was pretty much gone but he did seem to recall that a Rosie was involved.

The idea for a sister city is tabled for the present time.

Another possibility has emerged. Dewey has decided Hogshooter needs something special to call attention to our community. The new cell phone tower on the edge of town is not it. Maybe some kind of a festival is in order. Suggestions for the event include a pecan festival (no one is very nutty about that one, sorry), a duct tape festival (imagine that), a citywide fish fry in conjunction with a catfish noodling competition, a pumpkin smashing festival and cook off, a tornado festival and chili cook off, an Eastern Orthodox new year celebration (no we don't have any in town), or a canned meat festival.

Personally, I am leaning toward the canned meat festival. To me there is nothing more American than something high in fat and made from meat by products. I am not kidding when I say I love the stuff. I can serve the meat hot or cold, by itself or with other foods. And, the meat comes in a low-fat version. Hawaii leads the nation in per capita consumption. That is good enough for me. We might even be able to convince a city from over there to be our sister city. I can see our kids lined up for the 'all you can eat' contest. Hogshooter might even attract that little Japanese guy who eats so many hot dogs. The ladies could compete in the great canned meat cook off. Another contest could pit us against a Hawaiian town where contestants are required to run and flip pieces of meat in skillets. The local vo-tech could hold special grilling lessons for the community on unique ways to cook the meat. The kids could have a carving contest where each gets a hunk of the stuff and they have ten minutes to carve something recognizable. The losers have to eat the shavings. The FFA might have an attractive pig contest (no girls or guys allowed) with the judging criteria being which hog made the best meat. We might have a food drive to benefit the local food banks assuming one is found that would take the stuff. An ode to canned meat poetry contest is possible with different age groups being available. The Sensible County running club will agree to a "Cut the meat off 5 k run." The crowning event would be "canned meat" ball with the crowning of a queen.

I am sad to say to this point I haven't been encouraged with support for the "world of canned meat" theme. Si keeps mentioning throwing up when his ate a whole can when he was five. I tried to convince everyone a sponsorship might be in order and an appearance on a television show. I can see it now. The Chairman on *Iron Chef* announces the ingredient. I'm telling you that Hogshooter will be sorry if we don't jump on this one before some other town does.

That's It

I do believe the yellow notes of the hysterical society are better after my revisions. I am sure the kids of Hogshooter will be but they need to know and understand the significance of where they live. I don't know what'll happen if the school shuts down at the end of the year. Most likely all of our crew will be shipped to Violet. I hate to see that happen but it probably will.

We are a proud people and have an interesting history. I can't do any more right now. After I think about things maybe I will come up with something else. Or, I can just lie about things. There are only a few of those in this epistle and I ain't telling you where they are.

Go fish.

Oops!

I was afraid this would happen. There is breaking news in Hogshooter and Sensible County. The yellow notes need revising after this one. The buzz on Main Street is several options were taken on the vacant buildings down there and new businesses may be moving in. You will note I used the word may a lot. Anyway, I think it's important enough to open up this masterpiece to talk about the possibility.

Okay, maybe this is all a little premature but where there is seepage from the ground there is either oil or your septic tank is leaking.

I should tell you what brought this cascade (like this?) of excitement. Many people in the area are enthralled watching *Antiques Roadshow* on the local educational channel. Forget the fact that the PBS is one of the few channels many people can still get in Sensible County without cable or one of those little things you put on your house. And no, most out here can't afford that satellite stuff anyway. Burford (the brain) Bartles thought he discovered a new way to catch these "beams" from outer space. He went to the Wal-Mart store in Violet and he bought a bunch of pie pans and arranged them in a rather crude circle. He pointed them up to the sky, ran a piece of wire to his front window and in through a broken windowpane he forgot to fix. Burford tried to get Burl (the truth) to come out for the turn on but the editor was smarter than that. When the contraption didn't work, he blamed it on corporate America deliberating keeping the little guy down. Burford tried to get a grand jury convened but everyone lost interest after he paid for some donuts down at the café.

Oh, I guess I strayed a bit there.

Like I said, *Antiques Roadshow* has taken Sensible County by storm. The local low power television station, KPU, out of Violet decided to take advantage of the ground swell and produce a local program on Saturday mornings called *Your Smelly Stuff Doesn't Belong in the Junkyard*. It runs from 6 to 7 a.m. every week and is in Hogshooter. Burl (the truth) wrote a nice article and it got picked up on the national wire. Next thing we know the *National Inquirer* and other wonderful media are here to find out what's going on. Burl (the truth) insinuated a famous Hollywood Starlet left something of value in Sensible County and it turned up on the *Smelly Stuff*. He forgot to mention it was Irvina Irvin's pig, Porkchop. Porky was a double for Arnold the pig on *Green Acres*. Irvina had some droppings bronzed for posterity.

Next thing we know, tourists are popping up on Main Street and actually buying things. The increase in sales tax revenue led some to propose we actually look into getting a real stop light again. Anyway, this activity is leading to the interest in the vacant buildings downtown. There is even talk of commissioning a mural of Porkchop on the side of one of the buildings. The high school art class volunteered to lend their artistic license to the project.

I suspect the first question that pops up is why isn't Violet interested in hosting the television show? KPU indicated Hogshooter is a more rustic location for the event. I believe the people over there feel they are too good for it since they now have a Wal-Mart. Snobbery is a cruel thing. They believed us hicks would fall on our faces after a couple of Saturdays. Looks like to me they stepped into a big pile of it and we smell like roses and they are stinking like...

After Burl's (the truth) article was picked up, another significant national news item happened on the road leading from Hogshooter to the state line. Big Al's Circus and Carnival spends its winters just across the line. When it isn't on the road, they are centered there. Well, the troop was returning between gigs when the elephant truck was side swiped by Benny (the breath) Burgess. The first thing the circus workers did was to get the elephants out to make sure they were okay. When the highway patrolman got there, Benny was lying in the road laughing hysterically saying he was so drunk he saw elephants. The incident made the "American Spirit" segment of the CBS Nightly News. Big Al's sued Benny because one of the elephants had whiplash.

What does this have to do with the television show you ask? During the elephant story it turns out someone mentioned *Smelly Stuff*. The next Saturday, there must have been fifty people in line for the one-hour show. Since then, lines became a recurring problem. The television time was extended from 6 to 8 with the show being rerun on Tuesday evenings. Many of the items are not only being appraised on the spot but purchased for resale in Bubba's Baseball Card and Donut Shop. He has bought the building next door and knocked a new entrance into it.

As soon as the program is over, most of the people who came that morning adjourn to Bubba's for donuts and coffee. Then they are free to examine what he has for sale in the shop. I can attest quite a crowd is showing up at his place. He reports that a sale of "stuff" from the show is brisk. Ever the entrepreneur, Bubba has created *Smelly* tee shirts, thimbles, miniature spoons, taffy, and sports bras. He believes he has found someone to reproduce earlier shows for resale. KPU is delighted because the station gets a cut.

The appraisers are a diverse lot. They include Miss Mildred of her namesake rummage and estate sales. Her motto is "I only deal in high class junk." You will remember me mentioning "Low Dollar Joe" a ways back. Well, Joe appeared as a guest on the program but became such a hit he is now full-time. No one in Sensible County has a better knowledge of junk than he does. When something special appears for discussion, Joe jumps to his feet and does a little soft shoe. Burl (the truth) recently wrote Joe has quite a future in show business if he lives that long. He is able to limit himself to one nap per show. The furniture expert is Coach Warbucks from Violet High. Coach is the shop teacher there and his family used to own a secondhand furniture store. The jewelry expert is Lettie Virginia. In her younger days, Lettie was quite the jewel thief but governor pardoned her after one year in jail. Since then, she has gone straight or at least we think she has. Special guests are brought in to deal with specialty items. Si McIntosh has appeared several times to examine duct tape creations.

Each week a list of the items appraised appears in the disappointment. On those days, the circulation increased three-fold and with many of the edition mailed. Among the recent items listed:

One of Elvis' baby teeth. Comes complete with a shoestring that was used to pull the tooth and then later used in an emergency when one broke on his blue suede shoes.

An unused 19th century shoe. It supposedly was the one that was worn on the peg leg of Captain Ahab as he chased after the white whale.

A matched set of men's and women's union red flannel underwear. The men's pair includes unidentified spots on various locations on the fabric. The women's suit is pristine. The buttons on the ass flaps are made of the highest quality mother of pearl.

A hairbrush full of hair was used by Timmy on the television show, *Lassie.*

A lug nut off the winning 1925 Model T Ford found after the competitors came through Hogshooter during that year's transcontinental race.

Certified copies of the valedictorian speeches delivered during the 1940's from Hogshooter High School.

A Bible autographed by Evangelist Aimee Semple McPherson the night before she disappeared in her stunning fall from grace.

Chester Something's finger bitten off by his little brother, Simple (preserved in alcohol).

Mevinia's autographed basketball shorts from the Lady Gorillas' 1972 state championship team.

A picture of the professional wrestler, the Strangler, without his mask on.

A preserved piece of Grandma Smith's prize apple pie called a slice of heaven by the county fair judge.

A jar of pickled pig's feet allegedly belonging to Porkchop, the television star.

A signed Pinkie Lee hat.

The marble collection of Rennard (shooter) Ricochet, the 1952 Sensible County Agate Open champion.

A Masonite painting by Marvella (the wiz) Brush reported to be the Grandma Moses of Hogshooter.

A signed copy of Miss Marie's 1932 award winning poem, *Fleecy Clouds Up in the Sky.*

Chopper Marine's dishonorable discharge from the Army for poisoning all the troops in Company B on Wake Island because of his tainted still.

A slug taken from John Dillinger's body.

A six-foot long synthetic rattlesnake skin.

A stuffed billy goat said to be the champion brush eater for three years running during the Sensible County fair in the 1940's.

Miss Nilla's favorite seashell taken from the New Jersey shore when she was four years old.

A fake leather steering wheel cover from the first Edsel car sold in Sensible County.

An empty suitcase with a likeness of George Washington stained on the inside leather.

A signed illustrated comic book of the classic story of *Ivanhoe* by a namesake of Sir Walter Scott, Sir Walter Scott from Joplin, Missouri.

A napkin supposedly used Gypsy Rose Lee to blot her lipstick.

George (mughead) Morris' collection of cups from all fifty states except Alaska (he swears it is still owned by Russia).

A complete five-year collection of the disappointment.

Travis Tremble's playing card collection from all the casinos in Laughlin, Nevada (one of them has water damage when it slipped into the stool while Travis was shuffling them).

An exact reproduction of the udder from Smoky Jones' prize-winning Jersey that held the record for producing the most milk in Sensible County for three years in a row. The state agriculture college recently returned it.

Highway Patrol Trooper Josh Cruiser's autograph collection featuring five of the ten most wanted men's signatures for 1962. Extremely rare since two were executed and another was later killed in a shootout.

A photo of the girls' locker room at Hogshooter High taken by a transvestite posing as a basketball player from a visiting team.

Old man Adams partial plate which is recognized by folklorists as the first one made of a combination of wood, nails and animal bone and held together by super glue. The government turned down his application for a patent.

And, a set of unidentified men's and women's skivvies found at the lake. Hopefully, DNA testing will solve this mystery some day.

I think you now can see why the show has been such a tremendous success. I am hopeful the trend of these wonderful items will continue.

With this, I really am going to close this down.

Oops 2

By golly things have gotten REAL busy around here. Hogshooter and Sensible County is busier than a one-legged man in a butt kicking contest. Breaking news will take precedent over my mere wants and desires. I genuinely tried to avoid a couple of subjects in this epistle. They are politics and lawyers.

You know the difference between roadkill and a lawyer? There are skid marks before the roadkill. Sorry.

I still hope to avoid the politics aspersion but I can no longer keep from commenting about lawyers. Oh, I know I mentioned about some earlier lawyers in Sensible County but that was different because that discussion was strictly from a historical perspective.

I can't let old Judge Glen Buttocks go. The controversy started about a year ago when one of the locals at the county courthouse complained the judge sexually harassed her. That in and of itself didn't really cause much of a commotion because the judge has been known as "Dirty Glen" for years. Most of the women down at the courthouse viewed him as a pest and some felt slighted if he had not made lewd comments to them. His suggestions were nothing new from what they had heard all their lives in Sensible County and at home. Miss Blessed Commotion was new to the area and stated she didn't have to put up with this nonsense.

Technically, I suppose she was right but the county commissioners had a heck of a time getting Old Glen to run for the office. He was unopposed now for years.

That reminds me...An attorney died, went to heaven and was met with a stack of trial files by St. Peter. He handed them to the attorney and told him his trials would start in a week. The lawyer said that was what killed him and asked what happened if he turned them down. He would go to hell. So, the attorney went to hell and the devil handed him a stack of files and said he started the next day. Why the next day he asked and pointed out heaven gave him a week. The devil replied they had more judges in hell...Sorry.

Anyway, things got bad when Blessed began to hear strange noises from behind the bench during trials. The bailiff confirmed the noises. After conferring with the district attorney, the DA issued a search warrant. It seems Judge Buttocks used a penis pump during the trials. Further search warrants including DNA samples from his robe, chair and carpet confirmed the unsavory acts.

After an indictment, a jury convicted him. The former judge served time in the state pen. His family tried to get him released early on the grounds he needed to help run the family's car wash business. The request was denied. A rumor from prison said he was a popular man there. Those rumors are unconfirmed.

That reminds me...a doctor, minister and lawyer were stranded on a desert island. There was another one just a short distance away. They used up all the food and needed to get to the other island. The only problem was the channel between was full of sharks. Finally, the three drew straws and the doctor won the right to swim across. He started and before long the sharks swarmed and red foam engulfed him. The other two held out a little longer but finally they drew straws again. This time the lawyer won. He started to swim over and the sharks formed a circle around him as if protecting him. Once he got to the other side, the minister yelled and asked why the sharks had left him alone. The attorney yelled back, "professional courtesy." Sorry again.

The boys over at the café debated the disgraceful actions of the judge for some time. A couple of them didn't really believe there was such a thing as a penis pump and didn't think one would work. There was talk of taking up a collection to see if they could buy one at Miss Scarlet's Creams and Inducements over at Violet. They gave up the idea when they couldn't agree on who would get to use it first.

About the same time a big gambling scandal broke. Illicit gambling had been going on for years in Sensible County. Homer (odds) Baccarat took bets from around here for as long as anyone can remember. Half the attorneys in this part of the state paid for part of their tuition from betting football. Anyway, one of the leading line setters from Las Vegas is actually from Hogshooter. He, like me, decided he wanted to retire back at home. He married a showgirl (feathers) and Big Al settled out in the country west of here. His old buddies from around Las Vegas wouldn't leave him alone. Course, I have heard all the excitement in Sensible County finally got to the couple and he started making book again. I also heard a feather was seen dancing out behind their barn to stay in practice. That report came from Rip (the ripper) after he said the aliens put him back at the wrong farm after one of his breeding trysts. Florida says he mixed the batch too strong, had a momentary lapse of memory and a touch of blindness.

There is an old saying in the law that you never mess with the feds. Next thing we know there are FBI agents everywhere. Big Al is indicted and a special prosecutor is brought in all the way from the east coast to try the case. There were three others indicted including one from Kansas City, another from Chicago and a third from Vegas.

The old federal courthouse in Violet hosted the trial and lasted two full weeks. Burl (the truth) came in every morning for a couple of hours, took a nap and then wrote a marvelous article on what took place that day. Because of the nap, there is some doubt as to the truth and veracity of the story but who cares. Burl (the truth) is an institution and this trial series just might finally get that reporting prize he always wanted.

The mob brought in its own attorney from Kansas City to represent Big Al. The reason I heard was to make sure nothing came out that they didn't want to come out. One of the attorney's father was a hit man for organized crime up there. I guess in many ways there isn't much difference between a hit man and an attorney.

The highlight of the trial came during the closing arguments. The defendant from Las Vegas (Lobo Wolf Woofington) was represented by an attorney who had been disbarred once. Every night he put his trial file in the defense table so he knew where it was the next morning. When the court was in recess, he'd tell the US Marshalls that he would be in his "court." Of course that meant the Court of the Three Brothers, a local bar.

Every day Big Al showed up impeccably dressed in a suit and tie. He looked like a businessman and not a bookmaker. Lobo on the other hand looked like the hood he was. He was about five foot tall, weighed about 250 lbs and came to court with his shirt unbuttoned with gold chains hanging out. He should be convicted for the way he looked and his stupidity.

Anyway, during closing arguments, Lobo went to sleep. For those you who think trials are exciting, think again. Next thing we know the Wolf falls over backwards out of his chair and hits the floor. The judge, No-nonsense Harper, is holding the trial folder in front of his face to keep from letting the jury see him laughing.

Well, all the old boys got convicted. They were guilty. Big Al served a little time. That was okay with him. He stated to Burl (the truth) his term and probation were up the day before pre-season football started. I guess that is one way to look at the situation.

About the time the big federal gambling bust came down, the Sensible County sheriff, Moonbeam McCool, felt like he had to do something to attract attention because of a tough reelection campaign coming up. Now the sheriff got his name because the man from time to time isn't connected to this earth. His sense of reality was a little warped. In an article in the disappointment, Moonbeam stated his office was just a good as "those federal fellers." Somehow the man was able to secure a search warrant for several local businesses seeking gambling materials. Moonbeam knew they were there because he was one of their best customers. Dirty Glen was the judge that signed the warrant. I don't know, maybe Moonbeam gave him a penis pump to sign the thing.

After the raid, the sheriff displayed the computers and disks he confiscated. Moonbeam proudly announced to Burl (the truth) that the names on the disks would be prosecuted to the fullest extent of the law.

That was the last we heard of the deal. I have it on good stead that the names of the gamblers were the leading citizens of Sensible County. In fact, Moonbeam was defeated in his reelection campaign by a 10 to 1 margin by a fellow whose name is supposed to be on the list.

The feds never returned to Sensible County for any more gambling investigations. Maybe they are concentrating on real crimes now.

Do you know why lawyers are buried ten feet deep instead of six? The deeper the better...Don't want to take any chances with them getting out...Sorry.

I ain't making any promises about this being the end because things are moving fast in Hogshooter...

About the Author

Dr. Joe Dillsaver is a Professor Emeritus of Criminal Justice from Northeastern State University in Oklahoma. He is also a retired Air Force Officer and lawyer. Current published novels include "The Ghost," "Cedar County," "These Bones Shall Rise," "The Old Man Chronicles," and "The Old King is Dead." He is a retired Elder from the First Presbyterian Church of Tulsa. Dr. Dillsaver served as a professor/instructor or administrator at the University of Missouri, University of Vermont, Oral Roberts University, Northeastern State University and Rogers University.